The Coin

By Alex Bloch

KIP - Kotarim International Publishing, Ltd.

KIP – Kotarim International Publishing, Ltd.
Edited by: Anna Mowszowski
Graphic Design by: Laura Gryncwajg

Publisher: Moshe Alon

ISBN 978-965-7589-15-1
Printed in Israel 2014

*Dedicated to all those
who were forced to deny their heritage,
be it during the 15th Century or whenever.*

Contents

Part I

CHAPTER 1

1998

It was pure chance that brought Joanna and Michael together. Neither had meant to be in Manhattan that day, but last minute changes in each of their plans had led them to stand at the corner of 42nd street and Fifth Avenue, waiting for the light to change. It was 11:30 AM on a cool, cloudy April Saturday. Joanna had taken the train from Bridgeport to Grand Central with the aim of going to the New York Public Library across the corner. As usual, she had postponed going until a couple of days before her final exam in English Literature. She was in her senior year at University of Connecticut's school of education, majoring in history. She had meant to go the week before in order to have enough time to discuss Shakespeare's *Henry V* with her instructor. She felt the need to clarify several lines in the text. Joanna had been in the last car, having come at the last minute. Michael, who lived in Norwalk, had taken the same train sitting in the front car. He was to meet his roommate from his years at Northeastern in Boston. He had graduated from NU two years before with a B.Sc. in Mechanical Engineering. His friend, Henry, who lived and worked in Detroit, had called him the other day to tell him he was leaving that night for London on a business trip and they could meet in the city in the afternoon.

Both Joanna and Michael had reached the intersection of 42nd and Fifth at the same time. Just at the moment the light had changed, and as they had gotten off the curb to cross the street, a tremendous crash stopped them and others from proceeding further. A bus jumped the light and a small Toyota had crashed into it. For a second it seemed the world had stopped, an unnatural quiet reigned with nobody moving, but then cries and shouts resonated in the air, with some people rushing to the scene, but most others going quickly on their way, a few of them looking around guiltily to see the reaction of other. Two cops standing at the corner immediately went into action, running to the spot with one calling for help. Both Joanna and Michael were among those who went to help but could not do anything as they were blocked by others who had reached the place before them. Within minutes, two police cars arrived on the scene and officers began asking bystanders to sign affidavits describing exactly what had occurred. Most declined with various excuses, Joanna and Michael were among the few who agreed. In the meantime, three ambulances came to take the seriously wounded driver of the car and those on the bus hurt by the crash. Traffic on 42nd Street, as well as on Fifth Avenue, was blocked for miles.

Michael half-turned toward Joanna, after both had finished their deposition, and said in a barely audible murmur, "Gee, I could use a drink after seeing that, this could happen to anyone!"

Joanna, not sure the remark was addressed to her, hesitated a few moments before saying, "You know, that's a darn good idea. I have plenty of time anyway. There should be a bar around here." Michael now looked directly at her, surprised not only to hear from her but especially at her response to what was not meant to be an invitation. Shook up from the scene, he actually had just uttered the phrase to himself. Only now did he fully register the girl who stood before him. He would never have dared to pick up a girl like her; he was much too shy and conservative to have done it. The first thing that struck him was her eyes, a hazel color flecked with green, rather widely spaced on her oval face. The black hair framing it was gathered tightly in a ponytail with some strands falling down her forehead. She was fairly small, maybe 5'6", but well built with a nice bust and the most beautiful legs Michael had ever seen. He managed to stammer out a few words saying he was glad to meet her, and was pleased she would join him. Joanna, on her part, did not mind going with this young man whose appearance she rather liked. His face had an open feeling, his brown eyes looking out mildly at her without the stares she often had encountered. He was dressed casually; jeans, a light blue sweater and a dark blue windbreaker.

Michael, a small embarrassed smile on his face, said after a long pause, "Ok, let's go and look for a place. I'm afraid I don't know any bars around here. In this city, there should be one on just about every block. By the way, my name is Michael Berk, what's yours?"

"Mine is Joanna, Joanna Aguilar, nice to meet you." With that, she extended her hand to Michael who felt the firm pressure from her warm palm. He was even more captivated by her, seeing her fleeting smile that was at once open and yet somewhat restrained.Michael turned back east with Joanna following. As they walked, they kept some distance between them. Sure enough, just a couple of stores from the entrance to the Station was a bar, its bright green neon light flashing making sure it was not to be missed. The smells of alcohol emanating from the door made sure that the passerby knew what place it was without the sign. The bar was not very crowded, the people there perched on stools were mostly separated from each other by empty places around the vast counter. Michael suggested they sit at one of the small tables in the back, wanting the chance to get to know her in the semi darkness of the place without her noticing his nervousness. The bartender came out to ask what they wanted. Joanna, without hesitation, asked for a whiskey sour while Michael, thinking for a while, said that he would have the same. Neither knew how to start a conversation until Joanna said,

"Wow that was some accident. It's terrible what happened to the young woman in the car; who would think the bus would go through a red light? I hate to drive in the city. Did you get to see her when they took her out of the car?"

"I sort of saw her. You are so right about the traffic.

Unfortunately, I have to drive here twice a week to go to Columbia, where I hope to get my Masters this June. After that, I won't do it anymore."

Michael was glad he was able to tell her, without obviously bragging, that he was going to Columbia.

"Why can't you take the train? Didn't you do it today?"

"I'd waste a lot of time waiting for the train. I take off from work in the early afternoon, from Stamford. And on the return trip, I want to be home at a reasonable hour, I always have plenty of work to do. I can't study on the train; it's always crowded at that hour with commuters, mostly drunk."

The waiter came and set the drinks on the table. Joanna was the first to pick up hers, said "Cheers" and took a sip. Michael followed suit, wondering how to get the conversation going. Finally he said, "So where did you come from?"

"I came from Bridgeport just to go to the library here to look up a few things," she replied, without going into further details.

"Is this in connection with your studies, if I am not too nosy?"

"I am a senior at the School of Education at the University of Connecticut," Joanna said, wondering if she should expand on her activities. Finally, she decided Michael seemed nice enough to go into some personal aspects, and she liked that he kept his eyes fixed on her.

"You see, I want to be a high school teacher of History. I've always been fascinated with the past, like why things were done the way they were and what might have been if something had not taken place at a certain time. Right now, I have to prepare for a test on one of Shakespeare's plays. His plays dealing with history are wonderful, but don't always reflect what actually occurred. I should add that Bridgeport is my home but I live in the dorms at the university," she said with a slight smile.

"And I'm from Norwalk, working in Stamford as a mechanical engineer. My parents live in Boston. I took a job there since I wanted to be near New York. Norwalk is nice, not too far to get in for a play and also inexpensive. I pay half for my rent than I would in the city."

A long pause ensued, both looking down while sipping their drinks. Finally, Michael asked, "How far is it to Storrs? I've never been to that part of the state. And how do you like the university?"

"It's too far to commute, unfortunately, about 80 miles. But I do get home some weekends and, of course for holidays. I don't have much more to go. I'll graduate in June and then I'll look for something in the Bridgeport area." As an afterthought she added, without really thinking what she was saying, "It's beautiful country up there, you should come and see it sometime."

"I'd love that. You have to tell me how to get in touch with you."

Joanna hesitated for a moment; *Do I really want to continue to see this man? Why not? He seems nice enough.* "Well, yes, you can reach me at this number in my dorm. I share a room with another girl and you can leave a message with her if I'm not there."

"Gee, thanks, I'll certainly be in touch and would like to visit some time. It's strange, isn't it, how this terrible accident led to us meeting?"

I hope he does not make too much of us being here for a drink. Maybe I should not have said what I did. Oh well. I can always claim to be busy with exams if he does call.

They sat for a few more minutes, having finished their drinks, when Joanna got up, saying, "Nice meeting you, Michael," and turned abruptly and walked out from the bar. Michael followed her slowly. *I guess I will never understand women. Here I thought she wanted to see me again, so why this sudden turnabout? Now I don't know if I should call her or not.*

CHAPTER 2

Michael waited for two weeks, debating time and again whether to call Joanna. *She is an attractive girl, and I would love to get to know her. But after her abrupt departure I don't really know if I should. What the hell, why not? All that could happen is she'll say she's busy.* He finally screwed up his courage and called but was answered by her roommate who said that she was out. She suggested he call back in half an hour. Joanna returned to her room a few minutes after Michael had called, and was told about the call. *I thought he had forgotten about our meeting. I don't see why I should refuse to meet him, if he does call again. He seemed rather nice. This wouldn't be the first date to turn out to be a dud.* Half an hour later, Michael called.

"Hi, this is Michael Berk. Do you remember me? We met after the accident on 42nd Street."

"Why sure. How've you been? It took me a while to get over the awful scene we saw."

"Yes, me too... I was wondering if you would like to get together some time. I just saw in the paper that *Richard III* is playing in the New Haven Playhouse two weeks from Saturday. Their performances are usually quite good. I could pick you up from your parents in Bridgeport if you're staying with them that weekend. How 'bout it?"

"Wow, you sure make it attractive. I'd love to see the play. I can, of course, stay at my parents whenever I want. We live on the corner of John and Main Street. Get off the turnpike at exit 24A, which takes you to Lafayette Blvd. Take a right on John Street. We are the first building on the right at the corner of Main. You shouldn't have any problem finding it. What time will you come?"

"I suppose 7 p.m. would be a good time. We won't have to rush and maybe can have a cup of coffee before the play. I'll order the tickets. It's a date."

After hanging up Joanna reflected for a while on what had just transpired. *Well. This was a surprise. I did not expect it. He seems a bit shy, but so what? Better than those guys who start pawing you on your fist date. What do I have to lose? The play should be nice.*

In the intervening two and a half weeks, Michael often thought about Joanna. *I really know nothing about her. I've met her, but it's still like a blind date, which I hate. I can't go back on it now. The play should be good. Should I pay for the tickets and the refreshments? She paid for her drink after the accident. Guess I will have to play it by ear.*

Michael pulled up at Joanna's house at 7 o'clock sharp. The door was opened by a good-looking woman in her forties, obviously Joanna's mother, appearing as her daughter might look twenty years hence.

"You must be Michael, Joanna has told me about you. She will be down in a minute. I'm her mother, Reyna. Come into the living room for a minute, I know you won't want to be late for the show but how about a cup of coffee in the meantime?"

"Thank you very much, maybe another time."

Reyna led the way down the small entrance hall into a spacious living room furnished in a style unfamiliar to Michael. A special attraction was a tall wooden cupboard with a great many small doors each inlaid in various colors. Wood dominated the sofa and easy chairs, which did not look very comfortable. The walls, covered in an unobtrusive flowery wallpaper, were quite bare with only two small watercolor paintings. Michael did not get a chance to look closely at them when Joanna came down the stairway in the far corner of the room. He walked towards her, then shook her hand very formally saying how glad he was that she agreed to come with him to the play.

"Well, I must thank you for such a nice idea. I had to study *Richard III* last year and it's a fascinating play. I hope the acting will be good. Have you read any reviews? I understand it's been playing in New Haven for a while."

"No, I'm afraid not. Just saw the advertisement. I love Shakespeare's plays, although I've only seen a couple beside the *Henry V* movie with Laurence Olivier.

I must admit I find it very hard to read them. But let's go, we don't want to be late."

With that, Michael turned to Joanna's mother, thanking her for her hospitality. He waited impatiently for Joanna to put on her coat and lead the way out the door.

The drive up to New Haven took a bit longer than expected, nearly forty minutes, due to heavy rush hour traffic on the turnpike. They decided not to stop for coffee but to go after the performance for a bite to a nearby restaurant. It was a long performance, the full five acts with no noticeable omissions as often done. Walking to the car, they exchanged views on the play.

"What did you think of it, Joanna? You're the expert. I rather liked it. Especially Richard, who gave a very believable performance."

"Come on. I'm no connoisseur, I've just studied the play in class. Yes, he was good but some others were, too, like Clarence and Anne."

"Let's first decide where to go. Do you know of any decent place, not too far?"

"I've heard of the Barcelona restaurant, in the Omni Hotel, not far from Yale, near an entrance to the turnpike. I must confess that I've wanted to go there for a while to see what it's like. It's not cheap but we'll of course share the bill. You see, my father owns a Spanish restaurant right around the corner from us on Main Street, and I want to tell him about this one."

"Ok let's go there. I've never had any Spanish food

and I'd love to try it." *I hope it won't be too expensive, so what, she said we'll share the bill.*

The drive to the restaurant did not take long. The place looked impressive, with a long bar on which various small dishes were displayed. Michael was not familiar with their contents. A huge selection of alcoholic drinks crowded the shelves on its back wall. Along the opposite wall hung landscape paintings and travel posters from Spain. Round tables with red checkerboard tablecloths, with seats for four people, were dispersed on the floor. Candlelight provided an intimate ambiance.

"These dishes here at the bar are called 'tapas'," Joanna explained. "I personally like the one with cauliflower, capers, and anchovies. There are various kinds of sea food, as you can see, as well as dishes with all sorts of vegetables and potatoes, some in a spicy sauce."

"It looks very good, but is this all there is to eat here? Not that I am very hungry."

"Oh no. Come let us sit at a table where we can also talk a bit. I'll ask for the menu but just to see what they offer. I'll just have some tapas and a beer."

"Me too. I will follow your recommendation. Is there a decent Spanish beer you can recommend? I'd also like some bread with the tapas."

"Not too many. I'll ask what they have here. If you like dark beer, a good one is Alhambra Negra, while a lager is Mahou Five Stars."

Just then, a waiter approached with menus. Joanna looked through hers with considerable attention and said,

"It looks pretty good, except it seems to be geared for American tastes, not quite as authentic as what my father presents. You might like Spanish food, Michael. You know, don't you, that we have our dinner much later than is usual here. Even though my family has been here for generations, we never have our dinner before eight and that is much earlier than in Spain."

"I may like the food but I would be starved waiting that late! What are you going to have?"

"Like I said, some tapas and a beer. Come, let's pick out want we want at the bar."

Waiting for the waiter to bring their order, Joanna asked Michael to tell her a bit about himself other than what he had told her in New York.

"Not much to tell. I grew up in Boston, or more specifically in Brookline. My parents still live there, as I may have told you. My father is a physicist teaching at Northeastern while my mother's somewhat of an artist; some of her paintings have been exhibited in galleries but not too many have been sold. I must have inherited some of her artistic talent – at least I can draw fairly well – and my curiosity to see how things work made me go for Mechanical Engineering. I didn't have to pay tuition, as my father is a professor there. Though Boston is really a nice town, I wanted to be in or near New York City to see what it's like. I got this job in Stamford at a medium-sized company making military ground support equipment. I told you that I'm now also going to Columbia but I'm taking Industrial and Management

Engineering. I want to expand my horizon; a Masters in Mechanical Engineering will not be of much benefit. There you have it."

"Ok, I expect you want to hear a bit about me too, then?" Joanna said after digesting for a minute what she heard. *From what he said it seems he is ambitious. Not a great talker though.*

"As you can tell from our name and my father's occupation we are of Spanish heritage. My great-grandparents arrived in this country in 1919 from a place called Aguilar de la Frontera, not far from Cordoba. That's where our name comes from. As I understand it, at the beginning of the century conditions in Spain were very poor, harvests were insufficient and many people were out of work, so many came here. I have, by the way, two younger sisters, one is eighteen and hasn't decided yet what to do and the other is sixteen."

"You know, I can also claim a bit of Spanish heritage, but it's very far removed. My mother's maiden name is Calderon, which is Spanish as I was told. Hers seems to date back to the time of the expulsion of the Jews from Spain in 1492. After the edict, the family appeared to have wandered all over and finally settled for a long time in Lithuania from where they eventually came to this country. We are Jewish, obviously, but not Orthodox."

The waiter brought their order and the conversation stopped for a while.

"This is real tasty, Joanna. Thanks for suggesting this

place. I can't get over this bread, it has such a special flavor."

"Glad you like it. Yes, I think their stuff is pretty good, except for the prices. The food is certainly no worse, and half the price, at my father's. The bread, by the way, is made with olive oil and therefore the special taste."

"I didn't tell you that I have a sister, she's twenty five, lives with her husband in San Diego and has a two-year-old daughter.

"You'll be surprised to know that we're not Catholics, like most Spaniards or Italians, but Seventh-day Adventists. Have you heard about them?"

"Why, for sure. You keep the Sabbath as a day of rest, not Sunday, just like us. That's nice."

Joanna looked at her watch, a surprised expression on her face.

"Do you know what time it is? I wouldn't be surprised if my parents have gotten worried. Can you imagine? They don't know what I do and how late I am out when at UConn. But when I'm at home it's like I was still a little girl."

"So, let's go. I'll get you home quickly."

The drive back to Bridgeport took only twenty-five minutes since there wasn't any traffic at that time of night. Before getting out of the car, Joanna turned to Michael.

"It was a very nice evening, Michael. Thank you for suggesting it." She looked at him rather questioningly.

"I enjoyed it too Joanna... Can I call you sometime so we might get together again?"

"It all depends on my schedule; call me and I will see."

She left the car and walked quickly to the door of her house. *He's nice; I might go out with him if he calls. I never dated a Jewish boy, nothing wrong with it though.*

Michael drove back deep in thought about the evening. *I wouldn't mind getting to know her better. I think it was a good beginning. Beginning for what? Why not just let things happen as they come? Seventh-day Adventists, what do you know! I wonder what she and her parents think about dating a Jew. I know my parents won't be too happy should this develop into something. How relieved they were when Judy finally married Sam, who's Modern Orthodox.*

CHAPTER 3

A few days later, Michael was over for dinner at his friends David and Helen Gordon's house who lived in Westport. David, also a Bostonian, had gone with Michael to Boston Latin High in the same years but was not in the same class. Both had started in the seventh grade and gone through graduation. They got to know each other as both went to the same Sunday school and, for a time, were inseparable. They met again in the Norwalk Conservative Synagogue and picked up their friendship again. David had graduated from Harvard Law School and had joined a firm in Westport.

Helen opened the door for Michael; her face lit up upon seeing him, and kissed him on the cheek.

"Come on in and make yourself comfortable," she said, pointing to the easy chair in the corner of the smallish living room. "Dave will be with us in a minute, unless you want to join him in the kitchen where he's finishing his famous spaghetti sauce. It will be only the three of us, so don't expect anything fancy; you're considered family, and we don't need to impress you."

"It's just the way I like it. You guys are wonderful. I do smell something good emanating from the kitchen.

Maybe I'll go and see what Dave is doing." With that he went into the kitchen followed by Helen.

"Glad to see that you are doing something constructive, Dave," he said, putting his arm around his friend's shoulder while the latter smiled at him still stirring the sauce in the pot on the fire. "You lawyers don't really contribute much to society. It's just that the law has been purposely made so complicated that it needs people like you to interpret it. That's some way to make money."

"My, you're combative tonight. What's come over you? As for my profession, I think it's a lot better than engineering. After all, a lot of you people make weapons or things connected with them."

"Ok you guys, why all this needling? I suggest we adjourn to the living room as soon as you're finished, Dave, and have a drink. That'll relax you."

"Good idea, Helen. I'll be done in a minute. Why don't you pour something in the meantime? I'll have my regular."

A few minutes later, the three sat sipping their drinks and talking about current events.

"I'm furious Clinton was acquitted in the impeachment trial. The man is a liar. How can we trust him to take the right decisions – either in economics or war?"

"I think you're making too much of this, Helen," said Dave. "How can you compare what he's done with Nixon's foul deeds?"

"I agree with Dave. I think he should be judged on his

actions as President, so far he's been pretty good. One small slip can be excused."

"You guys are just chauvinistic pigs. That's all I have to say. And since we're on the subject of women, how have you been doing Michael? Any conquests lately? I think it's high time you settle down and start raising a family."

"Please, not so fast, Helen. It took you guys a while to tie the knot, and I don't see any offspring yet."

"That was the opening I was looking for; I didn't feel comfortable just blurting it out. You see, we're expecting our first in half a year."

"Why, congratulations! I'm so happy to hear it!" Michael got up and embraced both Helen and David. "As for a girl, I did meet one and took her out to see a play in New Haven just last Saturday, *Richard III*. I recommend it."

"So tell us something about her. How did you meet, what's she like?"

"Don't get so excited, Helen. I met her by chance in New York, and saw her just once more. She seems nice and is very good looking."

"Sure sounds promising. What else can you tell us?"

"Only that she's a senior at UConn, interested in history and is a Seventh-day Adventist."

"You don't say," David exclaimed. "You haven't gone out with too many non-Jewish girls. Actually, you haven't gone out with too many girls altogether! Your parents won't be too happy about her not being Jewish."

"Why are you making it into such a big deal? I'm not marrying the girl yet. We don't know each other very well. Why don't we change the subject?"

"OK, you're the engineer. What do you make of the Y2K scare? The millennium is just around the corner and people are afraid all computers will crash."

"I'm not a computer maven, and supposedly it is a matter of software. Something to do with the fact that only the last two digits of the year have been used and there is no year zero-zero. This has been known for years and I'm sure that it's been taken care of. No need to worry."

They sat around for quite a while, chatting amiably until Michael, looking at his watch, exclaimed that it was getting pretty late, as he had to get to work early the next day.

"Thanks for a lovely dinner and evening, guys. I'm sure excited about your wonderful news. I can hardly wait to see the offspring."

He left thinking about whether to call Joanna or not.

When he did call, Michael felt as if a burden had been lifted as Joanna readily agreed to meet with him a week from the following Friday.

"I'm glad you called, Michael. I think it's a good idea to meet in a restaurant so we can sit and talk over a leisurely meal. It would probably be best if it's at some place in Bridgeport so you won't have to drive back and forth. Do you have any suggestions as to a nice place?"

"I'm afraid I'm not very familiar with restaurants in Bridgeport, I do know the area of Norwalk-Stamford pretty well. But you're right, it'll be better in your town. Can you recommend a place?"

"Not really, but what do you think of eating at my parent's restaurant? At least I can be sure the food is good. *Why did I suggest this? I hardly know the guy, he might think I'm pushing things. Well it's done.*

Michael was astounded at Joanna's invitation, and hesitated a moment before replying that he would very much like that. *I wonder if she wants her parents to look me over, maybe see if I know how to eat properly. It's possible that Joanna never went out with a Jewish guy. From the little I know about Seventh-day Adventists, they are very strict Christians in spite of their few Jewish customs.*

It was with some trepidation that Michael drove to Bridgeport on Friday evening having put on his best, and only other, jacket, grey slacks and matching shirt and tie. This time it was Joanna who opened the door for him and greeted him an uncertain smile on her face.

"Good to see you Michael, come on in. Why don't we sit in the living room for a while before going around the corner to the restaurant? We'll meet both my parents there as they are working now. I'm sure I can scrounge something up to drink."

"That sounds just fine. From what you said, you people are used to having dinner at a much later hour. *Maybe I will have to get used to the idea if I keep going out with her.* So how have you been? I suppose you've quite a bit of studying to do these days, what with finals coming up."

"It's not too bad actually. I mainly have to work on my thesis. We're given a choice of writing a paper or taking the history final."

"That's interesting. Not so usual for a B.A. What are you writing about?"

"I'm taking a rather obscure work, *Historica Francorum* by Gregory of Tours. I'll try to show how we should analyze such texts in terms of the period as well as the writer and his background."

"It sounds really interesting. I must confess I've never heard of him. When did he live?"

"In the better part of the sixth century. He's actually considered one of the first historians after the Roman period. I'm afraid you engineers don't take enough liberal arts courses. Isn't that so?"

"You're absolutely right. We just have to take one liberal arts class a term – like music appreciation, history or art. Most people don't take them seriously since they carry little weight in terms of the professional evaluation. Personally, I've always loved reading historical novels, and I spent hours looking at encyclopedias as a kid. Today we have the internet of course."

"Feel like going to eat now? I know you are not used to our late hours."

"Sure. I really appreciate you suggesting we go to your parent's restaurant. I look forward to meeting your father too."

The small restaurant was nearly full of guests when Joanna and Michael entered. Joanna's father was talking with one of the diners but looked up and, upon seeing them come in, excused himself and came over.

"You must be Michael," he said, shaking his hand. "I'm Joanna's father. Glad to have you here. We've kept a table for you two; I hope you'll like our food. From what Joanna told me, you're not very familiar with Spanish cuisine. My wife is in the kitchen right now, by the way, giving instructions as she usually does. I believe you've met her."

"Glad to meet you, sir. Yes, I had the pleasure of meeting your wife and, as far as the food is concerned I'm sure I'll like it very much. Thank you for having me."

They sat at the table reserved for them with Joanna explaining the various dishes on the menu.

"I suggest we have a few tapas and, as our main course, the seafood paella. It's a very tasty rice dish made with saffron and all kinds of spices, laced with olive oil and cooked with the seafood. It'll take a while since it's prepared individually for each guest. The paella will come as a dish for two. As you see, we don't have too many desserts here. There are pestinos which are sweet fritters, Flao which is a cheesecake I highly recommend and arroz con leche, a pudding which also very good."

"Well, I see we won't go hungry, I must say the aroma here is heavenly and it sure works up the appetite, which anyway is present."

A waiter came over greeting Joanna familiarly, introduced himself to Michael and took their order.

"So how is your thesis coming along, Joanna? Working very hard?"

"Not too bad. It's almost finished, and I mostly have to proof it and add a couple of things that I only found out recently. Doing the research was a lot of fun, actually."

"Well, I'd be glad to read it if you want me to. Like I said, I am interested in history but don't know anything about the period you mentioned. Do you have anything lined up as far as a teaching position is concerned for the fall?"

"Not really. I've made some inquiries but will start to look seriously in June. I need a job since I don't want to continue living with my parents and being a burden."

"I can understand that. I was glad to move out, though I have wonderful warm parents. They were quite unhappy that by moving here none of their children are close by. Maybe I'll move back to Boston one day, it really is a nice town."

Just then, Joanna's mother came out of the kitchen to sit with them for a few minutes. Michael stood up, thanking her for having him.

"Nice seeing you again. I hope you will enjoy our food. Joanna said that you are not familiar with it."

"I'm sure will love it. The smell emanating from your kitchen is heavenly. It must be hard to run a successful restaurant."

"Yes, it was at the beginning for some years. Now I'm not cooking anymore, mostly overseeing everything. Together with my husband, we decide on the menu and do most of the shopping. He takes care of the administrative tasks. I'll let you have your dinner now."

The tapas came quickly to Michael's delight. He did not feel comfortable asking Joanna to talk more about herself, as much as he wanted to. *She seems like such a beautiful, smart girl who, I am sure, has plenty of admirers. What do I have to offer? Why am I always putting myself down?*

"You know, Joanna, these tapas are better than what we had after the play in New Haven… Tell me, have your parents always been in the restaurant business? It must be a very demanding job."

"Not only my parents; my family has been in the business for generations. In the old country, it was customary for the oldest son to take on his father's profession, and here many like us keep the tradition. I don't think, however, that I or my sisters will continue with it. Cooking is very creative but, like you said, it's a very tough and competitive business."

"I'm always impressed when people keep traditions handed down from generation to generation. Continuity is, I guess, comfortable. I told you we are not Orthodox, yet my mother lights candles every Friday evening to honor the Sabbath like it has been done for ages. At home, we always sort of kept the Sabbath somewhat special, not necessarily going to the synagogue but trying not to work and instead doing something enjoyable for the whole family."

"It sounds like what we do although usually one of my parents goes to church for Vespers on Friday evening and one or both will go Saturday morning. As a matter of fact, my mother told me that Friday candle lighting was a tradition in our family before we became Seventh-day

Adventists. I suppose it was one of the reasons we left the Catholic faith and became Seventh-day Adventists. It is, of course, not easy to run a restaurant and keep strictly to our faith. Obviously, we can't close on Saturday but we open only at 5 PM."

The paella finally arrived emanating a marvelous aroma that had Michael exclaim:

"Wow, I never had anything looking and smelling so good. It seems like quite a bit for just two people, but I'll try my best to do it justice."

It did not take long before they finished the paella. The Spanish beer was also very good.

"What about dessert?" Joanna asked.

"As much as I would like to, I'm just too full."

"How about sharing one? I love desserts. Let me suggest it: I mentioned the pestinos, flao, and ensaimada and a few more, if you remember what they are."

"I believe flao was a cheesecake, right? Why don't we have that, if you like it?"

"So how was it?" Joanna asked when they had finished the cake together with some strong coffee.

"It was delicious. It reminds me somewhat of what my grandmother used to make. She passed away four years ago."

They sat for some time talking about Michael's work and Joanna's school until Michael noticed people standing waiting for a table. He suggested they leave, which Joanna readily agreed. As it was not very late Joanna suggested they stop for a while at her place and listen to some music. *I wonder if it means something. Though she does not seem to be a girl looking for on-night stands. She really is nice and I don't want to spoil what may become a relationship by doing something rash.* "I would love to. What kind do you like?"

"I like mainly folk and country music. I hate the current loud booming pop and rock music. People at school think I'm odd, and maybe it's true."

"I'm with you on that. I also like classical music, the romantic kind; you know 19th century. I am also a little odd in that I like opera. I absolutely melt hearing one of the great voices."

They sat on the Aguilar living room sofa listening to Irish folksongs and Spanish flamenco while sipping some of the parents' brandy.

"You know, Joanna, once my good friends David and Helen took me to a flamenco show in some small nightclub in the village in New York. It was not just fascinating but it hit me emotionally. I don't know what it was which made me feel that way. I was told that the music draws on old Spanish, Arabic and Jewish sources. I suppose you might know something about it."

"Not really, though I grew up on it. I think the music itself is very haunting; the dance depends very much on the performer. You are right it can be electrifying when done well, but also boring when a poor performer does it."

Michael looked at his watch and said, "It's getting quite late, don't you think? I guess your parents will close up soon and I don't want to disturb."

"We wouldn't disturb them. They will be home any

minute but will go right upstairs to their bedroom.But I guess you are right, it's about time to say goodnight. I very much enjoyed the evening, Michael. Give me a call, and if I don't have too much work we can do something again."

Both got up and walked to the front door. Michael looked at Joanna questioningly for a few seconds when Joanna put her hand on his shoulders and kissed him briefly on the cheek.

"It was a lovely evening Joanna, thank you so much again." With that, Michael turned around, opened the door, looked back and waved at Joanna. *I guess most guys would have stayed and tried to go as far as I would have let them after what I said about my parents being upstairs. I don't know what to make of Michael; is he just shy with girls or maybe gay? I like him, he seems very nice. Let's see what develops.*

During the drive back to Norwalk Michael kept wondering whether Joanna had actually wanted him to stay. He could not of course come to a conclusion. He was home when another thought began to bother him. *Her family comes from Spain, and it seems they had kept, for some reason, a few Jewish customs. Now I read about the Marranos, those Jews who converted to Christianity to escape the prosecution of the Inquisition, and wanted to stay in the country after the edict of expulsion in 1492. Is it possible that they are descendants of our people? Maybe they don't know it themselves. I must talk to Joanna about it, but then she might think me too nosy, or that I'm trying to have them change their religion.*

CHAPTER 4

Michael had thought of calling Joanna to make a date with her for the following weekend, when he suddenly remembered that the coming Saturday was his father's sixtieth birthday, and he wanted to be home on that day. He anyway did not want to appear too anxious and decided to wait until later in the week to call her. He bought his father Thomas Friedman's book *From Beirut to Jerusalem*, considering his interest in Israel and its political and security problems. He drove up to Brookline on Friday after work; getting there, dead tired, about nine.

"Michael! We haven't seen you in ages. Come let me look at you. You must be tired," his mother said, embracing her son who reciprocated, kissing her warmly. "Ben, Michael is here," she shouted.

They walked towards the living room when his father, dressed in an old flannel shirt, chinos and slippers, came towards them and hugged Michael strongly.

"Hi Dad, you're looking good for your age. What's new in physics? Any new laws lately?"

"Still the wise guy. What you need is a good wife to teach you manners, apparently we haven't succeeded in doing that. How have you been, son?"

"Pretty good, am enjoying my studies, work is reasonably interesting, but could be more."

"What about your social life? Is there anything new that would interest us?"

"Why don't you ask it straight, dad. Yes, I am going out with a girl. No, I am not getting married yet."

"OK, you guys," Michael's mother interposed. "Enough of that. Come, let us eat. We've been waiting for you to come and it is getting very late."

Michael's sister, Deborah, arrived the following morning with her two-year-old, exhausted after taking the red-eye from San Diego. She came by herself, as her husband was away on a business trip. She went to sleep for a couple of hours while the parents and Michael tried to occupy the little girl, who was quite rambunctious for her age. It was only at lunch that the family finally got together, sharing memories, enjoying each other after many months of distance. The afternoon was devoted to preparations for the party that was scheduled for the early evening. Rachel and Deborah worked in the kitchen while Michael hung various decorations and balloons to give the place a festive look.

The guests started to arrive, bringing small presents, with some of the wives coming with home baked cakes and other delicacies. Most of the invitees were friends and colleagues of Benjamin, a few were neighbors. Soon the house was filled with noisy chatter, which increased with the quantity of spiked punch and other alcoholic drinks imbibed. Benjamin's good friend Prof. Amos Goldberg of Brandeis University gave a lengthy speech laced with a great deal of humor in honor of Benjamin's 60th birthday. After that, everybody went to partake in the rich buffet, trying to find a place to sit rather than eat standing up. Amos had noticed Michael standing in the back, and went up to him with his plate in his hand.

"Michael, I haven't seen you in ages. How's it going with you? Boy, does the time fly. I remember you still in diapers. How old are you, 22 or 23?"

"Hate to disappoint you, but I'm 25. I have been working four years now since I graduated from Northeastern."

"You're an engineer, aren't you? Married? Your parents mentioned that you live down in Connecticut and do not come up often enough. All parents say that, actually."

"Well, I try to come, but am quite busy with finishing up my Masters at Columbia on a part-time basis after work. No, I'm not married yet. These days most men don't marry as early as in your generation. We feel there is no rush; life expectancy is longer, and anyway the traditional institution of marriage has taken a beating with not only postponement, but also many one-parent families and gay ones. But tell me Amos, you're an expert on Jewish history, what can you tell me about the *Marranos*?"

"Wow, you sure are asking a five minute answer on a subject one can talk about for hours. What is your interest in this topic? You're not changing your field to history, are you?"

"Oh no, just a personal interest. I have a girlfriend who's a Seventh-day Adventist. She's of Spanish descent.

Some of her present religious practices, and those in her family when still Catholic, are to my mind distinctly Jewish. Could her ancestors have been *Marranos*?"

"First of all, let me tell you that the word *Marranos* is a pejorative one. Back in the 15th century, it denoted a pig. We prefer to call those Jews that converted to Christianity whether by force or choice '*Conversos*'. Secondly, there is no quick answer to your question. The prevalent idea that conversion started only when the Jews of Spain were given a choice of either leaving the country or converting is very wrong. Papal inquisition started with the re-conquest of Spain by the Christians back at the beginning of the 13th century. Towards the end of the 14th century vicious anti-Jewish pogroms took place in various cities like Cordoba, Valencia and Seville, which led many to convert for the sake of safety. The Spanish Inquisition was started in 1478 because it was believed that many converted Jews practiced their religion in secret. It was charged with finding these Jews and bringing them before their court. The fact is, many converted Jews reached high positions, which kindled jealousy and hatred amongst the Christian population. This found outlets in spectacles of public torture and burning of Jews convicted by the Inquisition. I should also mention that Jewish presence in Spain dates back a very long time. Many came from Palestine after the destruction of the second temple in 70AD and more after the defeat of Bar-Kochba in his revolt against the Romans in 132AD. There were those who came to settle directly in Spain while others first sojourned in Rome."

"It's interesting you mentioned Cordoba. This girlfriend of mine told me that her family, back several generations, came from a town not far from the city."

"It may be just a coincidence but it can be worthwhile to look into this. Not that I can tell you right now how to go about it. Speaking of your girlfriend, I don't think your parents will be very happy if this relationship gets to be serious and leads to marriage. As it is, our people are suffering demographically, many of the mixed marriages lead to a net loss in our numbers."

"Not to worry, Amos. I have been out with this girl only a few times, and I have certainly no intention yet to get married. But thank you very much for your informative review of the Marra... oops... *Conversos*."

CHAPTER 5

I wonder why Michael hasn't called me. Joanna thought. *Was I too forward for him? He's not one to pounce on a girl, so maybe he thinks I should be as straight-laced as he is. To hell with it, why am I so bothered about it? He's just a guy I went out with a few times.*

It was two days later that Michael called explaining he had to be in Boston for his father's birthday over the previous weekend while also finishing a big paper for school. "Are you free this coming weekend?" he asked. "There's a big new exhibit at the Met of Egyptian artifacts, as well as one of Chinese paintings. I could come up to Bridgeport and we could take the train into Manhattan or drive, whatever."

"Gee, that sounds like a good idea." *I better say I'm busy, not to give the impression that I'm too anxious to go out with him whenever he calls. Am I really anxious?* "Not this weekend, Michael. I have a couple of exams coming up. How about the weekend after, OK? Give me a call sometime at the beginning of the following week."

Michael drove up to Bridgeport on Saturday morning, getting to Joanna's parents a little before eight-thirty. They had just enough time to get to the station to catch the 8:53 train to New York. Knowing the wealth of the museum, they wanted to be there early before the huge crowds that normally come on weekends. During the hour-and-twenty-minute ride, they talked about school, work, museums and the weather; avoiding anything more personal that could be construed as wishing for a more intimate relationship. Arriving at the museum, they found it packed at that relatively early hour, and they had to stand in line for tickets.

The exhibits were everything they had expected and more. Most remarkable was a reproduction of a royal burial chamber with all its colorful hieroglyphic inscriptions. There was the head of Nefertiti, on loan from a museum in Berlin, mummies and sarcophagi, innumerable animal figurines of exquisite beauty, as well as gold ornaments that looked as if they were made in this century and were worn by wealthy women.

"Isn't it remarkable how beautiful this queen of Egypt is, she looks just like any beautiful woman today," said Joanna, to which Michael agreed wholeheartedly. Standing before the various displays, their hands touched occasionally while absorbed in viewing an object. It was after several such times that Michael finally built up enough courage to take Joanna's hand and hold it. *Do I really want to have a relationship with this man?* went through Joanna's mind. Her answer was clear; she left her hand in his and responded with a slight pressure. Still, they avoided looking at each other for fear of expressing too much. As planned, they then went on to the old

Chinese painting gallery, which took Joanna by surprise.

"Look at these scrolls," she said, "They actually show the life as it was long ago. It's better than reading history books. I am so glad, Michael, that you suggested we come here," she said, smiling at him affectionately. It was by that time close to 1PM, and they decided they had seen enough and, anyway, it was time for lunch.

"We can either have a sandwich here in the museum or go downtown to have something more substantial. What would you like, Joanna?"

"Look, it's such a nice day, why don't we have a quick sandwich here and go to the park and enjoy the sun. We don't have to be back early, do we?"

"I have no plans. Let's do it. And it might be a fitting way to end the day if we go later to Chinatown for dinner. What do you think?"

"Great, I'd love to."

The way to the exit brought them through a hall where a numismatic collection was displayed showing coins of the ancient Middle East. On display were cases showing those of Phoenicia, the Parthian, Seleucid and Byzantine empires, and others. The case with Judean coins caught Michael's eyes, and he asked Joanna to look at them for a minute.

"I have never seen these before. Look, there are coins from the Hasmonean and Herodian kingdoms, as well as those from the time of the Jewish wars against Rome. I believe it was around the first century AD the Great War took place that resulted in the destruction of the temple, and some years later the Bar-Kochba rebellion took place. I learned about some of this in Sunday school. Aren't these amazing? This coin of the Bar-Kochba period shows a structure depicting the Temple according to the explanation here."

"It's interesting to see all this. We didn't get to see them, unfortunately, in the history books I was exposed to. They should have shown just a few when discussing a particular period."

"You know what makes me mad, Jo? It's the denial of those Moslem rulers who not only claim there was no Holocaust but deny the existence of Jewish independence in what are now Israel and the West Bank. It is here to see, and also in various archeological excavations."

After a quick lunch in the museum cafeteria, Joanna and Michael entered Central Park just one block south at 81st street. They did not have to go far to feel the beauty and tranquility of their surroundings, not many people were to be seen at this hour. They walked for a while until their hands naturally found each other as they neared the turtle pond. They continued leisurely finding their way to the Shakespearean garden, where they saw a secluded bench and sat down in the serene place warmed by the early afternoon sun.

"My, this is wonderful, Michael," Joanna said, turning to her companion, an expression of pleasure on her face. Michael looked at her for what seemed a while, but was measured in seconds, and pulled her to him, kissing her deeply on her responding lips.

"You're such a lovely girl, Joanna; I feel good just being with you. Come, let's learn more about each other. You'll be graduating soon and move to Bridgeport, so we'll have more of a chance to be together than now." Joanna did not say anything for what seemed to Michael like an eternity until she replied. "I am fond of you, Michael. Let's try and see what develops. I've been disappointed before and don't expect too much at the beginning of a relationship, if we can call ours the start of one. I hope you're not such a romantic as to imagine us living happily ever after together."

"I must confess that I consider myself inclined to be romantic, but I'm also quite level-headed and don't get carried away by unrealistic notions. After all, I'm an engineer who, supposedly, is trained to evaluate things logically. I've had experiences that started out well but did not work out because of basic incompatibility. I will say that I don't like one-night stands, as they are meaningless. There must be more to making love to a girl than getting rid of one's desire. Does that sound very old fashioned to you?"

"Sure does. But you know what? I find it refreshing and attractive. It's also somewhat rare these days, unfortunately."

"I try very hard not to be a conformist, though I must be to some extent. Look, I chose a conservative profession rather than becoming an artist or something. I like to draw, I like music, but again, old-fashioned classical music. On the other hand, I hate repetition, doing the same thing over and over again. You see, I'm about to try a different direction in engineering. It's not much of a change, but still."

"Don't expect too much of me, Michael. I'm just starting on a career that I hopefully will like. I don't know what to expect out of life. I have good hard-working parents but cannot see myself living as they do. There must be something else, but I don't know what. Does that make sense?"

"Sure, at this stage none of us can have a clear idea of what is best for us, what are our possibilities, how we can contribute; in other words, who we are. Come, let's walk a little more. I hope we'll have plenty of time to try and sort things out. I saw a sign to a Swedish Cottage. Let's go and see what it is."

The cottage turned out to be a 19th century schoolhouse, to be viewed in a few minutes. They continued to amble along, exiting the Park and going over to Lexington Avenue and 86th Street to take the subway to Canal Street and Chinatown.

"I hope you're familiar with Chinatown, Michael. I've only been there once with my parents, and it was some years ago. Do you know of any recommended restaurants?"

"I've been down here a number of times. I can think of two right now. One is Ping's Seafood and the other is Wo Hop. Both are on Mott Street near each other. The first is fancier while the second is less expensive but crowded and noisy with shared tables. The food is good in both. What do you say?"

"Let's go to Wo Hop."

The restaurant was not only crowded, but a few people were even waiting outside to be seated. However, it didn't take too long before they were shown to a vacant table with two seats.

"My, the food is really good and I rather like the informality," Joanna said after they had finished their main course. "There is a good variety and the prices are reasonable. We didn't have to wait too long to be served."

"You are so right. But what I really want to say is it I felt so good and relaxing with you the entire day. It seems to me as if we've known each other for quite a while. With you, I don't feel like I have to try and impress you, I can be myself, it feels so natural."

"Well, it's a good beginning but let's not get carried away. I agree we've had a wonderful day, but it's time now to start heading home. It will have been a very long day by the time we get back."

"Sure, let's just get the check and go."

They rode back to Bridgeport in near silence, each going over the events of the day, and the possible significance it had for them.

"Well here we are, Joanna. It has been a wonderful day for me and I hope for you too. I will call you, OK?"

"Sure, do, and thank you. This day was your idea and I enjoyed every minute of it. I hope I won't be too busy now, with the end of the term in sight."

Joanna opened the car door, but turned to Michael, a serious expression on her face, and kissed him fleetingly on the lips before quickly leaving the car. She turned around and waved to him just as he started to pull away from the curb. *Am I getting deep into an affair with her?* Michael wondered. *I've known her for such a short time. She does seem like such a nice girl. What do I want? Let's see how things develop. What will my parents say if we really get serious? Hell, why worry about it now, maybe she does come from a Converso family. Wouldn't that be something?*

Chapter 6

A couple of days after their trip to New York, David called Michael asking if he was free the following evening to go to dinner and possibly to a movie, as Helen had gone for two days to be with a sick aunt of hers in Philadelphia.

"Sure thing, Dave. I have nothing planned; anyway I feel like taking off from doing homework in the evening. Why don't you come to my place, say around six thirty? Then we can decide what to do."

"Ok, it's a date."

David came promptly at the agreed time.

"Great idea, Dave. We haven't done this in quite a while. Not that I'm glad that Helen's aunt is sick, and she had to go down to Philly. Have you looked in the paper to see what's playing?"

"Yeah, I noticed that in the Bow Tie Regent, on North Main Street, they're showing *Shakespeare in Love*. Have you seen it?"

"No. As a matter of fact, I have wanted to go but never got around to it. Let's go. We can eat before the movie at one of the restaurants nearby in South Norwalk."

"Why don't we go to that little Chinese restaurant there? I haven't had Chinese food in ages. Helen isn't a great fan of it. Is that ok?"

"Sure why not, though I was down with Joanna in Chinatown this past Saturday and had a nice meal there."

"Well, well. So you are seeing this girl regularly?"

"Just a few times. Let's go; we can talk about it later."

The Chinese restaurant had been at the same location for a very long time. The present owner was the son of the chef who had worked there after its opening, and had taken over the ownership with his boss's retirement. It was quite empty when the two friends arrived. They ordered a set menu, which promptly started to arrive at the table.

"So how was your trip to Chinatown with your girlfriend? What's her name again?"

"Joanna. We actually spent the day in New York, going first to the Metropolitan Museum, then spent some time in Central Park and went to Chinatown in the late afternoon."

"That sounds real nice. I take it both of you have found some mutual interest in each other? What's she like and what about her religion, you said she was a Seventh-day Adventist?"

"She seems very intelligent and looks nice. What more do you want to know? Have I slept with her? That's none of your business. I'm not too worried right now about her religious beliefs. From where her family came from and the fact that they keep the Sabbath makes me think that they are possibly *Conversos*, although it would be very hard to establish this as fact."

"Well, good luck in your relationship. You know Helen and I would love to meet her."

"Sure, why not? But first let me see how things develop."

The conversation then switched to politics, with Michael bemoaning the fact that NATO had started to bomb the Serbian forces in Kosovo.

"I don't see why they, with the US in the lead, should resort to this kind of intervention. Sure the Serbians have done some pretty awful things but the Bosnians are no angels either. What makes it unacceptable to me is the heavy loss of civilian lives as a result of these bombings."

"How else can the Serbian atrocities be stopped? Sending in troops will cause a lot of casualties on our side."

"So you think it's better to kill civilians than soldiers? I always thought the reason we have armies is to fight the enemy when the cause is just; civilians should be involved as little as is possible."

"Who knows what's really going on there? The media sure isn't a truthful source for information. Maybe the extent of the killings of Bosnians have not been reported to avoid inflaming the situation further or maybe the situation on the ground is such that this is the quickest way to stop the slaughter, therefore reducing the overall number of civilian casualties. What I am more concerned with is the election of Barak as Israel's Prime Minister. Not that Netanyahu was so great, but I fear this macho general will offer the Arabs more than

Israel can afford without losing its capability to defend itself. Unfortunately, I don't see any move by the so-called Palestinians to stop their incitement and give up their aim to annihilate Israel. Israel doesn't appear on their maps at all."

"You know, American politics are bad enough, but for the life of me I cannot understand those in Israel. I believe it was Kissinger who said Israel has no foreign policy, only internal politics. I really cannot relate to what you said. I can only hope that people in Israel will be safe and the country will prosper. Do you know what time it is? We better pay the check and go to the movie if we don't want to miss the show."

They both enjoyed the movie and parted after Michael dropped his friend off at his house where David had left his car.

Is it too late to call Joanna now and try and make a date with her? Michael wondered when he returned to his apartment. He finally decided to do it in the morning. Joanna was just about to go to a class when he reached her.

"How have you been Joanna? Working hard? I hope we can get together sometime soon. I am pretty much finished with all the requirements in school. Graduation will be first week in June."

"I wish we could, Michael, but I have finals this week, I need to put some finishing touches on my thesis, which I have to hand in by May 31, the last day of school. It seems I have no time to breathe lately. My graduation will be a week after yours, on the 13th. How about a week from Saturday? We'll decide in the meantime on what to do. I will be completely free by then."

"Great, we'll talk about the details a few days before. Are you staying in the dorms or will you be going home right after school ends?"

"I guess I'll be going home, although I may stay a few more days here depending on what my friends will do. You can call me at home or I may call you, whatever."

"I sure look forward to being with you Joanna. Best of luck on the exams and the thesis."

Michael was in seventh heaven when Joanna called him a week later. He had thought about her a lot since they last spoke and debated with himself as to when to get in touch with her.

"Hi Michael, I'm relieved to have handed in my thesis before the deadline. Finals haven't been so bad, I only have one more to go. So how about getting together Saturday or Sunday? I will be home by then."

"I'm so glad you called. I'm free on Saturday; no more schoolwork. Sunday is my graduation. Do you have any suggestions on what to do?"

"Not really, why don't you come to Bridgeport in the morning, say around nine, and we'll decide. Sorry I forgot about your graduation on Sunday. How were your finals? I never asked you about your thesis. Will I understand the title?"

"You sure can. I wrote about the future of the US automobile industry after reviewing the various engines once used, technological developments and competitive industries in various countries. Right now, though, I'd rather think about our date! I've worked my tail off on this study, and I'm sure nobody will pay any attention to it anyway. I'll pick you up at your parents' on Saturday."

"I sure look forward to it. And, Michael, don't be so modest. Maybe some manufacturer will learn something from it."

"Any changes that must be introduced will cost a lot of money, all the various makers have a lot invested in their present equipment and facilities, part of which will go down the drain. It will take a lot of guts to make the needed changes. I'm afraid it won't come to pass until the foreign competition, which is taking a great chunk of automobile sales in the world, will threaten to reduce ours to a fraction of what it is now. I hope I'm not boring you with my sad story. See you on Saturday."

I believe Joanna really wants to enter into a serious relationship with me. I just have that feeling. Michael thought while driving up to Bridgeport on the rainy Saturday morning. *Is this what I also want? What am I afraid of? Is it her religious beliefs and how they would affect us? I must let myself be guided by my feelings, try not to always analyze things. Heck, what are we going to do today in this lousy weather?* Michael's thoughts wandered until he found himself in front of Joanna's house.

Joanna opened the front door just a short while after Michael rang the bell. A wide smile was on her face and both looked at each other for a few seconds before she stepped into Michaels outstretched arms and kissed him hungrily, their lips clinging together, their bodies searching each other as if they were meant to be one.

"Come on in," whispered Joanna turning around and, taking Michael's hand, guided him to the living room sofa. "My, you got wet just by coming in from the car. It really is lousy weather, cold for this time of the year. Want something warm to drink?"

"No, not really. Come, let us just sit here for a while. You are so beautiful, I feel I can look at you forever."

With that, Michael bent over Joanna and kissed her deeply, both exploring each other's mouth, their passion mounting. Joanna pulled back a little, looking at Michael, smiled at him and said:

"My parents aren't home, my middle sister, Vanessa, is at work in Brentano's and the little one, Eleanora, is of course at school. So we have the house to ourselves. We can go up to my room, Michael."

It took Michael a few seconds to absorb her meaning and then he looked crestfallen. "Joanna, dear," he said his voice almost inaudible. "I feel like a damned fool. I don't have any protection with me. I was not sure of your feelings. There is nothing I want more. What will you think of me?"

"I think you are very sweet, considerate and, like I said, a bit old fashioned. All of which makes me rather fond of you. You can remedy the situation, if you want, by going just two blocks to the drugstore; it's on the right as you come out. But let's wait until the rain stops."

Michael did not wait, he got up to go to the door

and Joanna quickly went to the closet and gave him an umbrella before he had a chance to leave. He was back in no time having run all the way and back. The mood, however, had evaporated by then and, at Joanna's suggestion, they sat in the kitchen drinking coffee and eating doughnuts.

"You know, Joanna, I like nothing better than being with you. I hope we'll now be able to see more of each other once we're finished with school."

"Yes, I'd like that. I also feel comfortable in your company and want to see how things will work out. What would you like to do now? Shall we go some place?"

In response, Michael stood up, took her hand and said with a big smile: "Yes, I would like to go upstairs. How about it?" Joanna rose, looked at Michael, her face serious, and responded with a throaty yes, pulling him in the direction of the stairway. At the entrance to her room, Michael grabbed her from behind, spun her around and enfolded her in his arms, kissing her passionately. Joanna responded willingly, her hands on Michael's back, pulling him closer, his manhood pressing strongly against her. Impatiently, they started to undress each other throwing their clothes all over and then tumbled on the bed, their hands discovering each other, their ardor increasing, until Michael suddenly sat up and looked at Joanna as she was lying on her back, her eyes questioning.

"I nearly lost my head, Joanna. You are so beautiful, I cannot take my eyes off you, it will be just a second," he said while fumbling with his trousers trying to take one of the condoms out. He finally succeeded putting it on his extended member. Joanna pulled him back down and he entered her forcefully. *What a girl.* Michael thought *Passionate, beautiful and nice to be with. I hope she feels good about me.* With that, he tried to restrain himself waiting for her climax, which soon came together with his. Michael felt himself lifted into spheres as yet unknown. Panting, they lay side-by-side holding hands, their eyes interlocked for what seemed a very long time. *I guess I am lucky,* went through Joanna's mind. *Maybe he is the man I was looking for. He is sweet, considerate and good in bed.* Joanna rested her head on Michael's chest while one hand of his was cradling one firm breast. They stayed this way, drowsily, for a while until Michael asked what time Eleanora was expected home from school.

"Oh, not until two thirty at the earliest. We are in no rush but maybe we should think about having lunch soon. I can fix us something and then we can go out somewhere."

"Is there anything to do in Bridgeport or should we think of something farther?"

"Well, Bridgeport is not an interesting a city. There are some nice parks, one can go deep sea fishing if you go for that sort of thing, there is the Barnum Museum, and the Discovery Museum. You might like the latter. I was there once, many years ago and it was quite interesting."

"OK, let's go there."

They got up, dressed and went down to the kitchen where Joanna quickly made a tuna salad and fixed delicious sandwiches in no time. They ate, drinking coffee, taking their time mostly looking at each other until Michael said; "You know, it feels so domestic as if we have been doing this forever. I like it."

"Me too, but let us not get carried away. There's no rush. It may work out but it's much too early to tell." Joanna thought for a minute and continued. "How about coming to my graduation? You've met my parents, but my sisters will be there, and one of my uncles, a favorite of mine."

Michael was surprised, especially following what she had said before.

"Are you sure? How about tickets? I only got two for my graduation. I very much would have liked you to come; you know that my graduation is tomorrow. As it is, my parents will come down by train from Boston. There will be about 7,000 graduates and there is no more room in the quadrangle than them and about 15,000 guests."

"No problem with tickets. UConn has that many graduates, too, but there are also several smaller campuses in different towns and Storrs sits on some 4,000 acres with huge lawns, so I was able to get six. You will make the sixth. You know, I would have gladly come to your graduation but I am glad you do not have enough tickets. I am a little afraid to meet your parents in these circumstances. At another time, gladly. You have met mine, anyway."

The visit to the Discovery Museum was a letdown. It was more suitable for kids. Only a few of the exhibits required explanations, which Michael provided. They decided to go to the Sea Side Park, the day being quite warm for the very beginning of June and it had cleared nicely after the rain.

"I love the sea," Michael said gripping Joanna's hand more firmly," and being here with you makes it just perfect." Joanna returned the pressure and they kept on walking until getting to the lighthouse. A bench there invited them to sit and rest, looking at the slight breakers coming into shore.

"I think I could sit here forever," Joanna said. "Would you believe it, I've never been on a boat. I'm a little afraid of being on the water. It's nice looking at it from here."

"Being on a ship is the greatest experience. It's hard to describe the feeling of being in the midst of the ocean with nothing but the sea around you. It is the most peaceful place to be when the weather is good. One can relax completely. My parents took my sister and me once on a seven-day cruise from Boston to Bermuda. We were kids then, and I will never forget the experience. I bet you would like it too. I would love to travel to different countries. Hopefully I'll one day be in a position to afford doing it with my family."

"Yes, going to different places and seeing other cultures are my ambition too. The first place would be Spain; looking for the roots my family has talked about."

"I wouldn't mind going there, either. I told you that my mother's maiden name is of Spanish origin. Unfortunately, I know nothing about her family's history. All I know is that they came to this country from Eastern Europe at the beginning of the century."

"I know a little about Jewish religion and history. We had a one-semester course on comparative religions. It was rather superficial. I learned about the expulsion, it happened in the same year that Columbus set out West and discovered America. I don't know much about what happened to the Jews in Spain."

"Yes, it's an important part of our history. Actually, not all the Jews left Spain. Many converted to Christianity in order to remain. Many of these conversions actually took place during a century or more before the expulsion because of the discrimination and persecution of Jews throughout the years. Many of the converted Jews actually tried to practice their religion in secret. Those who were found out by the Church were severely punished and burned at the stake. They were called *Conversos* or *Marranos*. Have you ever heard of these terms?"

"No, I never have. I really should learn more about our Spanish history. Unfortunately, in high school, we mostly learned American history and some Greek and Roman. In college, as a history major, I was of course exposed also to general European history, especially the Renaissance; the French revolution, the Industrial Revolution, Marxism and, naturally this century with all its terrible events."

"I can recommend some books if you have the time and inclination to read heavy stuff. One is *The Marranos of Spain: From the late 14th to the early 16th Century* by an author called B. Netanyahu. We should talk about it some more, but I think it's getting late. Would you like to have dinner some place?"

"Sure. How about coming to our restaurant?"

"It was wonderful, but I don't want to burden your parents again. Any place you suggest would be fine."

"OK, I know a little Italian place. It should be nice."

Dinner was pleasant; the atmosphere intimate yet both felt a certain let-down from the heights experienced earlier in the day. They held hands, looked at each other constantly, but were shy and reluctant to talk more about their feelings and hopes. After dinner, Michael took Joanna home, both finding it hard to part from each other.

"See you a week from tomorrow at UConn, Joanna. I will miss you in the meantime."

"Bye, Michael. Enjoy your graduation tomorrow. I'll be thinking of you."

Joanna called Michael Monday evening asking how the graduation went and telling him she was looking forward to seeing him on Sunday.

"In a way, I'm sorry I went," Michael responded. "It was terribly crowded, the speeches were no great shakes, and the only good thing about it was it gave me an opportunity to see my parents. We met in Grand Central and had a nice dinner after commencement was over. They planned to stay in the city for a couple of days to some shows and what not. I told them, by the way, that I wanted the two of us to come up and visit with them over some weekend whenever they're free. Is that OK?"

"Yes, why not. But don't you think it might be a bit too early? Sure, you've met my parents, but that was very informal."

"Absolutely not. No harm can be done. We want to learn more about each other. One's family is an important part, isn't it?"

"I suppose so. Well, we'll see each other on Sunday."

"I can hardly wait. What time should I come and how will I find you in the crowd?"

"Commencement starts at ten but there will be refreshments from nine, and we will be there. At least the weather forecast is for a clear warm day. You won't have any trouble finding us; everything will be marked very clearly."

CHAPTER 7

It was only a few days before her graduation that Joanna told her parents she had invited Michael to come to her graduation.

"Isn't a bit too early for that, dear?" her mother, Reyna, said. "You haven't known each other very long. He seems like a nice, polite young man, but we don't know anything about him. What does he do, what religion does he follow?"

"He's an engineer working in Stamford and has just received his Masters from Columbia this past Sunday. He's Jewish but not Orthodox. We seem to have a lot in common and enjoy each other's company. Isn't that enough for a good start?"

"I have nothing against Jewish people," Joanna's father, Manuel, butted in. "But I think it's much better for couples to have the same religious beliefs and background. That way there won't be problems when it comes to raising children, and we sure hope to have grandchildren."

"In this generation, dad, there is less emphasis on religion and more on compatibility. There are so many more intermarriages between Catholics and Protestants, Jews and Christians, than ever before. Also, I have not said that I was going to marry Michael. We're just getting to know each other better.

Michael was early to the commencement exercises at Storrs. Only a few people stood around the tables, which were weighed down with all kinds of baked goods, coffee, and soft drinks. He was getting impatient to see Joanna, but it was not until half an hour later, when it had become quite crowded, that he spotted Joanna coming with her parents and sisters. He went slowly towards them bidding each a good morning and congratulating them warmly on Joanna's graduation. Their response was quite cool, being just as polite as with a stranger. Except for Joanna, who showed some signs of affection, but was too shy to do more than that. She did try to warm the atmosphere by showing them around the campus with great enthusiasm until it was time to take their places on the huge lawn where endless rows of white plastic chairs had been set up. The graduates sat in the reserved front section, with a large table decorated with flowers the colors of the university before them on a raised platform, awaiting the faculty procession to arrive. This was followed by the usual speeches, which took quite some time before the diplomas were handed out by the president and provost to the undergraduates and Masters students graduating with distinction as well all those who earned their Ph.D. Joanna was among those who received theirs *cum laude*. All the other graduates received their diplomas in their schools after the end of the program, which concluded with the school anthem. Joanna was then surrounded by her friends and her parents and sisters, all congratulating her on her achievement, each offering some unasked-for advice as to her future plans. Only Michael, standing a little aside, refrained from doing so, only holding her hand for as long as he could and whispering his admiration. Everyone left soon afterwards.

During the drive back to Norwalk, Michael wondered about the rather cool reception Joanna's parents had given him. *I don't understand it. They seemed so nice to me in the restaurant. Why the change? Has Joanna told them anything that could have made them do so? I'll call her as soon as I get home.* He did so immediately, being impatient to hear her voice.

"Hi Michael, I was hoping it was you, otherwise I would have called you. I'm so glad you were able to come to my graduation. And I was very unhappy that my parents acted so formal and distant with you. I guess most parents react that way when they see their child in some new relationship, not knowing where it may lead. This is also why I'm a little afraid of meeting your parents, like I said. When will I see you?"

"Well, never mind your parent's attitude; I am not worried about it as long as we will keep our friendship. As to visiting my parents, I don't know what their reaction will be, but whatever, there is no need to be concerned with it. It will not affect our relationship. It's only up to us. We have the weekend coming up; will you be free Friday or Saturday?"

"I have nothing planned for this weekend. Do you have anything in mind?"

"We can always go down again to New York. Come to think of it, what do you think about spending the weekend there?"

"You mean staying overnight in some hotel? It's a great idea, but I have to think about my parents' reaction. I'll call you back either later this evening or tomorrow. I'd love to do it."

Two hours later, Joanna called. "Sure, let's do it. Will you make the hotel reservation?"

"Sure thing. I'm so glad you're able to come. When shall I pick you up?"

"No need for it. We were going to take the train in anyway, so why don't I take the train from Bridgeport, which stops in Norwalk. I'll be in the third car from the front. Why don't you look up the train schedules? I guess we should leave sometime in mid-morning."

"Wonderful idea. I'll take care of it and call you."

Late afternoon the following day, Michael called Joanna. "Hi, I checked the train schedule and the best will be for you to take the 9:53, which gets into South Norwalk twenty minutes later. I also made reservations at the Edison on West 47th Street, right in the Theatre district. I checked what's playing, and there are quite a few shows that seem good. We can decide on the train. Is that OK?"

"Sure! I can't wait. See you Friday on the train."

Michael's anticipation of the coming weekend rose with the passing of the rest of the week. He was afraid of getting stuck somewhere in traffic or meeting an unexpected problem on the way, and ended up at the train station very early. The train was on time and Michael, positioning himself at about the proper place, boarded quickly looking for Joanna. She had seen him standing on the platform and stood up as soon as he entered the car, waving to him. Seeing her, Michael tried to push his way past the two people who had boarded before him and now were walking excruciatingly slowly to the rear of the car looking for seats. He was unable to pass them and felt a growing frustration. The fear of not seeing Joanna on the train made him want to fly to her and hold her close. When he did finally reach her, he just kissed her chastely on the lips and sat down next to her holding her hand tightly in his.

"I'm such a stupid pessimist; I've been worried that one of us might miss the train or something else would come up to prevent us being together. But tell me, how've you been and what did your parents say about us spending a weekend together? I'd hoped they wouldn't mind."

"Please, Michael, don't think I'm a coward, but I didn't tell them and instead said I was going to be with my girl friend, Maria, who studies at NYU and lives in the Village. Nothing could keep me from coming to be with you but I didn't want to have a big scene with my parents at this stage."

Michael tried not to show his disappointment and just said that as long as they were now together everything was fine. There were a few moments of silence until Joanna, breaking the ice, said: "Have you looked into what play we might want to see?"

"I sure have. There are quite a few playing now, some are revivals. See which one you might be interested in: *Amadeus*, *Annie Get Your Gun*, *Death of a Salesman*, *The Lion in Winter* or *The Scarlet Pimpernel*. I haven't seen any of them but they all seem like they would be worthwhile. They're all in the vicinity of our hotel, and we can try to get tickets at the half-price booth in Times Square."

"Like you said, they all seem interesting to me except for *Annie Get Your Gun*. I don't really like musicals. *Lion in Winter* sounds good. It's about Henry II and Eleanor of Aquitaine. *The Scarlet Pimpernel* is also a possibility; I read the book ages ago. Why don't you pick one of them?"

"Let's try for *Lion in Winter*. Hope we can get tickets."

Both were shy, not saying much, while walking from Grand Central Terminal to the hotel. Though it was quite early, their room was ready. Upon walking in, they dropped their bags and were in each other's arms without realizing their actions, with Michael kissing Joanna's lips long and soft, thinking himself in another world, breathing in her soft sweet odor. Joanna responded more passionately exploring her boyfriend's mouth, her hands searching his body. Michael took her hand and led her to the king-size bed, in the process trying to undo her blouse, with which she readily assisted. They were ready for each other with Joanna taking the initiative, straddling her partner and adjusting the rhythm so both reached an explosive climax at the same time. Spent, she fell on his chest, both lying there in this blissful state for who knows how long, her face next to his. It was Michael who eventually said: "Jo, if we want to go to the theatre tonight, we better get down to the ticket booth before none are left. I'll take a quick shower; it will take just a minute."

"Me too. But you go ahead first."

"You go then, ladies first."

"Come on, let's go together. You can rub my back."

"Ok, but the shower here is in the bathtub, there is not much room. Oh well, we can try."

The shower was indeed not meant for two people, but it did not bother them, with each fondling the other and kissing under the heavy stream of water. Michael was aroused again and with Joanna's ardor rising she grabbed two towels with which they barely removed some of the water clinging to their bodies. Still damp they made love again, this time more tranquil than before, trying to please each other, feeling deep affection.

"Jo, I know I may be hasty, and say things without giving us more time, but I love you."

"I think maybe I love you too, but let's not be too certain… I love being with you and want us to continue being together. I've never really been in love before, and I really don't know what it means. It has so many faces. Of course I've had boyfriends before, but this is something new. Come on, let's get dressed quickly and go down."

The line for the ticket booth at Times Square wound around the entire concrete island that separated Broadway from Seventh Avenue. In spite of the large number of people, they waited only about forty-five minutes to reach one of the sales counters and were able to obtain the two tickets they wanted at half the price normally charged at the theatre. The play was at the Roundabout theatre at West 42 Street, just a few blocks from their hotel. Since the weather was pleasant, if a bit cool, they wandered around for an hour or so, looking at menus in restaurant windows until finally settling on a French one on 38th Street that was not too expensive. They still had more than two hours before the show but were in the mood for a leisurely meal sharing their thoughts and aspirations.

"You know Michael; my life experience is rather limited. I am all of twenty-two and was raised in a very conservative home. So despite living for four years in the school dorms, I still don't know what I am really looking for in life. That's why I don't feel ready to commit myself at this time. In our family, we still believe that marriage is forever, even though fifty percent of marriages today end up in divorce. That's one thing I'm sure I don't want, not for myself nor for the children I hope to have."

Michael, his hand on Joanna's on the table, looked at her contemplating his words.

"I certainly can understand that. Coming from a stable family with a similar outlook on marriage, I too look for permanency. I think the best way we can get to know each other is living together without any commitment.

Seeing the other person in such an environment, not just during a nice weekend, will make certain there are no surprises later on. I would have no problem with it, but I imagine your parents wouldn't look favorably on such an arrangement. Otherwise, we'll just have to try and see each other as often as possible."

"I know living together before marriage is now quite common. Two of my girl friends are doing it just now. But, like you said, as much as I think that it may be a good idea for us, my parents will be very upset and hurt if I should do that, too. I think we'll have to let them first get more used to the idea of us seeing each other a lot and then, perhaps, broach the subject."

"Yes, I suppose it is best under the circumstances. But come, I guess it is time to go to the play."

Sitting way back in the orchestra did not affect their fascination and enjoyment of the play. They left the theatre engrossed in what they had just seen and walked hand-in-hand out and along teeming Broadway.

"It was wonderful, Michael, I so much enjoyed it, and so glad you suggested it. I think Stockard Channing was perfect in the role of Eleanor of Aquitaine. She was just as I had imagined her to be when I learned about her. I think if she had lived today she could have been the President of France or the Prime Minister of England."

"You are so right. I think Fishburne was good, too, as Henry II. There's nothing like Broadway theatre. There's so much to choose from and much of it excellent. I'm also always amazed at the crowd here. You have to elbow your way through to make any headway. Where are they all coming from?"

"It's so alive. I love it. Our hometowns are so stale and boring. I wouldn't mind living here, if I could afford it."

"I would too, but Norwalk was more affordable. I wouldn't, however, want to bring up kids here. For that, there's nothing like a house and a yard. I think my parents did a wise thing by buying a house in Brookline where I grew up and where they still live today. The yard isn't very large, but we grew a few vegetables and strawberries there; and there was a sandbox and swing, which I loved."

They wandered around for nearly an hour, enjoying an ice cream on the way, before returning to the hotel. It felt almost natural to go to bed together, make love and have the whole night to themselves. They slept in late, with Michael waking up first and looking with wonder at the girl sleeping peacefully by his side, her dark hair disheveled, strands covering part of her face. *She looks so defenseless, so much at peace. I really don't know her so well but I am sure my gut feeling is right, that we are meant for each other. I wonder what she really feels.* It was not until close to ten o'clock that they were ready to go down, look for a place to have breakfast and go to the Guggenheim museum, which anyway opened only at eleven. They decided to check out and leave their bags at the concierge, since they did not plan to be back before check-out time. Joanna enjoyed the museum, but Michael did less so, as he was more conservative. He liked the impressionists and did not go for modern art. They went for lunch, then stopped for a while to sit in Central Park before returning to the hotel to pick up their bags. From there, it was a short walk to Grand Central. Boarding the train, they felt shy and nothing was said for a while until Joanna broke the silence.

"It was very short, this weekend. I felt good and I hope we'll continue to see each other often and maybe do this again."

"I was hoping you would say that, Jo. Now that we're both finished with school, we should be able to do it. I really would like us to go up one weekend to Boston to see my parents. They would be happy to have you. Boston is anyway a very nice place to visit."

"I don't know about another weekend soon. My parents will begin to wonder. Is it possible to go up for the day?"

"I suppose it could be done, but it won't leave us much time there. I think the train from Bridgeport to Boston takes about three hours. I'll check the timetable. It'll have to be on a Saturday or Sunday, of course."

"You do that. When will I see you again?"

"If it's up to me, tomorrow! Whenever you're free."

CHAPTER 8

As it was, they saw each other only the following Thursday. Joanna, in the meantime, had her good friend from college, Megan O'Connell, stay with her for three days. Megan lived in Hartford with her parents. Joanna was anxious to tell her friend about Michael and her feelings towards him.

"You know, Megan, I don't know what to make of it. I feel a closeness to Michael that I don't believe I've felt towards any other guy I've been with. I've met Jewish boys before but only on a superficial level, he's the first I've really gotten to know, and frankly it feels really good to be with him. We've seen each other quite a few times now and we spent last weekend together at a New York hotel."

"Well, it sounds exciting. But what can I tell you? I've never gone out with a Jewish man, not that I have any prejudice, but I don't think my parents would like it very much. Look, nowadays you hear more and more about interfaith marriages. The saying goes, by the way, that Jewish men make very good husbands. What about your parents? Have you talked to them about it?"

"They've met him. He was over at the house and we also ate at their restaurant. I haven't said anything to them about my feelings for him. They might not be too pleased if it comes to marriage, but I don't think they'd be so opposed as to make things difficult."

"So tell me more about him. What does he do, how does he look and how is he in bed?"

"Michael is an engineer who just now got his M.Sc. from Columbia, works in Stamford and lives in Norwalk. He's from Boston, where his father's a professor of something. I like his looks and enjoy being in bed with him. Is that enough?"

"Well, it sounds good for a start. I'd love to meet him. Don't worry; I'm not going to take him away from you."

"A fat chance you have. But let me call him. Can you stay over until Friday morning?"

"Sure, I'd be glad to."

"Hi Michael, how've you been? It seems like ages since that great weekend. Yes, my friend Megan is still here. She'll be leaving on Friday. What do you say the three of us get together Thursday evening, if you're free?"

"Sure, why not. Should I come up to your place, say, about seven and we can have dinner together somewhere?"

"That would be nice. You sure don't mind?"

"Why should I? I like to be with you whenever, and with anyone who is a friend of yours."

"Good, see you then."

Michael felt somewhat uneasy after their conversation. *Does Joanna want her friend's opinion of me? I hope that's not the reason for suggesting this date. I would think she wouldn't need some outsider's advice and could make up her own mind. Maybe it's just her friend's curiosity. I don't mind meeting her friend. It might be interesting to get to know what she is like.*

Thursday evening, promptly at seven, Michal rang the bell to the Aguilar home. Joanna opened the door with a big smile on her face.

"I knew it was you. You could set a clock by your timing. How do you do it? Come on in and meet Megan."

Megan, who had been sitting on the sofa, got up and walked towards Michael and extended her hand in greeting. Michael took hers and shook it warmly. *One can guess she is Irish. Her bright blue eyes and black curly hair are an indication. She seems nice, at least from such a cursory glance.*

"So glad to meet you Megan. Joanna told me about you, I'm glad to meet a friend of hers. I bet she told you about me so that no introductions are necessary. Have you girls thought about where we should go? I'm still not so familiar with Bridgeport, although I hope to become more knowledgeable with time."

It was Joanna who answered: "We actually thought to eat here at home. Between us we cooked up a few things. You don't mind, do you?"

"Of course not. I think it's a nice idea. I'm sure I will be impressed by the results."

"Good. Let's have a drink first. Megan you do the honors while I go for a moment to the kitchen to see how things are doing. You know what I like."

"Well, Michael, there is not too great a selection. Whiskey, Irish Cream, and Campari. I imagine there is also beer in the fridge. What would you like? I know Joanna likes Irish Cream."

With that, she poured some into a wine glass and some whiskey for herself.

"I'll have some Campari with soda water or orange juice or whatever there is."

Megan poured a small amount of Campari into a glass and went into the kitchen for the rest. She asked Joanna for soda water and when that was not available took orange juice from the refrigerator and filled the glass. "He does seem quite nice," she whispered to Joanna as she left the kitchen. Joanna followed soon after. The three sat in the living room, sipping their drinks quietly until Megan broke the silence turning to Michael.

"Joanna told me a little bit about you but what exactly do you do? She said you have a Masters degree but was not specific in what field. By the way, I roomed with Joanna but I took a degree in physics and now cannot do anything but try and go for the Ph.D., if I can make it. A B.A. is not worth a damn."

"My, that's interesting. I do not want to sound chauvinistic but I imagine there are not too many girls in your field. As for me, I'm a mechanical engineer now trying to switch to industrial engineering. I, of course, took some physics courses, but to tell you the truth, I use very little of it in my daily practice. I work at a plant making defense-related hydraulic equipment, and am Assistant Chief Engineer of a small 18-person department. It might interest you to know that we have three female engineers with us. I've been with the company quite a while and have begun to feel the need to change directions a bit, and turn more to technological management rather than stay in the pure design area."

"It sounds interesting. Will you be able to do it in your current organization or do you have to move to a new company?"

"I don't know yet. But I hear Joanna calling us for dinner, so let's go into the kitchen. Dinner smells great!"

Joanna had set the table and arranged the food. First, there was a large green salad followed by veal cacciatore, green beans and hash brown potatoes. A bottle of Chianti was on the table.

"Joanna, this looks and tastes better than professional. And not Spanish! I did not know you had this terrific talent. I always admire good cooking, it's so creative." Michael was so full of admiration that he would have gone on had Joanna not interrupted and said, "I've always liked to cook but don't believe for a moment that I would do it professionally. However, if I ever marry, I'll try to keep my hand at it since it gives me satisfaction to prepare something nice. Anyway, Megan here helped me a great deal so the compliments are due to her also."

The dinner concluded with big bowls of ice cream that left everybody well sated and in a relaxed mood. They had long talks covering the girls' college experience, Michael's interests, and diverse opinions on the situation in Bosnia, the coming millennium, and Clinton's sexual escapades. The latter was especially heated, as both Joanna and Megan thought Clinton should have been impeached and that it was disgusting for a president to have that kind of affair in the White House. Joanna said that she was no prude, and did not see anything wrong in positions other than the missionary during intercourse, but a quick blowjob in the Oval Office was demeaning for the woman. They both looked almost accusingly at Michael waiting for him to agree with them. Michael, however, said the president was not the only man with strong sexual urges and that he should have channeled his impulses in a better way. As far as he was concerned, the important part of the matter was whether the president was truthful in the investigation or not. He certainly expected honesty from his president. He added that he also did not think Monica Lewinsky was blameless. She apparently used her sex to obtain a promotion from the lowly intern she was, through the influence of the president. It was way past nine when they put the dishes in the dishwasher, cleaned up a bit and went into the living room. Michael suggested going to a movie or to a nightclub unless the girls had some other ideas.

"Why don't we stay in? We can listen to music, talk. Anyway it's late for a movie and I don't feel like going dancing. Is that OK? My parents won't be home till eleven at the earliest."

Megan and Michael agreed, it was now a question of what music to put on. Michael asked if there was any classical music while Megan preferred folk music. It turned out Joanna had a large collection of country as well as light classical and some jazz. They all agreed on country music, which Joanna put on the disc player. Actually, nobody really listened to it, as the conversation was lively, fueled by a few drinks. It was after eleven when Michael got up, remarked on how pleasant the evening was, how much he enjoyed the great dinner, and took his leave.

Well, that was interesting, he thought while getting into his car. *I bet they'll now gossip about me. I wonder what Megan is going to say. She is a pretty nice girl, actually, although you can't tell from one evening. Maybe I should do something like that and take Joanna to meet Helen and David, who are dying to meet her. What the hell, I don't need anybody's opinion. Whatever happens, it is my decision.*

"What do you think, Megan? How does he strike you?"

"Pretty much like you said, except I don't know his performance in bed of course. He does seem to be ambitious and, I guess, has decent prospects in his profession. What more can I say? Could I fall for him? It's possible, although this religious business still seems to be somewhat of a drawback."

"Yes, it bothers me a little too. Maybe more so because of my parents. I want to have their blessing when it comes to marriage. I certainly don't want to fight with them. The funny thing is that some of our customs as Seventh-day-Adventists are quite similar to those practiced by Jews. Michael mentioned something like that. He told me that many Jews ostensibly converted to Christianity in Spain, back in the 15th century, but kept their Jewish practices in secret. I don't know whether he is actually thinking that we are their descendants. But come, time to go to bed."

Michael called Joanna a couple days later, and told her that he checked the train schedule to Boston and found that on Saturdays they could make the round trip in one day, but it would leave them only about five hours in Boston. He still felt it would be better to stay overnight. Joanna was in a dilemma; she was ready to meet Michael's parents but was uncomfortable telling her parents about staying for the weekend. Michael suggested that since his parents' home had two spare bedrooms she could tell her parents about the sleeping arrangements and they would, of course, abide by it.

CHAPTER 9

Michael preferred driving up to Bridgeport on Saturday and leaving his car at the station, rather than taking the train in Norwalk and have Joanna get on and meet him like they did for the weekend in New York. He remembered how anxious he was that they might possibly miss each other. Joanna, uneasy about meeting Michael's parents, was somewhat pensive during the three-hour train ride. *Does my coming to meet his parents mean I am really serious about Michael? And what will be their opinion of me? I am so confused.*

Michael's mother opened the door, embraced her son for a brief moment and turned to Joanna.

"So good to meet you, my dear. You must be Joanna, about whom Michael's been telling us so much. We're so happy you were able to come; we were anxious to meet you. Come on in to the living room, I'll call Michael's father who, as usual, is in his study. At least he's not working, since it's the Sabbath, just catching up on his reading."

Michael's father came within a few minutes, dressed in rather shabby looking chinos, a tee-shirt and beat-up slippers. "Well, finally. So glad you have come. I must say, Joanna, Michael did not do you justice when he described you. And how are you, my boy? "

"Thank you for having me, Professor Berk. Michael has told me about his parents, and I'm glad to be able to get to know you." Joanna's words came out hesitatingly, her embarrassment was obvious.

"Stop this nonsense about professor, my dear, I'm Ben and this is Rachel. Do feel at home; you'll have to put up with us during the weekend and I hope it won't be too stressful. Let me show you to your rooms and feel free to wash up and relax. We have delayed our Sabbath dinner for a little. We usually have it midday, but an hour or so later is ok too. We knew you wouldn't be here until noon. I hope you won't mind that we invited some friends of ours. Only one couple, since others could not make it. We have this arrangement whereby most every Sabbath one of the couples invites the others for dinner. We have no plans for the evening, we can talk later about what to do. I understand you'll be leaving tomorrow early afternoon so that we will have time to show you around if you like. And now I'll also go get dressed a little better."

Michael stayed with Joanna in her room after they put down their bags.

"You seem a little uncomfortable, Jo. My parents really are quite nice and down to earth, so don't be worried, they will love you once they get to know you a little. I only hope you don't think that coming here is a bit too early; I just don't want you to feel under any pressure. We said that there is no commitment at this point. I do have deep feelings for you, Jo, but it's important we both feel the same and want the same."

"Oh, Michael, I'm so confused. You're very dear to me, but I don't know if this is the permanent relationship I've been hoping for. Let's see how things develop; in the meantime let's try and be together as much as possible so we both can be sure."

They went downstairs, finding Ben and Rachel in the living room, deep in conversation with a couple about their age. Seeing them, Rachel got up, introduced their friends as Esther and Robert Serman, after which she introduced Joanna, since Michael was already acquainted with them. She then urged everybody go to the dining room so lunch could finally be served.

Joanna looked with some curiosity around the dining room, noticing a large candelabra on the sideboard, paintings of biblical scenes on the wall, and the beautifully set table. Rachel noticed and told Joanna that the candelabra was an heirloom dating back to the time of her grandfather, who was born in the latter part of the 19th century and came to the US from Lithuania as a child of six years old. As for the table, they always had a special meal on Friday evening and at Sabbath noon, at which they were usually together with other people and a few prayers were said. After everyone had their wine glasses filled, Ben, wearing a skullcap, said a blessing over the wine and the special braided bread. It was a very satisfying meal. It started with a great green salad fortified with hard-boiled eggs, anchovies, feta cheese and olives. This was followed by baked salmon, sweet potatoes, string beans, and a red cabbage salad. The meal was concluded with coffee and an ice cream cake. "I hope you like fish Joanna," Rachel had said at the beginning of the meal. "Esther and Robert here keep a kosher house, and since we do not, they will not eat any meat except at home or in a kosher restaurant." The conversation during the meal was lively, with Ben and Robert arguing about politics until Rachel stopped them, turning to Joanna and asking her to tell them a little about her studies at the University of Connecticut.

"Michael told us you were a history major at the school of education. I have always been interested in things that happened in the past and often am sorry I didn't go and do what you did."

"I believe it is never too late to learn new things. I've been reading history books since I was a little girl and found my studies most interesting. My aim was to be able to teach history in high school, which I am now going to do. However, I would like, sometime in the future, to go back to school for advanced degrees to get a much deeper understanding of what motivated peoples and their leaders to do things that to us, in our environment, look strange. It's hard to put ourselves in such situations, as they existed many years ago."

"Well said," Ben remarked. "I told Rachel many times to do just that but she is always too busy with her paintings. I suppose it's hard to do two creative things at the same time and maybe one shouldn't really try to do it."

"Well, well. I hope to see you at Harvard one of these days, Joanna." Robert said. "I teach History of Science and Technology there and I know how hard it is to put inventions and inventors into the context of their time when we try to follow the progress of science and technology over the centuries. People worship the great inventors of the past, like Edison, Watt, Marconi, you name them. One forgets inventors usually stand on the shoulders of those who came before them. Science certainly isn't static and builds on past achievements, at times, it has to negate what previously was thought as certain."

Rachel switched the subject to more mundane topics, such as the plays now in Boston theatres, the coming season of the Boston symphony, and the like. It was well past four o'clock when Esther got up, saying what a wonderful meal it had been and how much she'd enjoyed the company. All got up; the parting took some time since the two older couples talked about going out together later in the week.

After the guests were gone, Joanna told Michael's parents how much she enjoyed the meal. Rachel suggested that there was still time for Michael to show her something of Boston. "He can take my car," she said. "Do you know our city?"

"Not really, my parents took me up here once when I was still quite small. I only remember how excited they were to see the historical sites, or maybe it's what they said later. I don't recall much of the scenes. Anything would be interesting for me."

Michael suggested that for an afternoon it would be best to go and visit Boston's historical sites by car. Most of them were anyway best viewed from the outside and a walking tour would have taken several hours. Joanna agreed to that enthusiastically. The site to see first was the USS Constitution Museum; it was open until six PM. The highlight of it was the warship built towards the end of the 18th century that had taken part in many battles. Joanna found it exciting to walk on the planks of a warship built nearly two hundred years before and be able to actually see the living quarters, the implements for war, and the complexity of a large sailing vessel. From there, they stopped by Paul Revere House, Faneuil Hall, where the old market place was, the State House, and the Old South Meeting House, where the Boston Tea Party began. They ended up in the Boston Common, which dated back to the 17th century with the adjacent Boston Park. There was still time to ride one of the famous Swan Boats on the pretty lagoon. It was there that Joanna held Michael's hand firmly and told him how nice his parents were.

"I was really scared, especially when I heard that other guests would be coming. Your mother really put me at ease. To think that I spouted history to a professor at Harvard. I can't believe it."

"I was sure, darling, that everything would work out fine. I had no doubt that everybody would love you. What did you think of our religious customs? Was it strange?"

"Not really. We do things different, of course, but the idea behind seems to be quite the same. I had a very homey feeling, frankly."

Since Michael's parents were invited to a birthday party for Ben's colleague from the University, the young couple spent the evening walking around downtown, going as far as the historic section and stopping for a bite at the Green Dragon Tavern, supposedly the oldest in Boston, having been established in 1657. Michael told Joanna that it was purportedly a meeting place for Paul Revere and his comrades. They returned home just before ten, and sat a while in the living room listening to Spanish Civil War songs from Ben and Rachel's collection of folk music.

"You know, Joanna, I think it's a terrible waste of an opportunity to go and sleep in separate rooms. To me, every minute together with you is precious, but we've promised your parents." Michael looked longingly into Joanna's eyes. "What do you say?"

Her reply was a long soft kiss; after which they sat looking at each other until Michael broke the silence.

"I think we must do as promised, as much as I don't want to. We have to be honest not just with each other but also with others, even if they cannot know whether or not we kept the promise. I'm sure your parents won't ask you if we slept in separate rooms, but that's not the point."

"You know, Michael, I was on the verge of saying let's forget what we promised, but you're right, we have to respect ourselves. Come, let us go upstairs quickly before we change our minds."

After a late breakfast on Sunday, the four went to the Isabella Steward Gardner museum, which for Joanna was, as she said, a heavenly experience. After an early lunch, Ben and Rachel took them to Back Bay Station where they said their goodbyes and parted with Rachel asking the young people to be sure to come again soon.

"It wasn't too bad an experience, was it?" Michael asked once they were seated and on their way.

"No, certainly not. You do have very nice parents; they made me feel very welcome. I'm glad we came. Still, I'm also glad it's over. I couldn't help feeling I was being evaluated as a suitable mate for their son."

"I can understand your feeling, although I believe both my parents are sensitive to other people's feelings. I know they tried to make you comfortable. I, too, tried to be on my best behavior when I met your parents, though they, also, were very kind."

The three hours to Bridgeport passed quite quickly, with both Joanna and Michael mostly engrossed in their thoughts about the significance of the weekend and its meaning for them. Michael then drove Joanna home, parting from her in the car after a long and passionate embrace, the kiss leaving its deep impression.

Joanna's parents were home when she entered, but after a brief greeting she went up to her room, not wanting to be questioned as yet about the weekend. She needed some more time to get her thoughts together now that she was away from Michael. She only went down for the light supper the family usually had on Sundays. Of her sisters, only Eleanora was at the table.

"So, did you have a nice weekend?" her mother asked. "How are Michael's parents? Did you like them?"

"It was very pleasant. Yes, they are nice people. It was interesting to see that some of their religious customs are very much like ours. You should see their beautiful candelabra. It's an heirloom dating back maybe a hundred years, having been brought from the old country."

"I presume you kept your word regarding the subject we talked about." Manuel said with a sideways look at Eleanora, who was intently following the conversation.

"Of course we did, Dad. I gave you my word, didn't I? I love Michael – he is the most considerate and honest person I have ever met. Just get to know him and you will agree."

"I see things have gone very far in a short time," Manuel said, his voice expressing his displeasure. All the while, Reyna had a worried look on her face. "You speak of love. Do you know what it means? How can you be so certain? Are you so sure Michael feels the same way? And what about the religious aspects? I told you that intermarriage leads to problems. No, Joanna, I do not like it."

"Dad, we are almost in the 21st century. Things have changed since you and Mom were married. There is also another matter. Do you know that many Jews who lived in Spain five hundred years ago had to convert to Christianity, but kept their customs in secret just so they could stay? Maybe some of our ancestors were such people. There is little difference between good people who believe in one God."

"Oh, so he's trying to make a Jew out of you, out of us? No way, I will not have it. I don't want you to see him again, ever. Do you hear?" he shouted.

Joanna started to cry and got up from her seat to go to her room, when Reyna asked her to sit down to hear what she had to say.

"I think what Dad means is you have made a decision that will affect your life without giving it the deep consideration it needs. Such a weighty decision needs considerable more time than you have given it. What I think is that you and Michael should stop seeing each other for six months. If both of you still feel the same way afterward, well, we may reconsider our present negative opinion. You'll go along with that, won't you Manuel?"

Manuel nodded hesitatingly, an unsatisfied mien on his face.

"And you, Joanna?"

Joanna got up again, tears still streaking down her face, muttering that she would think about it, and went upstairs. It took her a while to calm down and to call Michael.

"Michael, I need to talk to you. When can I see you?"

"What's the matter, darling? You sound upset, like you've been crying. I'll come whenever you like. If it's urgent, I'll take off work in the morning. Should I come to your place?"

"No, not at home. Let's meet at six at the Discovery Museum. You remember where it is, don't you?"

"I sure do. Meet you there. In the meantime, please try and take it easy. Whatever it is, I'm sure we can work things out."

I wonder what happened. It must be something to do with her parents, since she did not want me to come to her house. I really don't know her parents or what they think about our relationship. I do love her and should have told her so more often.

CHAPTER 10

Joanna was waiting in front of the museum for quite a while when Michael drove up promptly on time. She quickly jumped in and told him to drive to a place where they could park, her voice breaking while suppressing her tears. There was a supermarket not far and Michael drove into the lot. He turned to her, his arm around her shoulder, pulling her to him in a tight embrace.

"What happened, dearest? I love you and it hurts me to see you so upset."

"Oh, Michael, I felt good when I came home with the memory of our visit to your parents. The first thing my father asked me was whether we kept our promise. I told him we did and that I love you; it just came out. I hadn't even admitted it to myself, but it's so. Father was very angry, saying that we've known each other for such a short time and you want me to convert. He said I was never to see you again."

"How did he get the idea I wanted you to convert? I never mentioned anything like that."

"I just told him that your parents keep some of the same religious customs as we do, and also that many Spanish people may be descendants of the *Conversos*.

He just jumped to conclusions. But wait, mother knows how to handle him; she suggested that we not see each other for six months to see if we are still sure about each other. Father reluctantly agreed.It's still terrible. What are we going to do?"

Tears still running down her face she clung to Michael, looking up to him questioningly. It took a while for him to digest what she had said and respond.

"I will never give you up, my darling. There are really only three things we can do. I don't know if you can or want to simply refuse your parents' demand, knowing it could bring about a break in your relationship. After all, we want to have their blessing. This is one possibility. So we have two choices left; we can do what they have asked, which will be unbearable, or, two, we could meet clandestinely. I don't like the latter either since we aren't thieves who have to meet in dark places. I don't know what to say. You know your parents."

"My father can be very dogmatic; he is conservative to the core and views much of modern attitudes and behavior as immoral and that they should be condemned. Mother is much more realistic and understanding. Michael, I'm torn, I cannot see myself living with any of the options. Why did it have to come to this?"

"Let's not decide now, Jo. Think about what is best for you and call me tomorrow, at work or at home, whenever you can talk freely, OK?"

Joanna clung to Michael for a while, her sobbing having stopped. She finally agreed to do what he asked.

Coming home, Joanna was glad her parents were at the restaurant. She went into the kitchen, took some bread and cheese and a glass of milk and went up to her room. *It's not fair. I'm old enough to know what I want, what's good for me. Why can't they understand that? We are almost in the third millennium; we don't behave and act like a hundred years ago. It was not nice of Michael to make me decide what to do. Why couldn't he? I would not have this problem if we had never met, but I want to be with him.* Her thoughts went around and around. *I'll decide tomorrow morning.*

Driving home, Michael was in a quandary. *Poor girl; she's in an impossible situation. I now know she wants to be with me, but can she antagonize her parents? They are real old-fashioned people. But what can I tell her? Not to see her for six months is terrible, so what can we do? I'll talk to her tomorrow.*

"Michael, I don't know what we should do. I couldn't sleep all night. Please, tell me what to do, what do you think?

"Jo, darling. I too am in a dilemma, just as you are. Maybe we should give it a trial period. Here's what I think: We can, of course talk on the phone and communicate through e-mail. I suggest that we not see each other for two weeks, which will be terrible, but I am sure we can live with that. We will decide after that what to do. How does that sound to you?"

"Ok, two weeks; but then what?"

"That will give us time to think things through and see how we can handle it. I'd wait for you for a year, ten years, if needed. We aren't children who don't know what we want, what is good for us. Nobody else can do it for us. You know what? Maybe it's a good thing if we encounter difficulties on the way; we will come out of it that much more mature."

"I still don't like it, but OK. We'll talk to each other every day, yes?"

"Sure, darling. You'll have to call me unless you know for sure your parents aren't going to be home. How about your sisters? Will I be able to call if one of them should answer the phone?"

"There should be no problem with Vanessa. I'll talk to her. Eleanora, though, might say something to my dad. She, being the youngest, is his favorite and sometimes tells him all kinds of things to get back at Vanessa or me if she feels we slighted her. I'll call you for the time being, it'll be safer."

"I'll be waiting, Jo. It's going to be pretty terrible, I can tell you. I love you."

"Love you too."

The two weeks passed with daily phone calls between the two, none much different from each other. Michael, not knowing what to do, called his friend David, hoping to get some advice from him. The two met one evening in David's house, when Helen was in a meeting.

"So, what's the problem? You sounded awful when we talked and don't look much better. From the little you said on the phone, I think maybe we should have met when

Helen was home, she's a very logical person, not what you expect from women. I'm a chauvinist, aren't I?"

"You may be right, but I like to know what you think, what you would have done if you were in my position. I told you about Joanna's parent's demand of us. We haven't seen each other during the last two weeks now and find it intolerable."

"You put me in a difficult position, Michael. I don't know Joanna's parents and I've never met Joanna. Frankly, I'm surprised the four of us never got together for an evening. It could have been nice."

"You're right, David. I should have suggested it; I don't know why I didn't. Still, you must have an opinion; what would you do if you were in this sort of position? Obviously you and Helen did not face this kind of problem, as far as I know. But what if you had?"

"Look, Helen and I knew that we were meant for each other. Nothing would have made us agree not to see each other. At least, it's what I think. Ask Helen. Whether we would have seen each other in secret or openly in defiance of her parents is another matter, which I can't answer. Anyway, Helen's parents would never have suggested anything like this."

"Well, I agree I shouldn't have posed this question to you in the first place. But ask Helen if you don't mind."

"Sure, she'll want to know about your situation."

Maybe my parents are right, thought Joanna. *It won't be so terrible if I do not see Michael for a while. We really have not known each other for very long. I do love him, but both of us can bear a short separation, we can still talk to each other.*

Towards the end of the two weeks, Joanna suggested they go along for another two weeks before making a final decision. "After all," she said, "I promised my parents, and as hard as it is, I can't, at this stage, go behind their backs, and facing them is equally difficult." Michael's disappointment was obvious in his voice as he said he understood her situation and would, of course, honor it. "It is just as hard for me, darling," Joanna said. "But we will be strong and get through it, right?" Michael agreed, though again he sounded unhappy.

Why couldn't she tell her parents that she's not a child anymore and that she knows what's good for her? Oh hell, what if it were my parents who forbade me to see her? I must stop acting like a petulant child whose toy has been taken away. OK, we'll wait another two weeks. But what will we do after that?

It was a couple of days later that Joanna's mother told her that her good friend Maria mentioned that her nephew, a nice young man by name of Joseph, wanted very much to meet her, having heard good things about her from his aunt. He would call this evening.

"I don't want to talk to him, mother. Why can't you let me make my own decisions? I'm old enough."

"I did not say you shouldn't decide what is best for yourself. But it wouldn't hurt to meet other young men, would it?"

"Do you think I didn't meet men during my four years in college? What do you take me for? You met some who came home. Have you forgotten?"

"Just do this for me, Joanna. What can I tell Maria? That you have a steady boyfriend? She'll want to know about him, something I don't want to do at this point in time. Joseph is a mature person of thirty and has a good job at a well-known accounting firm. We have to think about your father. Things have to be done gradually and with respect. He only wants the best for you. As you know, he isn't an easy person to convince once he has made up his mind. It may help if he sees you are meeting other men now. Please, Joanna."

"OK, mama. But don't expect anything to come out of it."

Joseph called that evening, and Joanna agreed to meet him on Friday. He suggested they go bowling. *Well, why not. Michael doesn't have to know about it, and anyway, we aren't married yet and both of us are free to meet people of the opposite sex.*

Joseph arrived at Joanna's apartment a little before their agreed time of six o'clock. Joanna purposely had him wait a while until she came down to meet him. He was a good-looking young man. His tall, athletic body went well with his tanned face, blond crew cut, and nice blue eyes; the appearance marred only by a receding chin and hesitating speech. They went out to his late model Chevy and drove the short distance to Milford to the AMF Bowling Center on the Post road. At Joseph's suggestion, they went first to the bar, where they had beer and pretzels before taking their place at one of the lanes. It turned out Joseph was an excellent bowler who scored over two hundred points in each of his games. Joanna got only one half as much. After their games, they went to the restaurant for dinner. Having ordered their meal, Joanna looked at Joseph as he seemed to want to say something, but after a short wait she said:

"My, you're a good player, Joseph. I never bowled with someone as good as you. I used to play quite often in college. So, tell me something about yourself. My parents told me a little, that you work in an accounting firm, but I am curious to learn more."

There was some hesitation on the part of Joseph until he replied. "Yes, I have a pretty good job as office manager at the Connecticut Tax Company. It's a good-sized outfit, serving small-to-midsized firms in all of Fairfield County."

"Oh, so you are a CPA? Where did you go to school?"

"An office manager doesn't need to be a CPA. I'm planning to study for it, though, in the near future. What about you, Joanna?"

"I just started to teach history in Central High. I only graduated this June and am still a little nervous standing in front a class of kids trying to keep them interested, which, unfortunately, doesn't always happen. I work hard preparing my lectures, but so far it's too early for grading tests, so it isn't too bad, time-wise."

"Huh, teaching history? Isn't that rather dull? What do you want to know about what happened long ago? I'm interested in the here and now. I'm an active Republican. Unfortunately, people here only elect Democrats. Most of them are too far left, especially that Jew Lieberman. It's about time people who care for our country get into Congress."

"I really haven't been too interested in politics, but as far as I know my congressman and our two senators are American patriots. At least that is my impression."

"You should look more deeply into their speeches and their voting records in Congress, maybe you wouldn't say that."

"Well, I won't argue with you about this. Here comes our meal." Joanna lifted her glass of beer, said "Cheers," and started to eat.

There was little conversation while they ate and, after finishing, Joanna looked at her watch and remarked how surprisingly late it was, and that she still had some work to do for the next day's lessons. Joseph voiced his disappointment, saying he had hoped that they could still go to a late movie. Perhaps another time, Joanna told him. As she turned to leave his car he took hold of her hand, pulled her towards himself, and kissed her. She did not resist strongly but left the car hurriedly. Her mother, who was at home watching TV in the living room, asked her how she liked her date. "It was ok," she answered and hurried up to her room. *I'm actually glad mother had me go out with this guy. Now I can really appreciate how lucky I am having met Michael. Maybe I should meet a few more, not that I didn't have boyfriends before.*

A few days later, on Saturday, Joanna and Megan were sitting in the food court of the Arcade Mall after a bit of shopping.

"So how was your date with that guy your mother had you meet?"

"Don't ask. It was awful. Not worth talking about. He thinks teaching history is awful. Typical run-of-the-mill idiot. I don't know how I can stand not seeing Michael for another five months. The whole thing is so stupid."

"Frankly, I'm disappointed with Michael. I would expect him to insist to either continue seeing you or else break off the close friendship. To me, it indicates he's a man without a backbone, don't you think so?"

"You just don't know him. He's the most understanding person I have met, and as honest as they come. Doesn't that count for something?"

"Well, maybe. But in the meantime, why don't you see other guys? There is one who might just be a good possibility. He's the brother of a girl from school I bumped into the other day. She suggested I meet him, but right now you know I'm tied up with Dick. He's from a wealthy old family living in Westport. Don't laugh; his name is W. Timothy Ballard III. Doesn't that sound great? OK if I tell her to give him your phone number?"

"Fine, let him call. I'll think about it. Frankly, it sounds a bit bombastic to go around with a moniker like that, but maybe he's OK."

That same day, Michael was at David and Helen's for dinner. "You've got to snap out of it, Michael," Helen said in a somewhat forceful voice. "This isn't the end of the world. To wait a few more months isn't so terrible. You could also date other girls in the meantime. Don't you think David?"

"How can you say such a thing, Helen? If this would've happened to you while we dated, would you have said the same thing? I doubt it. Do you have any dates for Michael in mind?"

"As a matter of fact, I do. Just the other day, I was talking to the senior accountant at the office about some business matter. He's a very nice guy, by the way. Anyway, he told me one of his wife's younger cousins had recently broken up with her long-time boyfriend. His wife wants to introduce her to an eligible man; she spoke very highly of this girl."

"I suppose a date can't hurt," David said. "But if I were in Michael's position, I wouldn't give a damn about the girl's parents and would have it out with them."

"You sure sound great, but I know you would never have done it. But what do you say, Michael?"

"I don't know. If I had thought it was the way to go, I would have done something about it. As for seeing this girl, I'll think about it and let you know. Thanks for the suggestion."

"OK, why don't we go to a movie this coming Saturday? Let's make it for the afternoon performance and then go out for a bite."

David and Michael readily agreed and made a date to go and see an old movie, *Paths of Glory*, which was playing at the Community Theatre in Fairfield.

Michael, as usual, was a bit early to the theatre. He bought three tickets and waited in the atrium for his friends, hating the smell of the popcorn permeating the large entrance hall. His glance passed over the many people passing through or bunched together at the food counter, straying occasionally to the door in anticipation of his friends. Suddenly he stiffened, not wanting to believe what he saw. It was Joanna, coming through the door looking back at a tall, well-dressed, young man who then took her arm and guided her to the ticket booth. For a moment Michael was frozen, not knowing how to react, but then he turned around and stared blindly at the large placard at the wall. He jumped when David tapped him on the shoulder.

"What's the matter Michael? You act as if you've just seen a ghost. It's only us. Have you bought the tickets? Hey, you look like hell, what's the matter?"

"Just let me be for a minute. Yes, I've bought the tickets and we can go in."

Helen and David looked at each other with a puzzled expression but didn't say anything and walked after Michael. It was only after they sat for a short time in their seats, waiting for the movie to start, that Michael, his head down, said that he saw Joanna come in with some guy.

"Good for her," exclaimed Helen. "Do you expect her to sit around moping for half a year? I suggested a while ago you should go out with someone one else in the meantime, too."

"I thought you were on my side, Helen," Michael said in pained voice.

"I am! You're not married or engaged, so why not? Do you think that if it isn't her, you'll never meet another girl who might also be as good a mate? I think this is an old romantic idea that went out quite some time ago."

"Why don't you leave the guy alone, Helen, can't you see he's suffering? And anyway, I'm not so sure you're right."

The mood during the dinner after the movie was subdued. There was a little talk about the movie they had just seen as it left a powerful impression on them and not much more.

What should I do? thought Michael on the ride home. *I sure didn't expect it from Joanna. She never so much as mentioned she was going out with some guy. Maybe Helen was right, I should do the same. But how can I, after Joanna? I must talk to her; maybe tomorrow I'll call her... but what can I say to her?*

It was nearly a week after the movie episode. Joanna had been waiting all this time for Michael's call. *What can be the matter with him? He used to call every day.*

Could he be sick or away on business? It was actually pretty nice going out with Tim. He's a bit pompous but quite bright and seems to like the same things I do. It was a good movie. Maybe mother was right that I should date other men. I don't have to feel guilty that I did what she said. I really should call Michael if I do not hear from him soon. Joanna waited three more days and finally called him on his cell phone. Michael, realizing that it was Joanna calling from her home, hesitated a minute before answering.

"Hi Joanna, how have you been?" He tried to keep his voice on an even level, as he felt his heart pounding. "We haven't talked in a while."

Joanna felt as if she was hit by a heavy object. *What's the matter with him? Has he forgotten everything?*

"Are you well Michael? You sound so… so unnatural. Has something happened?"

"No, not really. But since you called, I might as well ask you about your new boyfriend. He certainly looks good."

Joanna was speechless for a while. "So that's it. Yes, I went out with a couple of guys. Is that forbidden? Are you such a jealous child and so insecure that you didn't want to talk to me anymore? Maybe it is just as well I found out now."

"Look Jo, I thought we had at least an understanding that we would tell each other about things that had a bearing on our relationship. Maybe I was wrong. True, there was no commitment, but it would have been much more honest to be open about such things."

"Well, I think you are making a big thing out of it, without any need for it. I think my mother was right. Let's wait until the six months are up."

"If that's the way you feel about it, it's OK with me." He hesitated whether to continue, not sure what exactly to say. Joanna, too, felt unsure; nothing was said for a while until Joanna said she hoped that they would be in touch.

CHAPTER 11

Much to Joanna's parents' satisfaction, she continued to go out with Tim, doing so quite frequently. Timothy still lived at home, working in his father's insurance company as assistant sales manager and member of the board, in anticipation of inheriting the presidency. Joanna was astounded the first time he took her home. Never had she been in a mansion as large, richly furnished, and decorated as his. It looked more like a palace from one of her history books. From the entrance hall, a curved staircase went up to the second floor, lined with large paintings that screamed bad taste. To make the whole appearance rather incongruous, an elevator door was next to the start of the staircase. The entrance hall was furnished with imitation Louis IV chairs together with a few pieces of Danish modern chests on which large Chinese vases were displayed. Tim had a whole wing of the house to himself and it was not long before they had made love in the privacy of his apartment. Meeting his parents was, however, not encouraging. She was cordially received the first time, but noticed on the second visit that his parents were rather distant, as if talking to a person occasionally met on the street. She didn't think much of it, and they continued to go out, mostly to expensive restaurants in the area, some movies, and occasionally to parties at the homes of a few of his friends. It was only several weeks later at a dinner, after another encounter with his parents, that Joanna asked him about this matter.

"Tell me, Tim, don't your parents like me? They seem so reserved whenever I meet them."

"Don't worry about it. I think it's just your imagination. They really are very nice people. We are from an old Protestant family, so maybe they have some deep-rooted prejudices, which are out of fashion these days. Don't pay any attention to it. Anyway, we aren't engaged to be married, so they can't say anything."

"And supposing we possibly will want to be engaged, at some stage, what then?"

"Like I said, don't worry about it. There's plenty of time for it. We're not in a rush, are we? And anyway, I'm sure my parents wouldn't say no to something I wanted."

"Well, I just wanted to know what you think."

Timothy dropped Joanna off at her parents quite early, as she had claimed she was not feeling well, maybe having eaten something that did not agree with her. She went upstairs to her room without so much as saying a word to her sister Vanessa, who was in the living room. *I like Tim, he is very good to me, and I can imagine that being married to him would be comfortable. There is something missing though. Being with Michael is more exciting, more challenging. On the other hand, never having to worry about money must be quite a thing, I could easily get used to it. But why am I toying with marrying him? He hasn't asked and I have a suspicion his parents would not be happy about it. Will he go against their wishes if it comes to that? He said that he can do whatever he wants. Would I go against the wishes of my parents? I am pretty sure I would if I knew that I was doing what was best for me, but would I? I really have known him for only few months. I did not know Michael for terribly long, either, and yet I fell in love with him. And now? Must I choose? How did I get myself into this situation? I don't want to think about it now. I must prepare the lessons for tomorrow.*

The feeling of confusion and indecision did not go away, not the next morning nor the following days. Joanna put off going out with Tim for an entire week on the pretext that she had a great deal of work to do for school. There was, in the back of her mind, also the hope of hearing from Michael. When this did not materialize, she decided to forego her pride and call him. This too, however, she put off for several days. Michael, in the meantime, had gone out a couple of times with the girl Helen had recommended, but his heart was not in it, and it was the girl who told him she did not think that she wanted to continue seeing him. When Joanna finally called, there was no answer. She left a message, asking Michael to call her before ten in the evening, as her parents would be home then.

Joanna was deeply depressed when two calls turned out not to be the anticipated one. At twenty minutes before ten, it was finally him. Michael sounded hesitant when he heard Joanna's voice.

"Hi, Joanna, how have you been?"

"I'm ok. What's with you?"

"Nothing much really... Listen, I've been thinking about you all the time, even when I don't want to. Let's stop playing a game. Either we want to be together or say loud and clear it was nice but finished. I know I may have acted childishly when I reacted after seeing you with that guy, but that's me. I'm not perfect; I do like things to be plain and open. Can you live with that?"

"Oh Michael, I didn't do anything underhanded. My parents pressured me to go out with other guys and I gave in. Can't you understand that? How could I say to you, look here, I am going with this or that person, would you mind? We only have two more months to go. We can do it."

"How?"

"I can't think now. I'm too upset. Let's meet for once next week and we can decide together, OK?"

"How about if I pick you up after school? I can take off a little early from work on Tuesday."

"Tuesday is fine but not from school. It can get back to my parents. How about at eight? I'll walk the two blocks to State Street and then go West, away from the river, and wait in the entrance to the beauty parlor there. It's about 100 yards from Main Street."

"I'll be there. And it is so good to talk to you again, Jo."

As usual, Michael arrived earlier at the meeting place than agreed. He looked impatiently at the right side mirror, trying to spot Joanna coming. It was raining hard and it was difficult for him to see people in the mirror. A bad omen, he thought. *We'll just have to see each other without her parents knowing, unless she feels comfortable about telling them that she is old enough and it's none of their business with whom she goes out.* The minutes dragged on when finally, without him seeing her, Joanna opened the car door and slipped in. It seemed like quite a while during which they just looked at each other until at last Joanna was in Michael's arms sobbing piteously.

"Why, what's the matter, darling? We're together now."

"I don't know what to say. I've rehearsed brave speeches but I cannot see myself standing up to my parents, especially my father. Meeting like thieves is also no option. We're not doing anything wrong."

"What can I say? Look, I am sure of my feelings towards you. I can wait. In fact, after I saw you with that guy, I went on a date recommended by my friends but it was no good. All the time I kept wishing it was you instead of her. Maybe it's not fair to ask you, but I will. Do you want to wait for these two months and then continue from where we were and see if it leads to something more permanent, or shall we decide now to, to… not see each other?"

"I'll wait," whispered Joanna and buried her head in Michael's shoulder. He did not say anything and just held her tightly.

CHAPTER 12

Joanna had been dreading talking to her parents about seeing Michael again. There were a few times when they were together alone in the living room, but she lacked the courage. She finally decided to talk to her mother first. When the two were in the kitchen preparing breakfast, Joanna said: You know, Mama, six months have passed since I last saw Michael; I have gone out with other men, but I still think I want to continue to see Michael and then decide if he really is the one for me or not. You said it was only for six months."

"You really had no contact with him for all this time?"

"I only spoke to him once on the phone, about two months ago, and that was all."

"What about Timothy? I've heard only good things about him and his family? What is wrong with him? "

"He may be a nice guy, but also is a bit of a stuffed shirt; his parents rather looked down on me. I was never comfortable there. Some of the others were pretty awful."

"If you marry Timothy, you do not marry his parents. Well, I'll talk with your Papa. He is not going to like it, but let me see what I can do."

The next morning at breakfast, Manuel did not finish his meal as quickly as he usually did but took his time looking deep in thought, his head bent over the cereal. He finally looked up at Joanna.

"Your Mama told me what you said to her yesterday morning and I am not pleased. I know I agreed to the six months hiatus after which you are free to see him. Still, if you do so, and I cannot stop you, you will be doing it not only against my wishes but against the best advice I can give based on years of life experience. You are legally of age, but I think still without the ability to know what is best for your future. Infatuations are common, but they don't last. Look at the great many divorces these days. In my days and before, when we listened to our parents' advice, the rate was considerably lower than now. Think about it."

It took a while for Joanna to reply until she said, "I appreciate your concern, Papa, and I'll certainly not jump into anything without weighing the pros and cons. Please, try and get to know Michael and judge him for what he is. He certainly doesn't want to convert me, never having mentioned the subject. His parents welcomed me as an equal, not like Timothy's parents who obviously looked down on me for what reason I do not know. Maybe, like Tim said, they consider themselves superior being an old Protestant family."

"I have not finished yet, Joanna. I have no wish to see Michael anymore; if you do decide to marry him, I will not give you my blessing and will stop considering you my daughter. It is up to you."

Joanna started crying, looking at her mother, hoping to hear some redeeming words from her. They were not forthcoming, as she had hoped. She just looked sad, and it was a few minutes before she said, "Papa is right. You said Tim was nice, if you think he is suitable then you should marry him."

Joanna got up, tears streaming down her face, and went to her room not to emerge until after her parents had left.

It was late in the evening when Joanna called her friend Megan and told her what happened.

"How could they do this to me? I'm not a child to be treated like this. What should I to do? Elope with Michael or see how it is with Tim? I can't do either."

"Have you spoken with Michael?"

"No, of course not, what can I say to him?"

"Look Jo, I understand your predicament. Looking at it objectively from the outside, I say if you are not madly in love with Michael – enough to go with him and say to hell with your parents – then forget about him! Anyway, I think Michael is not man enough. If he were, he would have told you that he would take care of you and not worry about your parents. There are plenty of other fish in the sea and you are an attractive and intelligent girl. You could also do worse than with Tim; besides being a nice guy, he is filthy rich and you would have no money worries in your future life."

"His parent's look down on me, thinking I'm not good or proper for him."

"I haven't said you should marry him. There will

be plenty others, but see how it goes with him and hear what he has to say about his parents. Think about it."

Michael was anxious. The last time he had talked with Joanna was before her talk with her parents and he was waiting for her call. When it did not materialize he was sure that it did not turn out well. He waited for the time her parents were usually in the restaurant and called. Her sister Eleanora, answered and said that she was not home, as instructed by Joanna. Only two days later, after ignoring repeated calls, did Joanna build up the courage to call Michael.

"Hi, Jo, I've been waiting to hear how it went with your parents. You cannot imagine the state I've been in since we last talked. So tell me."

"What can I say Michael? I'm torn, I haven't slept, and I've hardly been able to prepare lessons for my classes. My father will disown me if I marry you, that's what he said. Please tell me, what should I do?"

"Jo, I don't understand you. You should know what you want. You are a grown person; you have the right to decide what is good for you. I don't want in on my conscience if you later miss your family; it will make life miserable for us. On the other hand, your parents may eventually relent. So what do you say; are we together or not?"

It took some time for Joanna to reply, her sobbing continuing all the while.

"Please Michael; I have to do what my parents want. I'll feel awful if I can't have any contact with them. They supported me, encouraged me all the while, and I can't do this to them. I wish I could, I love you, but we have to break up. Maybe they'll come around one day and change their minds."

"I think you're making a big mistake. We could have a wonderful life together and you're throwing it all away. Do you think I can sit around and wait indefinitely until maybe your parents will know what is good for their daughter?" Michael's voice changed and became hoarse, hardly able to continue. "So it's goodbye, Jo… it was nice while it lasted… it…" he hung up.

It was only a few days later that David called Michael suggesting he come for dinner, as they had not been together for a while.

"So how are things with you? Aren't the six months you're not supposed to see your girlfriend almost over? It should be a great relief for both of you. How about Friday evening around six as usual, OK? And don't forget to bring her along."

"I don't know, I don't want to see anybody. Yes, the wait is over. It is all over. For good."

"You don't mean you've broken up, do you? Then you certainly must come, what are friends for?"

"Give me a couple of days, I'll get back to you, anyway today is only Monday."

Michael did go over to his friends place after much hesitation. It was a sad evening. David and Helen were not able to cheer him up and all their suggestions fell on deaf ears. He went home as depressed as he came.

Part II

CHAPTER 13

2006

It was Sunday. Michael and Caroline were sitting in their living room while a heavy February snowstorm raged outside. The trees in front of their house took on a strange white shape; their branches bent tiredly from the heavy load piled upon them in great clumps. The driveway had disappeared, making their house seem isolated from its surroundings. After reading their newspapers quietly for a while, only glancing occasionally outside to see how much snow had accumulated in the meantime, Caroline put down her paper and said, "We've been married almost six years and I've felt for a while now that it's about time we should start a family. I'll be thirty in a couple of years and I'd like to have a few kids around the house," she said, her voice somewhat shrill. "You are such a good Jewish boy. Doesn't it say in the bible that one should be fruitful and multiply? When do you expect to start?"

Michael looked up with a start and took a minute or two to reply, "We've been over this many times, Caroline. Why do you have to nag? We work all the time, hardly ever have time off, taking stuff home from work so that we hardly have free evenings or weekends. Now you want to jump right in and have babies to keep you up at night? That is not exactly what I expect from life. I miss friends, a cultural life, and having fun. I thought that is also what you wanted, at least that was my impression when we first went out together. Now it is only our career, coming home, beat, at nine or ten in the evening."

"Ok, ok, you may have a point. Look, I have a suggestion. We both have accrued a lot of vacation time. Why don't we take a good long holiday, say in Europe or wherever, and begin a family after that. What do you say?"

"It sounds like a good idea. I have been thinking about doing it for quite some time, although not in relation to starting a family; but you have a point there. OK, let's plan on a nice vacation; where we want to go, how long a trip, and of course look into the financial aspects involved."

"Sure, sounds good to me. Why don't you come up with a plan? I guess Europe would be best; there is so much to see there, and it is not as far as going to China or Japan. I never asked you if you have been abroad.

"I've only gone as far as Bermuda, I went there as a kid with my parents on a cruise. It was great, I always wanted to go again somewhere by ship. I don't want to do it now; I'd rather take the time exploring. I'll think about an itinerary, and we will talk about it."

Less than a week later, on Saturday when they were having breakfast, the subject of a vacation came up again.

They had made it a habit to have a leisurely meal together on weekends, as they usually rushed out on weekday mornings for work, each grabbing something quick.

"How long a trip do you think we should take?" asked Michael. "Some guys at work suggested a travel agency. I called, and got some pretty good ideas from them for what should be a comfortable but not luxurious trip."

"So, what did they suggest?"

"They, provided several options. I think the best one for us would be to concentrate on just a few countries."

"That sounds reasonable to me, too. No sense just running around from place to place only to say we have been there. Let's say we go for a month, what kind of money would we need for such a trip?"

"Going off-season would be best, of course; places are both less crowded and expensive. May or September is recommended. We must figure on at least two hundred dollars a day plus the airfare. For a month, this would come to about a little more than seven thousand. I would add another thousand just to be on the safe side."

"It seems like a lot of money, don't you think? We could make it a little shorter. Don't forget having a family will also cut into our savings."

"I thought the idea was for a long break as we had no real vacations to speak of. We have put quite a bit aside during all this time, and I think we can certainly afford it and still have enough left. Some of the families here on our street have kids on salaries certainly a lot less than ours. Take our neighbors, the Wideners for example."

"Well, OK, and where do you suggest we go?"

"Since we will be going in the spring or fall, I think it will be best if we go to southern Europe, as the temperatures there will be comfortable, whereas in the north it may be cold. It means to concentrate on France, Italy, Portugal, and Spain. In fact, even this may be too much. Maybe without Italy, though there is much to see there too. How does that sound to you?"

"It makes sense. We'll have to rent a car, of course. Let's make a detailed plan and make necessary reservations."

They left for Paris right before Labor Day to reduce the amount of vacation time taken from work. It had been an exhausting summer, trying to clear their desks and leave detailed instructions to their temporary replacements. Michael's job, as chief project manager, was to oversee the progress of the various projects in the company, allocate needed resources, as well as be in contact with customers. Caroline was a systems analyst, working in a large manufacturing company dealing in precision instruments for both civilian and military use. Both were unable to sleep on the night flight, talking about their concern about the work left behind and possible problems that may arise during their absence. They were thus chagrined to find the room in their hotel not ready at the early hour of their arrival. They sat for what seemed the longest time in the lobby until they finally could enter their room and sleep for hours.

The ten days they had allocated for France were, of course, insufficient. Paris was overwhelming. The beauty of the city and the strangeness of it left them gasping.

They had read up about it in their guidebooks, of course, but needed time to overcome the problems with local customs, language, food, and transportation. Before they realized it, they had to continue on their way. They were in Chartres, the Loire valley, and the Dordogne, each with their innumerable sights. Michael thought the most impressive of all these places were the Lascaux caves with the prehistoric paintings.

"I never imagined pre-historic people to be able to achieve works of art like that. The lifelike presentation of the animals, their magnificent colors, is unbelievable. They used the uneven stones of the walls to give the effect of bas-relief to some of the figures. What do you think, Caroline?"

"Well, they were nice. I never really thought much about these people. What do you mean by bas-relief?"

"It means the figure is not two dimensional but yet not completely three dimensional. It gives you a more realistic impression. Just look at the head of Washington on a quarter and you'll see what I mean."

They arrived in Barcelona after a long drive south, going along the Costa Brava and stopping at the Dali Museum in Figueres, and in Gerona with its Jewish quarter in the old town. On the way, Caroline complained she was getting tired, as they had no time to relax for a few days in a nice resort.

"But Caroline, we planned the itinerary together, and we made hotel reservations accordingly. We can't change it now. Don't we want to see as much as possible in the time we have? We could have done just one country in the month but you didn't want to do it that way."

They checked in to their hotel at the Plaza Cataluña and rested a while, after which Michael suggested they go and explore the city.

"Why don't you go by yourself? I'll stay in, maybe sit in the café downstairs, and just take it easy. Be back by seven so we can go for dinner. Maybe you'll come across a nice place."

"I'll be back before. From what I know most restaurants here do not serve dinner before nine. Maybe we can find some who cater especially for the tourists, but those will be less authentic, I guess."

"I don't care! We are used to eating at seven, and even earlier. We had no problem in France so why should we change now?"

"OK, I'll look around and see what I can find."

With that, Michael left the room. He came back well before seven full of excitement at seeing the cathedral, discovering the Picasso museum that was unfortunately closed at that hour, the Rambla with the hordes of people just walking along. He also mentioned a Tapas restaurant, across from the Plaza, which was open.

"Let's go there. I remember a Spanish restaurant in Bridgeport that had these wonderful dishes. I bet you'll like it."

"I don't know much about Bridgeport; it's such an old industrial town. It seems to me as rather an odd place to have a restaurant of this kind. We have very nice places in Westport, as you well know, or in Darien."

The Tapas restaurant was not a great success. The dishes were too exotic for Caroline, the place too noisy. She was especially annoyed to see the people sitting at the bar throwing cigarette ashes and butts on the floor.

"How can people behave like that? It's disgusting! Tomorrow we should maybe try the restaurant in the hotel. I guess it'll be a little more civilized."

Michael agreed, albeit not vey enthusiastically.

After a couple more days in Barcelona, they drove to Madrid and checked into a small hotel near the Plaza de Espana. It was an excellent choice, being close to the Royal Palace, right on the Grand Via. Dinner was again a problem. Taking no chances, they decided to eat in the hotel. When going down, they found the doors closed as Michael had said, and were told they could eat as early as nine o'clock, to Caroline's great disappointment. The following morning, they went to the Royal Palace and the El Greco museum where they saw the famous painting of Toledo. They decided to take it easy in the afternoon and sat in a café in the Plaza Mayor. Caroline was astounded at this huge arcaded and decorated rectangle with innumerable fancy stores and cafes. She could not believe it was built in the 16th century.

"Why, back home anything two-hundred years old is considered ancient. Here and in France it would be practically modern. It's really very interesting."

"Yes," Michael agreed. "History comes alive in all the places we have been to. Can you believe right here, at this place, many an *auto-da-fé* was conducted by the Inquisition and many of our ancestors were burned alive at the stake? Not only here, of course, but also in many places in Spain. I think we made a great choice in coming here. There is so much to see and learn."

After sitting a while, enjoying a leisurely coffee and pastry, they got up to walk around the square to look in the shop windows. Just a few minutes later, Michael saw a woman who looked familiar, standing at the next store looking at the displays. It took only a few seconds to realize it was Joanna. He took Caroline's hand and pulled her along towards where she was standing. Michael softly called her name when they were nearly behind her. Joanna turned around, the surprise on her face turned into a big smile.

"My, it's you, Michael. I haven't seen you in ages. Where have you…" Here, she stopped, looking at Caroline still holding his hand. Her face now composed, only a questioning look left.

"It sure is a surprise seeing you here," Michael said. "How is your husband, isn't he here with you?"

"No, I've come to explore my roots which you know are here. It took me too long to do it. And you?"

Michael had in the meantime turned to Caroline and said, "Caroline, meet Joanna, an old friend of mine. Joanna; this is my wife Caroline."

The two women looked at each other briefly before extending their hands politely to shake that of the other.

"We're on a long overdue vacation. We were in France for ten days and have now started Spain, after having been in Barcelona. We'll be heading south to Granada the day after tomorrow. Are you planning to stay here long?"

"Oh, I guess about two-to-three weeks. I thought of going down to Granada on Tuesday. Why, it's the day you're going south, too. I decided to take the train rather than drive by myself these long distances."

"Then why don't you come with us? Where are you staying? We're near the Plaza de Espana."

"I'd love to come with you. It's better than riding alone. I'm staying not far from you. I am near the Plaza Puerta del Sol."

Michael did not notice Caroline's rather displeased expression when he said, "Great, give me the exact address, we'll come to pick you up. We'll have to decide at what time and will call you later."

"It's very good of you, but rather than have you drive around town, I'll take a taxi and be at your hotel at the time you want. Where are you staying?"

"We're at the hotel Senator Espana on the Grand Via."

"Again, thanks so much. I'll be waiting for your call to tell me when to come. Please leave a message if I'm not in."

Maybe it was because of the rain that started to come down, but hardly a word was exchanged between Michael and Caroline on the way back to their hotel.

Only when they were back in their room did Caroline, with an annoyed expression on her face, say, "Was she a girlfriend of yours? You've never mentioned her."

"Did I ever ask you who your boyfriends were? What difference does it make if she was a girlfriend or just an acquaintance? As a matter of fact, I knew her when she was at UConn. As far as I know, she married a wealthy guy. Does that satisfy you?"

"You still didn't answer my question, but forget it. Just tell me why you had to invite her to drive south with us?"

"I thought it was a nice thing to do. Wouldn't you have done the same thing if it were somebody you had known back home?"

Joanna was at Michael and Caroline's hotel promptly at nine on Tuesday morning, waiting for them to come down. They did so after a short time, then took the car out of the garage and started on the road to Granada. There was little conversation at first, as Michael was busy following the GPS directions for getting out of the city and onto the correct highway. Joanna, who had sensed Caroline's displeasure and Michael's withdrawal, tried to break the silence by mentioning her impressions of the various sites in Madrid and Toledo.

"I think what left the most indelible impression on me was the approach to Toledo. I saw El Greco's painting of that city, which he did more than four hundred years ago, just the day before, and it seemed as if time stood still. I should also mention that I feel at home here, though my parents hardly ever mentioned the country of their ancestors."

"But your parents have a Spanish restaurant and you seemed to be very familiar with Spanish tradition and customs," Michael said before he realized that it might have been a mistake.

"That's true; I must have absorbed some of it. Maybe that's why I was so interested in what you told me about the edict that forced Jews to convert to Christianity, or expelled those that refused in 1492."

Michael wanted to know whether she had studied this part of Spain's history any further but refrained from asking and concentrated on his driving.

They arrived in Granada after about four-and-a-half hours, dropped Joanna off at her hotel and checked into theirs. They hardly talked during the late lunch at the hotel, as Caroline kept wondering about her husband's and Joanna's past relationship. It was only when they were up in their room, trying to rest from the trip, that Caroline sullenly asked why they had to make a date with her for dinner at the restaurant she recommended.

"I think it was the polite thing to do. What reason was there to refuse? And anyway, she knows Spanish restaurants better than we do, so why not?"

"I have a hunch she was more than just an acquaintance of yours. Why is she here by herself without her husband? Didn't you notice she doesn't have a wedding ring?"

"No, I didn't notice, and what do I care about it? OK, so we went out together a couple of times and she introduced me to a Spanish restaurant in Bridgeport. What's the big deal? As for her husband, how should I know where he is? I don't care. Please honey; let us take it easy, there is no harm in seeing her. I guess we will part ways after Granada anyway."

Dinner was pleasant enough. The food and the wine impressed even Caroline. They met again in the same restaurant the following evening after they, separately, visited the Alhambra. Their reservations had been for different hours. Joanna was able to enlarge on what they had seen, being more knowledgeable about the history of the extraordinary fortress, which was erected in the 14th century. They agreed to jointly explore the city the following day; visit the summer palace of the Kings of Granada, called the Generalife, the Cathedral quarter, and a famous Carthusian Monastery. They again enjoyed dinner that evening, and parted amiably, with Michael and Caroline driving to Malaga and Joanna taking the train to Cordoba.

CHAPTER 14

It sure was a shock to see Michael all of a sudden in Madrid. There was a time I thought a lot about him, the mistake I made in marrying Tim and not him. Now he's married to this uptight girl. Why did he ever do that? I didn't think he was the type. I'm sure he still has feelings for me, as he tried to hide it. Would I still want to marry him? Sure, if he's still the same Michael I knew six years ago. What about my parents? I don't care anymore. They made a big fuss about my marrying a Protestant, though they had encouraged me to go out with him in the first place. I'd never realized how prejudiced they were. I'm so much older now and know that I don't need their approval. I wonder what it'll be like in Cordoba and Aguilar de la Frontera. Why is it so important for me to find out if our family really has Jewish roots? The more I've learned about the Jewish religion the more it seems that our customs have a lot in common with it. But it's not only that. The morality of Jewish religion and the emphasis on the here and now, rather than the hereafter, seems very attractive. All these thoughts went through Joanna's head while she rode the train to Cordoba, looking at the varied scenery. The beautiful sunshine made the poorest hamlets look magnificent.

They passed vast olive oil groves, where the branches on these gnarled, unique tree trunks were covered with leaves that shone silvery in the wind. Isolated haciendas were dispersed every which way, with each seemingly living in a world of its own. All these impressions caused her bothersome thoughts to remain in the background.

Arriving in Cordoba, Joanna checked into the Hotel Conquistador, in the heart of the old Jewish quarter, the Juderia, next to the Cathedral that used to be a mosque in the times of the Moors. It was built at the end of the eighth century but converted into a church after the conquest of the city by Ferdinand III of Castile in the 13th century. After lunch and the customary Spanish siesta, Joanna went to the Cathedral. It was of the most unusual construction, with its innumerable golden multi-lobed arches. Walking inside was like being in a hall of mirrors. She learned that some of the marble pillars had been part of an earlier Christian church at this place and were taken from Roman and Visigoths buildings.

In the evening Joanna went to a nearby Tapas Bar crowded with young people talking noisily so that it was nearly impossible to hear the music of the lonely guitar player. She was the only single woman in the crowd. There were girls sitting together at some of the tables, but men were in the majority. No sooner had she started on the various dishes the waiter had brought her, that a man who seemed to be in his early thirties approached her table and asked if he might join her as she seemed rather lonely. He introduced himself as Enrique Sanchez Marques. He was a rather good-looking man; his high forehead and full shiny black hair, parted in the middle and falling down to nearly shoulder height, giving the impression of an artist. After only a short hesitation, Joanna agreed and introduced herself.

"From your speech I understand you're not from here, although your Spanish is very good. I can't place your accent."

"I'm American, but my ancestors came from around here three generations ago and I picked up the language at home. Naturally, it's no longer as good as yours. I teach history in a High School at home."

"That's a coincidence: I'm at the University here in the faculty of Philosophy and Letters, studying for my doctorate in history. How long are you going to be here? And, I should have asked, what brings you here in the first place? I hope I am not too nosy."

He seems to be a nice young man. I was warned to be careful of Spanish men, they think they are the greatest gift on earth and want immediately to take you to bed. "I wanted to come here for a long time, just curious what it's like. I want to learn more about the history of this area, so maybe you can teach me a little. As for staying here, I figure I'll be in Cordoba about four or five days. I also want to see other parts of the country."

"It would be my pleasure to show you around, if you wish. My time is quite flexible except for the hours I am working as an instructor in undergraduate classes.

Tomorrow, for example, I'll be busy in the afternoon." Just then, he saw the waiter bringing his order to his table and motioned for him to come to Joanna's. He also ordered a bottle of wine.

So maybe he wants to get me drunk so that I will be more amenable to his advances? Not yet anyway. He's attractive, but let's see what develops. In the meantime, I may be able to learn a great deal from him if he really is what he claims to be. "I sure am looking forward to you showing me around a little, I hope you'll be able to spare the time also from your studies. How far along are you?"

"I pretty much finished with my course requirements and am working on my thesis."

"Can you tell me what it is about?"

"Sure, I'm looking into the change from Moslem to Christian rule in al-Andalus, and the effect on the local population and their attitudes. There was, as you may know, a large Jewish population here, some of whom were in high positions, others contributed to the cultural life as mathematicians, philosophers, and poets."

"Yes, I've read a little about it but would like to learn more. Would it be impertinent to ask about your religious affiliation?"

"No, not at all. Like most everybody here I am Catholic, but not a very observant one. Many young people here don't take their religion very seriously. I imagine you also must be Catholic from what you told me about your background."

"Well, not exactly. We are Seventh-day-Adventists, if you have heard of it."

"I'm afraid not. Please tell me."

"It's a Protestant Christian denomination. We keep the seventh day of the week, the Sabbath, as the day of rest, not Sunday, and our emphasis is on the imminent second coming of Jesus Christ. But like you, I am taking my religion rather lightly."

During the rest of the meal they conversed about all sorts of trivial matters until, sometime after they had finished, Enrique asked if Joanna would like to go to some nightclub in the area where good music was always to be heard.

"I think it might be nice another time, Enrique, but I'm a little tired tonight, I walked my feet off today after coming from Granada. I was in the Cathedral and then all over. Another time maybe would be fine."

Enrique called the waiter for the check and pulled out his wallet to pay. Joanna, her voice raised a little, protested sharply, "We are going to split the bill; otherwise I won't go with you anymore. How much is it?"

"There we go again, you are obviously an American who cannot relax and accept the way things are in other places. If you insist, I won't argue this time. Better let's talk about tomorrow morning. I suggest we go to the museum here. It's not the greatest, but you might find things that are of interest. It opens at nine, except for Tuesday, so we can spend a lot of time there and maybe at some other places. I don't have to be at the University until four. Where are you staying?"

"I'm at the Conquistador. I'd love to go to the museum

and have planned to do just that. It's very nice of you to suggest it. Why don't you come a little before nine. I'll be down in the lobby by then. "

"So why don't I accompany you to your hotel whenever you feel like going? It is not very far."

They walked slowly to the hotel, their hands occasionally brushing against each other. Joanna assumed it was deliberate on his part with the intention of holding hers. She made sure it this would not happen. Upon reaching the hotel doorman she extended her hand to Enrique's, shook his, and with a quick "See you in the morning," turned around for the doorman to open the door for her. *I'm going to have a problem with him, and will have to figure out how to handle it. He's attractive and does seem pretty nice. He can certainly teach me a lot about the history of this part of the country.*

It was past nine and Enrique had not come to the hotel. *Maybe he's given up on making an easy conquest,* thought Joanna. *If he doesn't come soon I'll go to the museum by myself. Too bad, I'd hoped to learn a lot from him.* Just as she was about to leave, Enrique appeared, quite nonchalantly, greeting Joanna profusely and saying how well she looked in the morning after a rest. Their first stop was the Cordoba Museum of Archeology. They viewed the Roman collection that included mosaics, sculptures, and architecture. There was also a collection of Moorish artifacts found nearby. It was interesting, but not what Joanna had been looking for, and they left after not spending very much time there.

The next stop was the Tower of Calahorra. The tourist brochure claimed it was built in 1369 by Enrique II of Trastamara to defend the city against his cruel half brother Pedro I. As they neared the sight, Enrique told Joanna that it certainly was an interesting site but the advertisement was historically wrong.

"I don't understand why they have not changed it. First of all, my namesake defeated his half brother in 1369, and became King of Castile and Leon after him. Therefore, he didn't need to defend the site against him. He only restored an older fortress built by the Moors in the twelfth century and added a third tower. Also, Pedro was not as cruel as it is implied. He was very good for the Jews; maybe this is why the Christian population did not like him. Enrique, on the other hand, I am ashamed to say, was the one who ordered the killings of many Jews because of their religion."

"I've read a little about the persecution of the Jews in Spain, culminating in the expulsion, but really don't know very much. I was told about the *Marranos*, or I should rather have said the *Conversos*, but am curious to know more about them. Especially if there are those now in Spain who believe they are the descendants of these converted Jews, and maybe want to revert to their religious origin."

"Well, this is a big subject, I hope I'll be able to see you some more during your stay here so we can talk about it. I see you know *Marranos* is a pejorative term. Not many people do. Come, let's go and see the audiovisual presentation of how life was here around the 10th century when Christian, Moorish and Jewish cultures lived peacefully side-by-side. It's done very well, you may like it."

"It was a well done presentation," Joanna said when they were sitting in a café having sandwiches for lunch. "But it seems to paint such a wonderful life of togetherness. It does not seem to have happened before or after ever again, in any place. Was it really so?"

"I also think that things were not quite as wonderful as that. We know that Moslems never accepted Christians or Jews as equals. People adhering to these religions always had to pay a certain tax from which Moslems were exempted. Historians actually do not agree on the dates of the so-called Golden age. This is the name given to this era. It was marked especially by the contribution of Jewish philosophers, poets, and physicians. There was Maimonides, Yehuda Halevy, and many others. It started possibly in the eighth or nineth century, and when it ended is also debated. This occurred, most likely, in the twelfth century, either with the end of the Cordoba Caliphate or possibly with the massacre in Granada. By the way, Christian sects who were persecuted by the Catholic Church in Europe found refuge in Moslem Spain. As for the Jews, they were here long before. Supposedly, some came as early as the time of King Solomon. It is certain that a fair number came as a result of the Roman conquest of Judea; we are talking hundreds of years before the Golden Age. Have you studied Roman history?"

"To tell the truth, very superficially. There is so much I would want to know."

"Well, you must at least know about the might of the Roman army. What you might not know is that those stubborn Jews gave them a hard time. The Great War against Rome started around 66 AD. In 70 AD, the Jewish Temple was destroyed and with it the rebellion was nearly over. A few holdouts remained; the last one was Massada, the desert fortress that fell in 73 AD. There was another rebellion around 132AD led by Bar Kochba. During both wars, coins were issued to indicate the country's independence from Rome. It is interesting that in Israel today they use the Shekel and the Half Shekel named after those issued during the Great War. The results of both revolts were tragic for the Jews. Many were killed, others exiled. After the Bar Kochba revolt, the previous name of Province Judea was changed to Syria Palaestina."

"I heard about these revolts against Rome and saw some of the coins the Jews issued during those wars in a museum in New York. It was very interesting. My, but you know a lot about Jewish history in Spain." *I wonder if he is a descendant of Conversos. It would be interesting to know.* "Tell me, does anyone know how many Jews lived in Spain at the time of the expulsion, and how many remained as *Conversos*?"

"The exact numbers are not known. There are various estimates, ranging from a quarter million to 800,000.

One can assume that there were maybe 300,000 before the expulsion, about half left the country and the rest converted. What would be interesting is if DNA studies could be made to see how many Spaniards today carry Sephardic-Jewish genes. I bet the number could be very high. But I must leave now for the University. Can we meet for dinner later?"

Joanna thought for a moment and then agreed. "Ok, where and at what time?"

"Let's say at nine thirty at the same place as yesterday. It was nice."

Enrique was again late, coming to the restaurant twenty minutes after their agreed time. Joanna, believing in punctuality, was annoyed and showed it.

"I've been waiting for quite a while and was ready to order dinner. Why are you always late?"

"I can always see you are American. We are much more relaxed than you people are. Nobody is excited about little things; I think we are much happier because of it."

"Oh well, let's forget it and order. I'm starved."

The food was very good again, and with the wine ordered by Enrique they spent a pleasant couple of hours talking about their respective backgrounds, world politics, preferred music and more. Finally, Joanna said she was feeling tired and thought it was time to part. She suggested meeting the following day, or the one after, as she wanted to learn more about local history.

"I'd love to see you tomorrow again, but only in the afternoon. But look, it is really not very late. Again, our cultural differences come to the fore. Why don't we at least go for a short nightcap in the bar I mentioned yesterday? I bet you'd like the music there."

The bar, located just a block away, was a lively place. Joanna was pleased to hear a classical guitarist was playing; but the noisy crowd did mar her enjoyment, and she said so to Enrique.

"I see we are never going to overcome our cultural differences. This is a bar, not a concert hall. Listen to the applause he gets. The people enjoy both their conversations and the music. But let us go."

Again, as with the dinners, they argued about Enrique wishing to pay for both, which Joanna did not accept and insisted on sharing the expenses. They walked slowly, with Enrique getting hold of Joanna's hand as they neared the hotel. *I know he wants to come up, what do I want? He seems OK. I have not been with a man for a long time and miss it. There have not been many since Tim and I parted. He wasn't so great actually, thinking mostly about himself. Let me see how Enrique will broach it.*

As they were at the entrance, Enrique asked if she would mind if he came up with her, as he was very much taken by her and would like to see if they could get closer.

"I have met only few American girls, but they were superficial, only interested in what they could buy, saying the fashion here was not as nice as back in the US. None had any interest in history or any deeper subject.

You should've heard them complain that dinner was not ready at half past six in the afternoon. No understanding of cultural differences. Not like you."

She answered simply by pulling him along, nodding to the doorman, and going up to her room. As they entered, Enrique put his arm around Joanna's shoulder, turned her towards him and kissed her strongly, trying to have her open her lips and let his tongue enter to meet hers. Joanna was reluctant at first but soon relented, their kisses becoming more passionate.

"Not so quick, Enrique, we have time. She pulled him to the sofa and sat down. Enrique looked deep into her eyes and said, "I wish you would stay here longer, or maybe come back forever. I have at least two more years to finish my doctorate."

"It does seem nice to be with you, but I've known you just a couple of days. Let's not make too much of it."

In reply, Enrique started to unbutton Joanna's blouse while she, in turn, unfastened his tie. Their ardor increased to a fever pitch, with Enrique having a hard time removing her bra. Joanna finally undid it, allowing him to bend his head, and suck gently on her erect nipples. The rest of the clothes followed quickly and they were standing holding each other close, his erect member pressing hard against her, when Joanna suddenly said: "Good lord, Enrique, where is your condom? We can't do it without."

"Why? It's so much better without this artificial membrane. I'm perfectly healthy, no HIV, and I imagine you do not have it either."

Joanna had withdrawn in the meantime to the sofa, holding some of her clothes over her, looking at him angrily.

"You should know better. How could you think of doing it without protection? Please go. I am sorry you turned out this way."

Enrique was still standing, an uncertain expression on his face, his member still erect. Only after what seemed to Joanna a long time, did he acquiesce, put on his boxer shorts, picked up his remaining clothes and said, "I see you're no different from the other American girls, after all. I actually thought you were."

"I see you have known many of my compatriots. Well, try again with somebody else. I've been warned about Latin men and should have heeded the advice. Sorry, I thought you were different. Goodbye!"

Enrique finished dressing quickly and left the room without a word. *Phew, I guess I was lucky; at least he was a bit refined. He could have easily raped me; nobody would have heard my shouting. And I was in the mood for a good fuck. It was so good with Michael; he was gentle, yet dominant, and so considerate.*

It took a long while for Joanna to relax and finally go to sleep. She watched TV for a while, thinking about how Spanish programs were no better than those at home.

Her mood the next morning was still rotten and did not improve until, after a good breakfast, she went out into the bright sunshine and started walking around town. As she had planned to leave the following day for Aguilar de la Frontera, she wanted to see as much as possible of the city. First on her agenda was the synagogue on the Calle de los Judios. It was built in the beginning of the 14th century and was the only one remaining of three. As there was no Jewish congregation in town, it was designated a museum and reopened after restoration in 1985 on the occasion of Maimonides' 800th birthday. Not far was the Statue of Maimonides, hidden away in a lovely small alley, a profusion of flowers pouring down from the numerous flowerpots on the window sills. Walking in this neighborhood of narrow streets, the plain white-washed houses leaning on each other, she felt transported back in time, feeling a nostalgia she could not understand. Occasionally, Joanna would cross an open door through which she saw beautiful courtyards with a great deal of colorful vegetation, leading apparently to the apartment of the owner. One such courtyard had a small fountain splashing gaily in a basin decorated with multi-colored mosaics. Cordoba was a good-sized town with numerous sights. She walked to the ruins of the Moorish castle, which was built in the ninth century, four hundred years before the Christians conquered the city. Moslems and Jews continued to live there after that, but the relatively peaceful coexistence never returned, as she was told.

By then, Joanna felt it was time for lunch and stopped at an outdoor café, as the day had become warm and sunny. She ordered a sandwich and a glass of beer when the woman sitting at the table next to hers bent over to her and said, "Please excuse my intrusion, but you have an English guide book, yet you spoke so fluently with the waiter. My curiosity just got the better of me. Where are you from?" The woman was well dressed. She had a pleasant looking face, mostly unlined except for the beginning of the smallest wrinkles at the eyes, maybe in her forties, her smile inspiring confidence.

"I'm American, but know the language well, being of Spanish heritage. Do you live here in Cordoba?"

"I sure do, as has my family for very many generations; since the 13th century. My name is Maria Delarosa Iglesias, by the way."

"I'm pleased to meet you. I'm Joanna Aguilar. It's very interesting to me that your family has such ancient roots here, as I'm anxious to learn more about the history of this country. My family came from here at the beginning of the last century but my parents didn't know much of our family history or of their hometown. At least that's what they said."

"You mean you have the same name as our neighboring town? That is extraordinary. Then, your people must have come from around here. I am afraid, though, that you have to be more specific as we cannot cover the entire history of Spain, and I am not qualified to do that. But do come and sit at my table, it will be more comfortable that way."

Joanna moved over but hesitated a few minutes before she said, "I do know a little about the history of Spain. What has interested me lately in particular is what I've learned about the persecution of the Jews by the Church and the expulsion of those who did not convert at the end of the 15th century. I'm not Jewish, by the way. I'm curious: Do you know if there are any people here who identify with being the descendants of those who converted and remained here?"

"I am sure there are, but you will have to dig deep to find them; there is still a reluctance to admit it openly. Did you know that the Inquisition was abolished in Spain only in 1834?" Maria took a long look at Joanna and continued, "You look like a nice young woman, why don't you come over this evening to my home and we can talk there at leisure. I live on 7 Calle Lucano, not far from the corner with Calle de San Fernando. Ring the bell with my name on it; my apartment is on the far side of the courtyard as you enter. Would you like that?"

"Why, certainly. That's very kind of you. What time would be convenient?"

"Make it eight; we will have a light supper."

Maria finished sipping her wine while Joanna thanked her again and took her leave. *This sure was unexpected. I have the feeling that she knows quite a bit about Conversos and just did not want to talk about it in the café. Whatever, it should be nice to see how people live here.*

She continued on her tour of the town; went to Posado del Potro, where Cervantes had stayed, the Roman bridge, and the Episcopal Palace, returning exhausted to the hotel.

Looking at the map of the town, Joanna noticed that Maria's apartment was not very far from the hotel, and arrived there promptly at the appointed time. The entire block in which her place was located looked somewhat run down, seemingly built a very long time ago. The large stones of the buildings appeared to have grown out of the earth, like this was where they belonged. There were a few fashionable stores located on the block, intermingled with what seemed to be private residences as seen from the bells with names on them. The door opened upon her ringing the bell marked with Delarosa, leading Joanna into a gorgeous courtyard. The sight of the myriad of potted flowers hanging from windowsills and planted in soil all around the beautifully tiled floor was overwhelming, especially when compared with the contrasting exterior. Before reaching the designated door, it was opened by Maria, smilingly inviting Joanna in, welcoming her warmly. The interior, too, was most pleasing. The small living room was furnished with what seemed to be antique pieces, including a deep red and blue oriental rug, which gave a feeling of warmth and continuity. Several kinds of heirlooms were displayed on the shelves of a breakfront including a beautifully crafted silver candelabrum. It appeared, though, that many years ago people paid less attention to comfort than beauty. Joanna soon found out as she sat on the sofa next to Maria who placed herself on the easy chair, which seemed to be her usual spot. Joanna also noticed that there was no TV in the room, only a High-Fi system and a great number of CDs.

There were a few moments of silence until Maria said, "Let us talk for a little while, as I think it is a bit too early for supper, if it is all right with you." Joanna readily agreed. "I have become used to these late supper hours, as I'm almost two weeks in Spain. I don't remember if I mentioned that my parents own a Spanish restaurant, but they have, of course, to keep to American mealtime hours. You have a beautiful place here, how long has it been in your family's possession?"

"Not very long by our standards, only about 120 years since this whole section of town was built. You asked about *Conversos*, although you did not use this word. It is common knowledge here that a good percentage of people in Spain are descendants of those Jews that converted, be it voluntarily or under pressure. Most people do not want to be bothered having to think what it would mean for them to know they are indeed of Jewish extraction. Since you are not Jewish I find it puzzling you are so interested in this subject."

"Well, my family belongs to a certain Christian denomination and we keep several customs that can also be found in the Jewish religion. We are called Seventh-Day Adventists. I was wondering if we might have some Jewish roots."

"I am not familiar with your denomination, but no matter. I can tell you that I have been brought up in what may be called a normal, Catholic family like most of the people here. It is based on tradition more than deep religious beliefs. I have always wondered about certain customs we had in the family that were handed down from mother to daughter over the generations, such as the thorough spring-cleaning of the house just before

Easter. Not a speck of dust was allowed to remain. We also had this custom of bathing and putting on clean clothes on Friday afternoon. The most peculiar practice in our family was to go out on Saturday nights, when there were no clouds, and see who would be the first to spot three stars. So I went and studied the Jewish religion and practice, privately of course, and found distinct similarities that led me to be quite certain my family had their roots in the converted Jews who remained in this country after the expulsion. Only my intimate friends know what I have just told you, and some of them have told me of similar experiences in their families. Right now, I have no interest in pursuing it any further or have any desire to delve deeper into my apparent Jewish roots. But come into the kitchen, I have talked quite a while, it is time for us to eat something."

The kitchen was enormous by modern American standards; it was notable for the large number of brightly shining brass cooking utensils hanging on the wall besides the most modern equipment. The large table was set for two, and the smell emanating from the covered pot simmering on the stove was enticing. Maria invited Joanna to sit down, and went to the refrigerator to take out a big bowl of Gazpacho, which she ladled into the soup bowls. She also poured a generous amount of wine into the goblets, raised her glass, and wished Joanna a long life. This, by the way, she said, seems also to be a Jewish custom. They now say "to life" when raising their glass for a toast. The Gazpacho was tasty but not as thick as she remembered from home. The seafood paella that followed was heavenly. It was better then what she remembered from home, and she complimented Maria highly.

"Thank you so much, the paella is the best I've had; I'll be very grateful if I can have your recipe for it, since I would like to give it to my mother. I also appreciate what you told me about your family's apparent Jewish customs. Someone else had told me about the feeling that many here are of Jewish heritage. I'm beginning to think that as we are also Spanish, that maybe we also had some of these customs in my family, and that made my grandparents convert from Catholicism to Seventh Day Adventists. We do keep the Sabbath and light candles on Friday night."

"I certainly cannot voice any opinion on what you just said. I do have the feeling, though, that you have a more personal reason for your inquiry. Is that not so?"

Joanna blushed a little, and after a slight hesitation answered. "Well, maybe. I had a Jewish boyfriend some years ago, and from him I heard about the persecution of the Jews in Spain and their expulsion, something I had not known before. Mind you, I'm a history major and teach this subject in High School. I visited his family and noticed that some of their religious customs seemed similar to those in our faith."

"I gather you are no longer with this young man. Have you thought how to further your inquiry into this conundrum? Let us say you do find that you are a descendant of these *Conversos*, what will you do about it, if anything?"

"Frankly, I haven't thought that far. I suppose it'd depend on what I'll discover. Tomorrow I plan to drive to Aguilar de la Frontera and see if there are any old timers there who can shed some light on my family. I think I have taken enough of your time and hospitality, and will take my leave. Thank you ever so much and please do not hesitate to visit me if you ever come to the States. Here is my card so you can get in touch with me. I hope you do."

"Well, my dear Joanna, I was certainly glad to have made your acquaintance and wish you all the best. Good bye."

CHAPTER 15

It was a short drive to Aguilar de la Frontera, just about 30 miles away. Joanna wondered what if anything she would find to remind her of the few stories she heard from her parents about the ancestral town. These she had heard when still a little girl. After all, about a century had passed since her great-grandparents had left the old country. At that time, Spain was a backwards country, its economy mostly agrarian, and quite primitive with an uncertain climate, little modern machinery and poor road transportation. Spain had also been recently defeated in the war against the US at the very end of the 19th century in which it lost Cuba and the Philippines. Poverty drove many Spaniards to emigrate; many to South America and others to the US. Joanna, now, saw a different country; modern with advanced technology and a reasonably high standard of living.

Aguilar de la Frontera was a small town, less than 15,000 inhabitants, in a rural area where the inhabitants mainly grew grapes and olives in the surrounding fields. It seemed to have stood still in time, many of the small homes looked sad in their disrepair, having been built a great many years ago, but still emanating a certain charm of antiquity. The ancient character was reinforced by the many remnants of Moslem architecture, notably the ruins of a castle built in the ninth century. One needed a great deal of imagination to visualize it as it was in its glory. There were also a number of mansions, dating back to the 16th and 17th centuries, looking their age, poor but proud. There were also two convents and churches dating back to that era.

Joanna asked at a gas station for the location of hotels or pensions in town and was told that there was only one, the hotel Malvasia on the A-45 auto route leading to Malaga, at the other side of town. Others, better ones she was told, were located ten miles or more away. As she wanted to get to know some of the inhabitants of the town, she decided to check into the one close by. The Malvasia was a small hotel that had seen better days. The national flag attached over the entrance hung limp and tired, with broken slats in many of the dark brown shutters and peeling paint attested to the indifference of the owner to attract prospective guests.She parked in front, took out her suitcase and bag, and entered the reception area. It was deserted; most of the room keys hung at the small number of cubbyholes behind the empty reception desk. There was only a small bell, a telephone and an old leather-bound book on the counter. A beat-up sofa and two mismatched easy chairs were the only furniture in the lobby. It was only after Joanna rang repeatedly that the receptionist, an old lady wearing a colorful old housecoat, came shuffling out of a back room looking inquiringly at Joanna.

"I'd like to stay here for a few days. Can I have a room please? I'd want to see it first, if I may, before I decide on staying here."

The woman looked Joanna over, seeing her well-dressed with handsome luggage, and said rather obsequiously, "Certainly, take this key, it is for room number four on the first floor. It is a very nice one, with a shower and toilet, and also has a beautiful view. You will like it. It is the best we have."

It was indeed a large room with a magnificent view over the verdant landscape, part of the town, and the distant hills. The furnishings were rather basic with no TV or make-up mirror. Joanna decided to take it and went down to the receptionist.

"I knew you would like it. Please sign your name and address here in this book and let me have your passport." She opened it and looked astonished. "Ah, you are American; I would not have thought so. Is this right? Your name is Aguilar. How is it possible?"

"Quite simple, my family came from here many years ago. I don't know if it was their original name or if they said so at Ellis Island upon arrival to remind them of the ancestral home. I've come here to learn a little about the place where my family came from. Do you know anyone who has lived here a long time and would be willing to talk to me?"

"I wish I could help you myself, but I was born in Cordoba and came here only thirty five years ago when I acquired this hotel. It has seen better times, unfortunately, as newer and fancier hotels have sprung up. People don't mind driving a few more miles for more luxury, they are all spoiled nowadays. You might get in touch with the Rosales who have the bakery on Calle de Silera, near the main square. This, itself, is a great attraction. Another possibility is the Gutierrez family who live on Calle del Carmen. You can call them from here. They are very nice people."

"Why, thank you very much. I will certainly do that."

Joanna went up to her room to freshen up a bit before going out to explore the town.

As small as the town was, it nevertheless needed a good amount of walking to breathe in the ancient atmosphere emanating from the old buildings and ruined remnants. One could feel the continuity of the centuries. As the day turned out to be very warm, Joanna grew uncomfortable in the midday sun beating down without mercy. By this time, she had reached the octagonal central plaza and thought of resting on one of the benches there but saw no shade, only a few leafy shrubs that were scattered all over. Looking around, she spotted the bakery the hotel owner had mentioned and decided to enter and introduce herself. The smell inside was heavenly and she first asked the girl behind the counter for some pastry to take back for a snack and then asked for the proprietor. The girl explained she was the daughter of the owners of the bakery and said it would be best if she came in the morning when both her father and mother would be in the store during those busy hours. Joanna continued on her walk past the four churches, one built in the 16th century and others earlier, but they were closed at that hour. She continued to the ruined Moorish castle that dated to the end of the first millennium and then returned to the hotel tired from the long walk in the heat.

The first thing the following morning, Joanna went to the bakery to talk to Mr. Rosales or his wife. Entering the store, she found it full of people getting their morning bread and rolls, so she waited patiently in line for her turn. It was Mr. Rosales' wife, Alicia Rosales Martinez Flores who was free. When Joanna introduced herself, telling her her name and what was on her mind, Mrs. Rosales invited her to come back for lunch at one thirty as the store was closed from one to four. They lived upstairs.

Lunch was on the table when Joanna arrived at the Rosales home. After a few words with Mr. Rosales, they sat down at the table. Mr. Rosales said a few words of blessing before the meal and raised his wine glass welcoming their American guest. The meal was simple. It started with a very tasty garlicky *ajoblanco* soup, followed by a plain white merluza fish, browned potatoes, and a small tomato and cucumber salad. It was only after the meal, for which Joanna thanked them profusely, that Mr. Rosales asked if Joanna or her parents had ever been back to Spain, and Aguilar de la Frontera in particular.

"No, this is my first time and as far as I know my parents and grandparents never visited the old country. My great grandparents left this town in 1919 and came to America. I studied history in college and wanted to know more about my ancestral land and this place specifically. I know that after so many years it will be hard to find anyone who actually knew my great grandparents or heard of them. Still, to hear about what things were like here after World War I would be interesting."

"The fact that your surname is Aguilar makes it quite certain that your people came from here, as it was common for people to take on the name of their town in addition to their first names and that of their mother. Your name would most likely have had another name after Aguilar denoting the woman's name. As the American practice shows only one or two first names and the man's family name, I assume it was changed to just Aguilar when they came to America. Unfortunately, I have never met anyone who had such a name as part of his. What I will do is ask some of my older friends if they have ever known or heard of such a family. How long will you stay in our town?"

"I thought of being here for four or five days, but more if needed. I'm staying at the Malvasia, as I've mentioned. You are very kind to have invited me. If it's agreeable, I'll stop by the bakery in a few days to see if you have any information for me."

His wife, who had sat quietly the whole time, now said she was also glad to have met Joanna, but now they were going to take their siesta before returning to work in the afternoon. She wished Joanna a pleasant stay and hoped to see her again.

The next day, Joanna called the Gutierrez family and talked to Mrs. Carmela Gutierrez Mendez who invited her to come on that afternoon.She found the house easily enough and was welcomed by Mrs. Gutierrez, a stooped old woman, her snow-white hair framing a face amazingly nearly free of wrinkles, smiling at her guest through old-fashioned horn-rimmed glasses.

"Welcome, my dear. I was wondering what you were like with such an American accent yet with the name of our town. I understood that you want to hear about our history. So come, let us sit here on the sofa and tell me what you want to know."

Joanna decided this time to come right to her real interest and not just hear about the general history of the place. "Being a history major and a teacher of this subject, I've always wanted to learn more about what happened here years back after the Christian conquest of Spain. I've read, in particular, about the acts of the Inquisition and the expulsion of the Jews in 1492. I understood that between one hundred and two hundred thousand of them converted and stayed here. There must be many of their descendants living here now, I've heard it said that as many as twenty percent of the Spanish people today are of Jewish extraction. Mind you, my family belongs to a Protestant sect, my grandparents having converted from Catholicism."

"Well, well, you certainly surprised me Joanna, if I may call you that. I had not expected this. I am glad that my husband went to play chess with his friend and is not home. You see, he would not like to hear what I am about to tell you. I have thought many times about the origins of my family and that of my husband. You see, throughout the generations we have had a few odd customs like bathing a lot, especially on Friday afternoon. We also always had our big meal on Friday evening rather than at noon as usual. The reasons were never explained. I was curious, and I tried to learn about the Moslem and Jewish religions if, maybe, we took some of their customs. It was then I came across the terms *Marranos* and *Moriscos*, meaning, as you may know, Jewish and Moslem converts. I firmly believe that we are descendants from these *Marranos* and would like to see if other families here have the same feeling. My husband, however, wants me to let it go, and not make a big story out of it. I am really torn now, as I am terribly curious. I am telling you all this since you are a visitor and I trust that you will not share my feelings with other people here."

"You may rest assured that whatever you tell me will not be disclosed. I actually will try to talk to other people here and maybe in other places and see what I can find out. By the way, did you know that the term *Marranos* is a pejorative, meaning pigs in ancient Spanish? The literature now uses the words *Conversos* or Crypto Jews."

"No, thank you for telling me. It seems the problem in our country is that anti-Semitism is still very prevalent and people are afraid of being identified with being Jewish or being of Jewish ancestry. I have read there are places in Portugal where a number of people have gone back openly to their Jewish roots. I wonder if it will ever happen here."

"Well, I'll see what I can find out in my travels here. I may get in touch with you if something of interest comes up, if it is OK with you."

"Why certainly, Joanna, do call me whenever you like. As I said, I am interested in the subject."

They continued to talk for a while, sipping tea and eating from the cake Mrs. Gutierrez had baked. Joanna told her about life in the US, a little about her family and their business. Mrs. Gutierrez in turn described their life there in Aguilar, having come some forty years ago, her husband being a mathematics teacher in the local school. They parted kissing each other, Joanna thanking her profusely for her hospitality.

When Joanna came back to the hotel, she found a message from Mrs. Rosales asking her to come to the bakery the following morning as she had thought of some people for Janna to talk to. One of whom, a Mrs. Lopez, would be there right at the opening hour as she was wont to do every day. She would also give her the telephone number of a Mrs. Benavides. Joanna hated the thought of having to get up early enough to be at the bakery at 7AM but decided to do so. She managed to get there just as Mrs. Lopez had finished her purchase and was ready to leave.

"You must be Ms. Aguilar, no mistake about it. Margarita told me about your interest in the history of our town since your family is from here. Why don't we meet in the Great Lion bar for a bite in the evening, say at nine? It's right here on the other side of the square, opposite the bakery. Would this be convenient for you?"

"Why thanks a lot, Mrs. Lopez, it's very kind of you. I'll be there punctually."

The Great Lion bar was not that great. In fact it was rather small, a bit run-down with the usual cigarette stubs and ashes on the floor. There was just one old man sitting at the bar, deeply engaged in a conversation with the owner who paid no attention to the new customers. Joanna sat at one of the few tables and waited for Mrs. Lopez, who came about ten minutes after her, greeting her warmly.

"Please call me Rosa and you are Joanna, I understand. Alicia told me your family left here after World War I. But first let us order something and then talk."

With their food and beer, Rosa mentioned that she personally had not known any one by name of Aguilar but heard her grandparents speak of a Maria Calderon de Aguilar who might be her great grandmother.

"I should add that I was born here these many years ago, as you can well see. My late husband, too, was from here. There are not that many old families left here now. Many of the old ones either died out or left for other places, and new ones came."

At hearing these words, Joanna felt goose pimples down her back hearing for the first time a name of what might be one of her ancestors who lived here. She anxiously asked Mrs. Lopez to tell her more of what she knew of her.

"I really do not know too much. It is only some gossip, which I remember as it made quite an impression on me as young as I was. You see, my grandparents often talked disparagingly of a Maria who was then a young married woman. I believe it was sometime towards the end of World War I." Here she stopped to drink of her beer. "I hope you won't be offended by what I heard." She continued. "It seems my grandparents knew, or heard from others, that Maria and her husband had some peculiar habits, which people said might mean that they secretly kept Jewish customs though they were ostensibly good Catholics and attended church regularly."

"What were these customs? I'd be interested to know."

Mrs. Lopez looked almost accusingly at Joanna and said. "You would not be Jewish by any chance, are you?"

"No, of course I'm not." Joanna paused a minute and continued "I'm a history teacher in a High School at home. Obviously, I also studied Spanish history and am familiar with the problems here throughout the centuries."

"It was said that Maria always went to the public bath every Friday. It was also considered strange that some of the house shutters were closed on that day during the summers when it was very hot here. Some said they detected the flickering of candles behind these shutters.

Other things were said that I do not remember now."

"Do you know what happened to this Maria and her husband? What was his name, by the way?"

"I do not remember his name. It seems that after a short while the gossip about them stopped as they may have left town."

"Well, this might be a coincidence, since as far as I know my great grandparents arrived in the US in 1919, which is not much later. I was actually told they came because of the tough economic situation then in Spain. Was this gossip the reason they left town?"

"I cannot be certain. I am quite sure that people did not like *Marranos*, and it appears very likely the community ostracized them. I understand people in America do not feel the same as we do. There were good reasons the Jews were expelled from here; they were responsible for all the ills that befell our country and it is better that those that secretly kept their faith should also leave."

Joanna thought for a moment about saying something on the benefits of freedom of religion in the US, but refrained from doing so. "Thank you Mrs. Lopez," was all she said, asked for a check from the waiter, paid for both and left.

Joanna had planned to explore the town some more after her meeting with Mrs. Lopez, but now she decided to go back to the hotel and relax for a while in her room. She had to think through what she had heard. Never before had she thought how she would feel if she found out her ancestors were *Conversos*, and now there was this possibility. She was also upset by Mrs. Lopez's obvious anti-Semitism, confirming what she had heard about the prevalence of this form of prejudice here. *What would Michael have said had he heard Mrs. Lopez's story. I bet he would be pleased to hear of my possible Jewish ancestors; but what difference does it make now? What about my parents? Can I ever tell them it is possible we might be of Jewish ancestry? Dad actually has the same prejudice as the people here. He'll never accept it.* It took a long time for her to calm down and finally go out for lunch, but not before calling Mrs. Benavides, who suggested she come to their home later the same afternoon.

Mrs. Benavides lived in a small house in the old part of town, the small yard was rather neglected and the house run-down, needing obvious repairs. The welcome was warm, however. Mrs. Benavides's deeply wrinkled face lit up upon seeing Joanna at the door, standing in the little dim vestibule.

"I've heard a lot about you, this is a small town and gossip travels fast. I was anxious to meet someone from America and hear about our people over there. Come, meet my husband, he is sitting in the living room; he can tell you more than I about the years gone by in this place."

Mr. Esequiel Benavides Castro was sitting in a wheelchair next to a sofa covered in old-fashioned floral design, the cloth showing signs of wear. He stretched out his hand in greeting and said, his voice hoarse and hesitant, "We are very glad you have come. We old people have few friends left so we are glad for company, especially such a nice young American woman. I know you want us to tell you what took place here, but we also would like to hear about your life in your rich and powerful country. So please sit down."

Mrs. Benavides went into the kitchen, brought out a tray with a cake and a bottle of red wine as well as plates and glasses, and sat it down on the coffee table. She poured the wine, cut the cake, handed each one the refreshments, and said to her husband, "You worked in the Ajuntamiento for many years; maybe you came across the name Aguilar. They obviously lived here if they kept the name in America."

"Yes, I certainly worked in our town hall, it seems forever. I started right after high school; it was… let me see… must have been about the time the War started. I do not recall ever seeing this name, but then my wife said your people left here right after World War I, meaning 25 years before. There might be records of them in the old files. If you go there and mention my name to one of the clerks, they may let you look and see some of the old files. What do you think, Alicia?"

"I think it is a very good idea. Other places to look are the churches. They usually keep records of baptisms, weddings, and burials. Have you been to some? There are four and all of them old. Especially the Parish Church of Nostra Signora. I believe it was established as early as the 13th century and rebuilt two hundred years later. The others date back three or four hundred years. I am sure they will be glad to help you."

"Your information is very helpful. I thought of staying here only four or five days, but I see there is yet plenty of work for me." Here, Joanna paused for a minute thinking whether to say something about her conversation with Mrs. Lopez and then decided to go ahead anyway. "I had an interesting conversation yesterday with one of the old timers here. She claimed to have heard about a family of my name but implied that they were *Conversos*, or shall I say, *Marranos*. They were ostracized by the community and left for that reason. Could that be true? I mean, were such people really persecuted, and what is the situation now? I am Christian by the way."

The old couple looked at each other until Mr. Benavides, in his slow husky voice said, "Yes, we have heard over the years of antagonism against people of the Jewish faith, or those suspected of Jewish ancestry. We have always tried not to get involved in that. Live and let live, we always say." Here his wife butted in, "As for the *Marranos*, it is very hard to be sure if someone was really one of them. People do keep all kinds of old customs that are handed down throughout the generations. Who is to say if these traditions are religious or not? Someone might think that we have a peculiar habit, but that does not mean anything. We would prefer that everybody could worship as he pleases without being forced to hide his religion. Someday maybe this will come to pass also here in Spain. Look, the Inquisition was only abolished here about one hundred and seventy years ago."

"It does seem as though there are beginnings of such openness, at least in Portugal," Joanna said. "I've heard about this town Belmonte, in the north of the country, where some of those previously hiding their Jewish ancestry have now come out into the open and have gone back to their original religion. I understand they also established a synagogue about ten years ago. So you see there is hope."

Mrs. Benavides again looked questioningly at her husband, pausing for a while, said, "We know people here in town who will not bid us good day. I do not know why, but fortunately there are not too many. We can only blame ourselves that we did not try and come out publicly against them when we were younger and stronger. Now we can only pray. But do tell us about America."

Mr. Benavides nodded vigorously, looking expectantly at Joanna. "Well, I hate to disappoint you, we may be perceived as a rich country but the economy has lately not been very good. It appears that the government is deeply in debt. We have rich people, some very rich, but many poor ones too. Take my family: My parents own a Spanish restaurant where both work very hard to make a reasonable living. I never knew real want, but then I wasn't spoiled by luxuries and always worked from the age of ten, helping in the restaurant. We can be proud of being a democratic country where everyone can follow whatever religion he or she believes in. My family belongs to the Seventh-Day Adventists, which is one of the many Protestant denominations. I've gone out with Catholic as well as Jewish boys, which is common practice."

"What you have said is very interesting," said Mr. Benavides "But what is that religion of yours that you mentioned? We have never heard of it."

"We are Christians who adhere to the New Testament but also deem the old one important and follow some of the rules laid down there, foremost the keeping of the Sabbath on the seventh day of the week as our day of rest. My mother lights candles on Friday evening to denote the beginning of this day."

The two old people looked with amazement at Joanna until Mrs. Benavides burst out and said, "You know, my dear that sounds to me like what *Marranos* did here. Only it was done secretly in this country, lest the Inquisition find out and punishes them. Lately, as we said, it is only that we... *they* are ostracized by most of the community." Here, Mr. Benavides quickly started to say, "We wanted to tell you about life here, around the time your great-grandparents must have left. Well, I was born in 1922, so you can tell how old I am; my memory is only from the late 1920s, and it is not that great anymore. From what my parents told me, and I certainly felt it later, there was an economic crisis here; there literally was very little food available. We went hungry at times. Socialism and anarchism grew, which led to the military dictatorship of Primo de Rivera, who assumed power in 1923. Times were very tough, and that may have led your ancestors to leave for the US. Don't pay much attention to this business about the *Marranos*. Frankly, I wish my parents had done the same as your family."

Joanna felt that old couple was getting edgy, maybe tired, and excused herself, thanking them and bidding them goodbye.

As it was too early for dinner, Joanna went back to the hotel to relax for a while. Asking for her key, the owner handed her also a letter that was in her box. She took it up to her room, puzzled as to who knew where she was staying. Looking at the envelope, she realized that only her name was on it, which only increased her surprise. Upon opening the letter she at first refused to understand its content. Looking again, she realized what it was: a threat. This is what it said:

"We not want you here! Go back, you Jew Marranos. This is Christian country – no room for Marranos." *Who could have written such a thing?* thought Joanna. *The only one could be Mrs. Lopez, but that is unlikely. Maybe she talked about me to some other people. The English is poor, but that, I think, goes for most people here. What should I do? Go to the police? They wouldn't do anything, certainly not during the few days I wanted to stay here. Could they hurt me physically? I am not going to run away. Certainly not.* Still, as Joanna was getting hungry, she hesitated a while before going out to a nearby restaurant for dinner. She purposely seated herself at a table at the far corner and only calmed down when she realized that nobody was paying her any attention. Waiting for her order, she decided to call Mrs. Gutierrez after dinner and tell her what happened. She felt a little better having somebody to talk to about this matter, and ate her meal with gusto. Mrs. Gutierrez seemed quite upset on the phone hearing Joanna's story and invited her to come the following morning when her husband would not be home.

Mrs. Gutierrez warmly embraced Joanna, leading her by the hand to the living room, where a large platter of lush-looking pastries was on the coffee table set with delicate plates and cups. Asking Joanna what she would have, she went into the kitchen to bring out a pot of tea and sat down next to her.

"Have some of this pastry. This time I did not bake and rather bought them from the Rosales bakery. They do make wonderful things, better than I could, and not expensive. You can tell me some more of what happened after we have some of that."

Joanna felt much better after this warm reception and pulled out the note she received the previous evening. Mrs. Gutierrez looked at it, her face showing anger as she looked at Joanna.

"Such a thing makes me furious. To think that there are people here who would do this in this year of our Lord and the world is supposed to be a global village! People have seen the result of wars, wars that have cost the lives of millions, caused by prejudice, avarice, and pure hate. Yes, I know that it is people like us who feel this injustice but are afraid to stand up for the rights of the persecuted and do nothing. Now we have the excuse of being old and powerless. Twenty, thirty years ago, we had the same problems here yet we also did nothing. All what I said is actually unimportant. I do not know what practical advice I can give you. Do you have to stay here at all and if so, how long?"

"I had planned to leave in three or four days. I want mainly to look at church records and see if I can find any mention of my ancestors."

"I really doubt bodily harm will befall you, but then I do not want to take responsibility if some crazy person would indeed hurt you. Do not worry, I do know the Chief of Police in our town; if you will agree, I will show him this note and tell him about you. Will that be all right?"

"Why, certainly Mrs. Gutierrez. I only hope this will not cause you too much of a problem."

"Of course not, my dear child. I will do it today and will call you at the hotel."

CHAPTER 16

Joanna was in no rush to leave the hotel the following morning, as she knew that nobody would be at work in the town hall much before ten o'clock. She decided to go to the Nostra Signora church, but only after the end of the morning mass. She was hoping to hear from Mrs. Gutierrez, before leaving her room, but no call came. She left for the church finding nobody there, to her surprise. As it was pleasantly cool inside she decided to wait a while, finding the quiet holy atmosphere calming, removing all troubling thoughts. It was not too long before she heard a door close to her right and a priest in a plain black cassock came towards her.

"What can I do for you, my child?" he asked. "Is there something troubling you, I would be glad to hear your confession if you like."

"Thank you father," Joanna said. "I've come to ask for help in finding the names of my ancestors that may have lived here one hundred years ago. My name is Joanna Aguilar and I'm an American whose great grandparents left this country right after World War I."

"Did I hear correctly, did you say your name is Aguilar? I never heard of anyone with that family name."

"Indeed it is, father. I hope that you'll allow me to look at the birth and death entries in your records during some forty or fifty years before the War. I would think that if my family is from here I'd find them listed there."

"Well, that is not easy. I will have to go down into the cellar and find the appropriate volumes. I do not know in what condition they might be, if they are at all legible. We have very few requests such as yours, and none that I can recall going back to the nineteenth century." He hesitated a few moments and added, "Come back the day after tomorrow around this time, hopefully I may have something for you. Go with God."

Having plenty of time, Joanna meandered through the narrow streets, looking at some of the old buildings that looked as if they were planted there by someone to give pleasure to the eye; like a set of beautiful teeth. Only, now, many were missing and instead ugly, square, structures rose up instead. She finally arrived at the town hall and went inside. There was no reception desk in the entrance hall, so she went into one of the corridors leading from the hall and knocked on the first door she encountered. As there was no answer, she continued trying those that followed until, finally, a man said something. Opening the door, on which a nameplate read 'Carlos Flores Jimenez', she saw a man, at least in his late sixties, reading the paper. He looked at her questioningly. "What do you want?" he asked in a gruff voice, indicating his displeasure at having been disturbed.

"Mr. Benavides recommended I come here to look at old records of people who lived here a century or a century and a half ago. Could you please help me?"

"Oh, how is old Benavides? Haven't seen him in ages. What is it now you want? Who are you?"

"My name is Joanna Aguilar and I'm looking for names of my ancestors in your records who, I think, lived here at the beginning of the last century."

"Aguilar you said? Where are you from? You don't sound like someone from around here."

"That's my name; I live in the United States and am here for a visit wishing to find the roots of my family."

"Well, well. I never heard of anybody with the name of our town, and living of all places in America. Ah yes, Benavides sent you so it must be OK. It will take me some time to find books you want that are so old. There are in deep storage. Not before a few days at least. Come back, say, next Monday. I should have something by then."

"But that is almost another week. I cannot stay here that long, could you not make it tomorrow, or the day after if that is not possible? Please, I beg you."

"All right, then. Since Benavides sent you. Be here on Friday, but not before eleven."

Joanna thanked him profusely and left. Back at the hotel, she called Mrs. Gutierrez to see if she had talked to the Police Chief. It turned out that she did and had received no support from him. "He told me," Mrs. Gutierrez said, "that it was probably done by stupid kids who do not know any better. This town is peaceful, nobody would deliberately make trouble. He said not to worry about it."

It was later in the evening that Mrs. Gutierrez called again, and told Joanna that there was another man living in town who might be able to help her in her quest for information about her family. "His name is Danilo Gonzales de Silva. We have known him for many years, but lately he lives in seclusion hardly seeing a soul. When I told him about you, he at first did not want to hear of you coming to see him. However, when I told him that you only want to find information concerning your great grandparents who may have lived here, he consented reluctantly. Give him a call and arrange to see him."

Mr. Gonzales lived in a ramshackle building not far from town hall, so that Joanna found it readily. Maybe because that neighborhood had mostly well kept whitewashed homes, almost all with lots of colorful geranium filled flowerpots on their windowsills, that the bare Gonzales home looked especially shabby. The paint on the walls was peeling and some of the window shutters, their wood nearly bare of paint, dangled from their hinges at odd angles. Joanna had nearly given up waiting at the door, after knocking loud and hard a number of times, when she finally heard shuffling steps coming. A small shutter opened in the door and she saw an eye of faded blue staring at her. Joanna gave her name and asked to be admitted. It took a few moments, during which she heard bolts withdrawn, for the door to open.

The man in front of her looked of considerable age, bent as he was, dressed in a well-worn bathrobe with warm slippers on his spindly feet. His craggy face was ill-shaven, with the few white hairs on his head falling every which way. He first looked at Joanna rather suspiciously, but then extended a gnarled hand and invited her to enter. The parlor was small with a few threadbare easy chairs, a low table and commode making up all the furniture. Only the Persian carpet on the floor, worn but still recognizable as of some worth, was a reminder of a more prosperous past. Mr. Gonzales sat down heavily in one of the chairs and invited Joanna to sit next to him. "You have to speak loudly so that I can hear you," he said, telling her that he had heard from Mrs. Benavides about her and her request to see him.

"I'm very grateful, Mr. Gonzales, that you agreed to see me. I hope that my request will not be too much trouble. You see, my great grandparents left this country for the United States after World War I and I wish to learn about the family. Mrs. Lopez told me that she knew of a woman that left this town around that time; her name was Maria Aguilar de Calderon. Do you know anything about this woman and her family, or anything else that could shed a light on my family here?"

"My dear girl," he answered in his hesitant raspy voice. "At my age the memory is not as good as it was. But first let me ask you your full name. It would help to know your father's and mother's family names."

"We, in America, do not have the naming system you have here in Spain. Most people at home have a first name, a middle name, which is actually a second first name, and then the family name. Some people do not have a middle name. I am just Joanna Aguilar."

"And what are the names of your parents and your grandparents? It will help."

"I know that my mother's maiden name, meaning her father's family name, was Calderon, while my grandmother's was Campos. My father's father was Aguilar but I don't know my grandmother's on my father's side. She passed away before I was born. Anyway, I think the family name became simply Aguilar after they arrived in the US."

"Good. So we have to look for the families of Calderon and Campos, in addition to Aguilar. Calderon is the name of the woman Mrs. Lopez mentioned, so there we have a clue."

"My gracious, why of course" exclaimed Joanna. "When she mentioned it I didn't connect it with my grandmother."

"Have you looked at the records in the churches and in town hall? Looking for only Aguilar might not be enough, you need also to find the other two names."

"I've been to the Nostra Signora church and to Town Hall. In both places they asked me to come back since they would have to find their old records. I'll do that in the next few days. But please tell me, do you know anything about families with these names that lived here at the beginning of the last century?"

"Personally, no! Do not forget that as old as I am, I was born in 1921; I could not have known anyone that left in 1919. You will not find anyone alive today that might have known your great grandparents. But there is always gossip. Let me ask you first. Do you know why I live here the way I do, and that there is hardly a person in town who will bid me good morning? I will tell you that my family has lived for generations the life of Crypto Jews, *Conversos*, outwardly good Christians but always following some old Jewish customs and rituals, hoping at one time to be able to return openly to the old religion. Now I never made it a secret that a long time ago my family converted, under duress as I believe. Unfortunately, this open declaration of one's roots is anathema to the many prejudiced people, those of pure Christian blood, and the many with *Converso* roots who are fearful of being found out and also suffer from the bigotry. I presume that you are a good Catholic; are you shocked by what I just said?"

"Oh please, Mr. Gonzales, of course not. I wish you'd lived in the United States. Naturally, there is prejudice there too, but we are free to worship whatever religion we wish, and associate with whomever we like. As a matter of fact, my family is Seventh-Day Adventist, a Christian sect that keeps a few rituals from the Old Testament. That is why I'm interested in the history of my family as I think that they, like you, might have been *Conversos*."

"Well, well. That is interesting. I do believe that in the not-too-distant future we here will also become more open and liberal. Ideas travel now much faster than in the past and societies change. Not in my time unfortunately, I am afraid. As for your family here, I have heard two of the names mentioned. As for the Maria Aguilar de Calderon,

I believe Mrs. Lopez should have said Maria Aguilas de Calderon since I think that was the woman's name. I think it was most likely changed to Aguilar when they arrived in America to better remember their hometown. Yes, my mother mentioned that name at home when I was seven or eight. She always wondered what became of her as she left very suddenly. My mother had only good things to say about her. I do remember also that I heard it said that not many years before she disappeared she had married a well-known man, a baker in town, whose name was Juan Aguilas Mendez; so when you look up the records, look for him too."

Joanna noticed that Mr. Gonzales' voice had become strained during the last minutes. It had become less distinct and hoarser than before. His head had sunk to his chest as he obviously needed rest. Joanna got up slowly from her uncomfortable seat and told Mr. Gonzales that she had taken too much of his time, asking if she could return tomorrow. He said that he wanted that very much as he still had plenty to tell her. They agreed on the late morning.

Before going to Mr. Gonzales' house, Joanna stopped at a grocery store to buy bottled water and milk and then went to the Rosales bakery for baked goods, including herb garlic bread, empanadas, and *conchas*. She arrived just after eleven, hoping that Mr. Gonzales had a good night's rest to be able to continue from where they had left off.

He welcomed her warmly, giving her a light kiss on both cheeks.

"What is it you are bringing my dear?" he asked, seeing her large packages.

"Oh, these are just a few things from the bakery and grocery store for you. I wish I knew what you needed."

"There is nothing I need, I lead a frugal, satisfactory life, and hope to do so until the good Lord will take me. It seems to be taking him a long time. But do sit down," he said, taking the packages from her, shuffling to the kitchen. Joanna waited for quite a while until he returned, carrying a plate with some of the baked goods, which he put on the table. He returned to the kitchen and brought the bottle of milk and two glasses.

"That was good. Here, have some, it smells heavenly."

They sat and ate for a while until Mr. Gonzales said, "I was going to tell you about Mr. Aguilas. Yes, he was well-known for his baking skills, but also as a man with a very short temper. My mother told me that she often heard him yell at someone in the bakery over something small, nobody else would have been offended. Especially when it came to matters of prejudice or untruth. He was a very honest and straightforward person, but people did not like that about him. At that time people thought ill of someone who was not like them, and they still do today. I believe he was considered a *Converso* and therefore was a convenient scapegoat to blame for all the ills that befell the community. I believe that at the time there was a severe drought in the country and there was a scarcity of food. Maybe he and his wife left for that reason, and not necessarily because he really was a *Converso*."

Joanna thought for a moment before speaking. "Do you think it's a reasonable assumption to say that this Juan Aguilas Mendez and his wife were my great-grandparents? I'm still a little confused though. If Juan Aguilas Mendez was married to this woman, why was she known as Maria Aguilas de Calderon? And another question, do you think they were *Conversos*?"

"As to the woman's name, it is customary here for a woman to keep her maiden name when she marries, and add it to that of her husband. Her family name is of course Aguilas. There can be variations to this, however. They can agree that she takes the name of her husband and adds it to hers. Now, if this couple had a son he would usually have the name of his father after his first name, and then that of his mother. You have it much simpler, but with you the woman loses her maiden name."

"Not always now. Often both husband and wife retain their full names, but that also may get confusing."

"You asked about your great-grandparents being possibly *Conversos*. Well, one cannot deduce that from the little we know about them, including the reason for their leaving the country. Judging by the names, I venture to say that the names Calderon and Mendez were common among *Conversos*, although some people of Christian origin might have had them too. Campos was not known among *Conversos*."

Joanna felt by this time that she had received as much information as was possible from Mr. Gonzales, and wanted to digest it quietly. She also saw that he was getting tired. She therefore got up and thanked Mr. Gonzales profusely for all the time he had given her. She was about to turn to leave when Mr. Gonzales asked her to stay for a moment while he appeared to be thinking of something, but then just said how glad he was to have met her and requested she come to see him again before leaving town. He said that he might by then remember something that could be of importance to her. Joanna promised to do so.

The next morning, not too early, Joanna went over to the Nostra Signora church. A few women were there praying, the small number of lit candles indicating a lack of worshippers. The priest was nowhere to be seen. She waited for some time in the back, all the while more women and a couple of old men started to come in, signifying the imminent start of the late mass. When she saw the altar boy come out of the side door, dressed in his red cassock carrying the chalice, she turned around quickly to leave before the priest would be able to see her. She went to a nearby café to sit until she could see people come out of the church. The espresso did not last very long and she started to think about what she had learned from the visit to Mr. Gonzales. *What possible reason had he to ask me to come again? It seemed that he had exhausted all he knew about the subject. I was surprised how much a man of his age did in fact remember. He was not sure about my great-grandparents being Conversos, maybe he did not want to say so not knowing how I would feel about it. According to the names it seemed quite possible that they were. So what am I going to do with this knowledge? Maybe I will learn more the next time I see him. I still have to see the records here and in the Town Hall.*

It took quite a while before Joanna saw people come out of the church, her patience nearly exhausted. When she saw the priest standing at the door greeting the worshippers, she quickly went over to the church to catch the priest before he might disappear again. She stood deferentially next to him as he shook the hands of the last ones emerging, their eyes squinting as the bright sunlight hurt their eyes used to the dark interior. When all were gone the priest turned to her.

"Oh, I see you have come to look for the records of your ancestors. It took a great deal of work to find those of the period you asked, and I hope that you will appreciate it. Come, I will show you."

With that, he led the way to his study, which was accessible through a door at the left side of the altar, past a large room with stored supplies of candles, hymnals, vestments, and other paraphernalia. The room was small with nothing on the wall except for a large cross and bare with just a bookcase filled with theological volumes in one corner, a table, and three plain chairs. Three large, leather-bound, dusty volumes were on the table.

"Here are the books I found. I will leave you here for about two hours during which you can do your search. Please do not leave before I come back."

Joanna started with the upper volume, the dates in which covered the years 1875 to 1910. It gave the names of people along with their birth, christening, and death dates. The writing was in ink, in an elegant hand fairly easy to decipher. Joanna found a mention of one Fidelia Campos who was born in 1877 but died in 1895. There was no record of a man by that name, nor that of a child. Joanna surmised that if she had a husband he was considerably older than her. She might have died in childbirth, quite common then. Joanna was just going to take a short break; her eyes were getting tired, when after about three quarters of an hour she came across the name of one Maria Calderon Trujillo, born on February 20, 1900, and baptized on March 14 of that year. *Wow, that might fit perfectly. She would have been nineteen if she were my great-grandmother who left here for the US in 1919. At that age she might have had a child, but I do not know if my grandmother was born here or in the US. To be sure, I have to continue looking to see if I do not find a death date for her.* That find gave her renewed energy to finish the one volume and start on the second, which covered the years 1910 to 1935. She was not half-way through, however – having not found anything – when the priest came in and told her that she must then leave as he had other business to do and needed to bring the books back into the vault.

"Thank you, father, I may have found my great-grandmother, but to be certain I need to look at these two volumes again," Joanna said, pointing to the needed books. "Please, let me come on Monday again. I am sure

I will then finish in two hours." The priest hesitated for a while and then agreed. "All right, be here like today, right after the late mass."

The next day was Friday, the day she was to be in Town Hall to look at their records. She arrived in the late morning as requested by Mr. Flores. This time he was actually doing something, shuffling through a mound of papers, looking up in some surprise as she entered his office. It took him a while to recognize her, asking her to sit in the one spare chair he had.

"Benavides sent you, is that not so? You wanted to see something."

"Yes, Mr. Flores, you were good enough to suggest I come to look over old birth and death records so that I could possibly find my great-grandparents, who might have lived here until 1919. Please let me see those volumes that cover the years 1880 to 1980."

"If they left the country in 1919, why should I bring all the volumes after that date? That is a big job."

"Because if I find that their names are listed as having passed away here at some later date, I will know that they were not my great-grandparents."

"Ok, but you have to come with me and help me carry them. I warn you, they will be pretty dusty and heavy. So come on."

They went down two flights, coming to a barely lit corridor that branched off into a number of rooms one of which, a rather large one, was filled to the ceiling with rows of open book shelves. Mr. Flores went down one of the aisles and stopped at a book. "Here, pull this one out, it covers the years 1870 to 1910. Take it and the one next to it, which is for the following forty years. I will take the third that will bring us up to 1990." Sneezing from the dust, Joanna was barely able to carry the leather-bound volumes up the stairs to an empty office, which Mr. Flores indicated was to be her room for the day.

"I will leave you here," Mr. Flores said, "You can be here until four, which is closing time. We will have to take the books down before you go. If you finish earlier, and I am not in my office, you will have to wait for me."

"Thank you, Mr. Flores. I certainly will not leave before seeing you." *What an inconsiderate person,* thought Joanna. *He could at least have told me where I can get a sandwich and water if I stay that late. I hope he'll not just disappear when I'll need him.*

It took less than an hour and a half until Joanna came across the name of Juan Aguilas Mendez, who was born on June 4, 1891. There was no death date given. *That must be him, the name of the baker. He must be my great-grandfather; Mr. Gonzales said that he married my grandmother. At least it appears so. Wait till Mr. Gonzales hears that. I still have to look further and see if I can find Maria Calderon Trujillo also here. If I find no death record of her, I will not need to go back to the church. But why is my great-grandfather not mentioned in the church records?* Joanna continued to look through the first volume, not finding anything further, and went on to the second with nothing there either. It was almost two o'clock by then and she was getting hungry and thirsty.

She thought of getting up to see Mr. Flores to tell him that she was going for a quick bite. She did so after a little while, but his office was locked, and she went back starting on the third book. It was just before four, her eyes getting heavy from the strain, when Mr. Flores came in telling her it was time to bring the books down to the vault. She had reached by then the year 1983 not finding anything, a year she was old enough to know her great-grandmother was certainly not alive anymore. Sweating in the stifling hot room, tired and hungry, she gladly picked up two of the volumes, and followed Mr. Flores down into the underworld of forgotten records of people that had lived there, some a good life while others fared badly.

Mr. Gonzales was glad to hear from Joanna and invited her to come to his place on Sunday morning. This time she had stocked up on Saturday on wine, fruit, and cheese to bring with her the following morning.

It again took quite a while before Mr. Gonzales opened the front door. He had not changed much from Joanna's previous visit except that instead of the ancient bathrobe he now wore a pair of old khaki slacks and a faded crumpled plaid shirt, the upper buttons of which were missing allowing some curly white hair to show. His face, however, glowed this time with pleasure upon seeing Joanna.

"Do come in please. I see you brought some things again; there is no need for it, as I told you. But please sit down and let me take the bag. My, it is very heavy, what have you brought?"

Mr. Gonzales went into the kitchen; all the while Joanna could hear the clank of plates, glasses, and cutlery as he apparently looked for all that was needed. He finally appeared, barely able to carry the tray that had all the food and utensils but without the wine. He put the tray down on the low table and went back into the kitchen coming out holding the bottle of wine and a cork screw. "Please Joanna, could you be good enough to open this nice bottle? I am afraid that I cannot do it anymore."

Joanna opened the bottle, and poured wine into the two glasses. They both raised theirs with Joanna wishing Mr. Gonzales a long and healthy life. Mr. Gonzales wished her a happy, productive life, finding satisfaction and fulfillment of her dreams. They both ate the fruit and cheese, with Mr. Gonzales praising the wine, saying that he had not had such a good one for a long time.

"I am very curious to know what exactly you found in the records," Mr. Gonzales said after they had munched for a while on the food. "There is also something I would like to give you this time," he added after a short pause.

"Well, as I told you on the phone, I found the name of Maria Calderon Trujillo, born in 1900 and that of Juan Aguilas Mendez, born 1891. What, I believe, is very important is that for neither of them did I find a death date. What puzzled me, though, was the fact that the name Juan Aguilas was only in the town hall records and not in that of the church. Now I only was in the church of Nostra Signora, there are the three others, so maybe he could be found there. I found the name Campos, a woman who died very young in 1895."

"It looks to me like these two could very well be your great-grandparents. I would not bother to look for records in the other churches. Do not forget that the church of Nostra Signora is the parish church, with the others of lesser importance. It is in the parish church that the records are kept. It is also the oldest of the four, having been founded back in the thirteenth century and redone in the sixteenth. So, are you satisfied?"

"I feel good to know who my great-grandparents were and that they lived here. However, I'm still uncertain as to their original religious affiliation. Were they *Conversos*?"

"I would say that there is a good chance that, indeed, they were *Conversos*. I believe I said that. The fact that the birth date of your presumptive great-grandfather was not listed in the records of the parish church may have some significance insofar as his parents may not have had him baptized. This, I must say, would have been a very dangerous act, so that his not appearing there may simply have been an oversight. We really cannot be sure."

"I really appreciate the interest you took in my quest. I realize that one cannot be sure when there is no actual witness to tell us. I don't know – I have the feeling that they were *Conversos*. I also thought about my parents and whether to tell them about my findings. It may upset them, especially my father who is somewhat prejudiced against Jews."

"I just remembered," Mr. Gonzales said. "There is something else that might strengthen the possibility that you come from *Converso* ancestry. There was a well-known Spanish musician by name of Don Fernando Aguilar who was the chief conductor of the Royal Barcelona Orchestra in 1497. He is known to have been a *Converso*. The story goes that he wished to hear the blowing of the ram's horn, which is usually done on the Jewish New Year in the synagogue. To make sure the Inquisition would not be aware of what he was doing, he arranged for a public concert on the Jewish New Year and composed music that included a great variety of wind instruments, including a ram's horn. The concert was attended by a great multitude, including members of the Inquisition as well as *Conversos*. It appears that none of those belonging to the Inquisition noticed the blasts of the ram's horn while he and the *Conversos* were able to hear them. Nice story, is it not?"

"Yes, it is," Joanna replied. "It would be interesting to know if he, or his family, came from here. I always thought that during the Middle Ages people took names that reflected on their profession or their place of origin. With that in mind, why then would my presumptive family have had the name Aguilas and not Aguilar as you said?"

"As to Aguilas, I believe it is the name as my mother told me. I could very well be wrong and it could have been Aguilar. Still, in spite of what you have found, and this little story, I see no point in telling your parents, as you have no firm proof, only a reasonable conjecture. But wait," Mr. Gonzales said as he saw Joanna getting up. "There is something I want to give you, and it will need an explanation."

Joanna sat down, wondering what he might have in mind, while Mr. Gonzales dug his hand into his trouser pocket and brought out some small object wrapped in tissue paper.

"Here," he said as he unwrapped the paper and handed Joanna what looked like an old coin. "This is a very old Hebrew coin, as I was told. It was supposedly minted about a century after the death of our Savior. As you can imagine, it is very precious to me and, frankly, I am loath to part with it, but my line is extinguished. My two children passed away untimely. My son in a car accident and my daughter was carried away by that cursed cancer disease. I have no siblings and thus no relatives I know of. I have the feeling that you will appreciate having it. So please, take it and guard it well."

Joanna was speechless for a while and just looked questioningly at Mr. Gonzales before replying, "My dear Mr. Gonzales, what can I say? I do not feel worthy of taking something so precious. But please, tell me how it came into your possession."

"It has been handed down to me from father to son, for at least a couple of hundred years with the explanation I just gave you. You see, until some generations ago the firstborn males of my family always engaged in pawn broking and, before they converted, in money lending. The story has it that one of my ancestors received the coin from another *Converso* who was afraid to keep it lest the Inquisition would catch him with it. My ancestor who accepted the coin must have valued it highly, and as a pawnbroker he could have all kinds of old artifacts in his possession without arousing any suspicion."

"Dear, Mr. Gonzales. I do not know how to thank you. Not just for giving me this precious coin, but mainly for the trust you put in me believing that I am worthy of it, and will know what to do with it. I have, by the way, seen a few similar coins exhibited in the Metropolitan Museum in New York. They are supposedly very rare and are very valuable. Am I to surmise from your giving me this old Hebrew coin that you believe my family has indeed *Converso* ancestry?"

"Not necessarily, although I said that there are good chances that this is so. I was impressed by your frankness and lack of prejudice. You have no wedding ring and have not spoken of a husband or children, which leads me to believe that you are unmarried. As yet, you have no children to hand the coin down to future generations, although I hope you will eventually find happiness in marriage. You seem bright and should you remain single you will find whom to give this inheritance. Go with God, my child."

Joanna embraced Mr. Gonzales, the tears and the emotion she felt only enabled her to murmur her thanks again. She turned and left.

Returning to the hotel, she told the proprietress that she would be leaving early in the morning the day after next, wanting to take a bus to Cordoba. She also requested to see the train schedule from there to Seville. The following morning, since it was the last day of her stay in this small town, she decided to once again walk leisurely all around and reflect on the great deal of meaningful information she had obtained. She stopped for breakfast at the nearby familiar café after a short walk and then continued, all the time wondering what to make of the possibility that she came from a family of *Conversos*. She was thus oblivious to the fact that for a while now two young men had been following her until they came abreast with one asking for her name.

"What is it to you? I am walking for my pleasure in this quiet town. It was nice knowing you." She continued walking with the two keeping pace with her.

"Not so quick, lady. If we are not mistaken you are Joanna Aguilar, a family name you have taken in vain. No miserable *Marrano* who spreads a false religion in this good Catholic town is welcome here. In fact, we ask you to come along peacefully with us, as otherwise you might get hurt. You would not like that, now would you?"

Joanna looked around to see if anyone else was on that narrow street; not seeing anyone, she started to run hoping to attract attention on another street.

PART III

CHAPTER 17

1449

"Have you heard the news from Toledo, Josue? It is too terrible to believe," Juana asked her husband once they finished saying grace after their Friday night dinner. Their three children had gone to bed. With rain pouring down on their house and occasional thunder and lightning seen through their windows, her black mood wasmore exacerbated.

"I certainly did, how could I not? I did not want to bring you the bad news just before the Sabbath. The Christians of Toledo went on a rampage killing and maiming hundreds, men, women, and children. Their hatred was supposedly against the *Conversos*, as they blamed them for helping their past coreligionists. Nevertheless, they killed Jews and *Conversos* alike."

"Do you think that this can happen here in our beloved town of Cordoba?"

"I would not rule that out. This fanaticism spreads like wildfire. Have you forgotten what happened right here in our town, when our grandparents were still young? Many of our brothers were killed or maimed, as were those in Seville, Valencia, and Barcelona. The question is what should we do?"

"What choice do we have? Do you think we should leave for another country?"

"No need for that, I think. Certainly not yet. I talked to some of our brothers whom I met in the market today. I went there to buy oil and other items I need for the shop. There was only one who said he might consider this possibility; the others said that they would wait and see. There is, of course, also the possibility of converting, but that also is too early to contemplate."

"How could you say that? It was against the *Conversos* that their hatred was directed. So you said."

"My dear Juana; you know very well that many of them did not properly conceal some of the ritual practices they had kept. Others openly flouted the prohibition of abetting our brethren. If one converts, it must be done so that not the least suspicion will fall on him or her. But come; let us forget about it for now. It is the Sabbath, and we will enjoy it as always."

Sleep did not come to Juana that night for a long time. She kept thinking about the future and it looked uncertain at best. *What will happen to my dear family?* she wondered. *Will we have to wander the earth to find a haven if the persecution reaches our town? How will we live? Josue will not want to give up his weapons workshop that has been in the family for generations. He has said many times that he is waiting for Mosse, our oldest, to start his apprenticeship there, and to eventually, when we get old, take over the ownership and support us. That might mean that we will have to convert, a terrible thought. Our religion is important to me, I cannot possible give it up, or even act a Christian. It is impossible that we should live a life of falsehood. Josue and I will have to talk about this, but there is time. Let's see how things develop.*

Many a time, during the following years, did Josue and Juana talk about the continually deteriorating condition of the Jews in Spain. Josue usually described the good position the Jews had occupied in the Caliphate ruled by the Moors. He suggested that all through history there were both good and bad times, and that there was no reason why under Christian rule conditions should not change again for the better. Juana was adamant that it did not look as if there would be an improvement in the foreseeable future. "Look," she said, "at what happened as long as ninety years ago here in our own neighborhood when the town of Aguilar was almost completely destroyed in the anti-Jewish riots there. Have things been so good ever since?" Their arguments became ever more heated after the establishment of the Inquisition in 1478.

"Look at us, Josue. We are old now, in another few years we will not be able to leave, even if we want to. The Inquisition will make life impossible for us to live as Jews in this country. It appears that our King Ferdinand and his wife hate us, even though it is said that he has Jewish blood in his veins. What should we do?"

"Juana, my good wife, we have lived a long and fruitful life in our town, we have children and grandchildren. Mosse is doing his apprenticeship and I trust that he will be running the weapons shop in a few years. I hope to be able then to act only as adviser and do some of the selling, if the good Lord will give me the time on earth. It has given our family a comfortable existence. Please, talk to Mosse and hear what he has to say. Do you think he will be willing to give up what has been in the family for generations? I see no way except to convert, as much as I hate the idea of leaving our age-old faith, even if only on the surface."

"But Josue, do you not know that the Inquisition has been established mainly to ferret out those converts that secretly keep the old faith and punish them horribly? At the same time, they will make it more and more difficult for us that keep the faith. Look at all the limitations placed on us. We have to wear distinctive clothes, cannot employ Christians, nor can our doctors treat them, and that is just a small part of the discrimination. We do not have to leave our beloved country where our ancestors have lived for many generations. We could move to some place in Aragon or Castile, many of our brothers are there."

"Please, Juana, do you think that I, at my age, could start a new business in a place where nobody knows me? I do not have the energy for it anymore and Mosse is too young and inexperienced to do it. Anyway, where should we go and who would welcome us, if we even found such a place? Do we have enough money for the expenses involved and the time it will take a new workshop to generate enough income to live on?It does not look good for us here as Jews. Like I told you, as long as we are careful, we can convert and keep our customs. So we go to church and mumble some things. Don't forget, the making of weapons is important to the Crown. They are less likely to go after us. I am sure Mosse agrees with me. As a matter of fact, he even told me that."

All their discussions stopped when it became known that soon all the Jews would be expelled from Al Andalus, which included, of course, the important town of Cordoba. Josue was adamant that they had to convert and would hear of no argument against this decision. Juana had to comply, as it was certain that Josue would not give her a bill of divorce if she wanted to leave the family. That would have been impossible anyway at her age with no means of support. The family was baptized just a few months before the expulsion occurred in 1483.

The months before the conversion were hectic, especially for Juana. She had to get rid of all things that had any Jewish association; dishes, candelabra, utensils, and even certain items of clothing. They could not have many pots and pans, or items of cutlery, which would give the impression of keeping a kosher home with separate meat and dairy dishes. They also had to acquire items of clothing worn by Christians and discard the typically Jewish ones. There was one object, however, that she would not part with, even at the cost of her life.

It had been handed down from generation to generation as an heirloom of infinite value, as small as it was. It was a coin, minted in the Holy Land about a millennium and a half before, by the Jews who had revolted against their Roman conquerors. It was called a *beka*, or half shekel, and on it was the inscription "Jerusalem the Holy" in Hebrew letters. She did not know how it came into the possession of her family. It may have been, as Josue once said, that Jews had lived in Cordoba or the surrounding country from early times. Some may have even come on the ships of King Solomon who sent them to Tarshish on the south coast, but that was before this coin was minted. Others came to Rome after they, or their ancestors, had left Judea because of the conquest of their land by the Romans; with greater numbers arriving there as slaves after the destruction of Jerusalem and the temple. Many of these Jews were later expelled from Rome as they were undesired there, and were sent to Spain to colonize the land with people who would not join the rebellious local tribes. One of them might have had this coin to remind him of the old homeland. It signified to her that at one time her people were free in the land promised to them by God and that God willing they would return there one day. From the little religious teaching she had received as a child, she knew that each Jewish person in the Land of Israel had to give such a coin, once a year, to the temple. It was used both as a support for its upkeep and as a means of census since, according to the bible, it was forbidden to count people directly. Many an evening, the family sat together and quietly discussed what rituals they could secretly keep and what they had to do to give the appearance of good Christians. Juana had her children swear that whatever would happen and wherever they would be, they would keep the secret rituals to remind them and their offspring of their Jewish faith. Sarita, their oldest daughter, had also to swear that she would guard the precious coin with her life and hand it down to her offspring. "My mother's name of Gonzales should not be forgotten together with her beliefs in the eternity of our race. The coin will be a reminder throughout the generations," Juana concluded.

They soon found out that their new life was anything but easy and often in the quiet hours of the night, they talked about their past life full of meaning through their long-kept faith. This was so especially during the last months before their friends, who had moved rather than convert, ostracized them for abandoning their age-old faith. It was strange, indeed, to have to go on Sundays and holidays to Church, to learn all the customs and prayers, and to appear as devout Christians. That, however, was not all. They could not bathe every Friday in the bathhouse, as was their wont. This was a Jewish custom and would have given them away immediately. It was hard for Juana to throw the night's soil from their chamber pots outside the windows as the Christian women did; she was used to disposing it in a discrete manner. All these precautions did not eliminate the suspicious stares of their neighbors. There were even those who, under some pretext or other, would come to their house and look around for signs of Jewish customs, books, or artifacts with Hebrew letters on them, or kitchen utensils not common in Christian households. It was no less hard for the children, especially for Nina, the youngest. Juana had to sit with her for hours to teach her how to behave outside or when strangers came to the house. She did not let Nina go out by herself for months until she was sure that nothing untoward would occur. One of the hardest tasks was to find a safe hiding place for the precious coin. If it were found, it could land them on the stake after the most horrendous torture. Finally, after much deliberation, they decided to hollow out one of the table legs, put the coin inside, and close the hole with wood shavings and a layer of glue. They thought that this place would be preferable to a hollowed-out wall or floor, since they might possibly have to move at some time.

Life continued more or less on an even keel, interrupted much too often with news of *auto-da-fés* in which mainly *Conversos* were burned at the stake after being accused of keeping their old religious customs or assisting Jews in various ways. These events took place in various towns all over the country. Many times, they heard of Christians going on rampage in areas outside of Al-Andalus, killing and maiming men, women and children, ransacking shops, and public establishments. At least Cordoba was spared of these happenings, only a few *Conversos* came to harm. Their workshop was left untouched. Josue passed away in 1486. As much as he advocated that they convert, he never got over the shock of the actual baptism and the consequent life of deceit. He deteriorated greatly during those few years. On his deathbed he voiced a declaration of guilt for having abandoned his age-old faith. He exhorted his children to pass Jewish teachings to their offspring and return openly to their heritage whenever that might be possible. It was only six years later that the Crown published the edict for all the Jews to convert or be expelled from the entire kingdom. Half of the *Conversos* in Cordoba left the country realizing that that there was no chance for things to revert to earlier better times. Those that kept some Jewish practices in secret and stayed took extra care to hide them. Juana, seeing so many of her former co-religionists leaving, wondered what Josue might have done. She thought that his guilty feelings would have been too great for them to stay. Mosse had no such qualms. He told his mother that they had done the right thing and was pleased that the shop actually prospered under him. He even expressed ideas of expanding and moving to a larger place. Being at an advanced age, he left it for his son, Miguel, to do.

It was Sarita who made sure that her family knew their heritage and kept their ancient customs to the greatest possible extent. She took the table with the coin with her when she moved to her husband's house upon marriage and eventually initiated her oldest daughter into the secret. Cordoba did not escape the eye of the Inquisition and *Conversos* were subject to persecution over the years. Racial laws were promulgated, at the instigation of the *hidalgo*, the nobility, which forbade high positions to be held by those who could not prove their Christian lineage for at least three generations. The New Christians were closely scrutinized for proper adherence to all religious precepts and anyone who, for example, would miss a Sunday service was questioned. Sarita's husband was recognized in town as a master craftsman and his jewelry shop was frequented by the highest Cordoba society as well as members of the clergy. Maybe because of that, the family was less bothered by intrusions into their private life than many other *Conversos*. The table was handed down until it came into the possession of Sarita's great-granddaughter Juana. The economic condition in Spain had improved tremendously with the arrival of gold and slaves from the newly conquered countries of South America. All those in high places were, of course, the first to benefit, and with their almost unlimited funds went about buying the best of everything available. This also included armaments. Juana's husband, Jose, specialized in the making of helmets and shields, the latter beautifully decorated with the family heraldic emblem emphasized in full color. He had to hire additional workers to keep up with the great demand. With the additional income, the family lived comfortably and purchased many new items for the home such as linens, furniture, and tableware. Much of the old was thrown away. One day Juana noticed that the old table, handed down through the generations, was missing. She asked Jose if he knew what became of it and was horrified to learn that he had asked some poor people to come and take a few of their old things.

"Did you not know what this table meant for me?" asked Juana in an agitated voice. "We were told to safeguard it with our life and you just gave it away. How could you do such a thing?" Jose was very angry with his wife for talking to him in this disrespectful way, and shouted at her to mind her ways. "You never told me what was so important about this ugly old table," he said. "It serves you right."

"Please, Jose, do you know the people that took the table? I will give them a lot of money just to get it back."

"And who do you think will give you this money? I will not give you, not one maravedi. So forget about it."

"How can you be so cruel? I will sell my earrings or whatever I own just to get the table back."

"Why do you attach such great importance to this piece of junk? You should have told me."

"My great-great-great-grandmother hid something in it and had her oldest daughter swear to keep it faithfully and hand it to her oldest daughter, and so on throughout the generations."

"Well, well. I am beginning to understand now why you have been keeping these odd habits like going for a walk on Saturday evenings on a clear day to look at the sky. You always bathed more than I, which I found odd. You told me that your family converted to Christianity many generations ago and I believed it. But now I am beginning to think that you did keep some of the old Jewish customs. Is that not so? Do not worry; I will not report you to the Inquisition. Most likely they would then also suspect me and our children would also suffer. But you must stop doing these things and be a good Christian. I forbid you to try and find the table. I will not have any incriminating thing in our house. Do you hear?"

The plague broke out in 1647, at the time when Jose and Juana's eldest granddaughter, Reyna, had married Fernando, who had just finished his apprenticeship in his father's jewelry workshop. At first, there were only rumors about some people getting sick with an awful disease. Not much attention was paid, as illnesses and death were a common occurrence. There was much else to worry about. King Felipe IV, on whom much hope was placed after the disastrous reign of his cousin, proved not much better, spending most of his time with his innumerable mistresses rather than attending to affairs of state. Many of those who went to fight for the country did not return after the defeats suffered in the battles against the English, French, and Dutch. It was only after the outbreak spread and details of the terrible suffering of those afflicted became common knowledge, that fear began to increase. Whenever a surgeon was seen walking on the street, a long stick in his gloved hand, totally covered from head to toe, his face covered by a beaked mask containing herbs and spices, people would pray that he was not on his way to a neighbor as the danger of contagion appeared very great.

Fernando, seeing the almost complete stoppage of business and the great danger in catching the disease, decided to take his bride to Montilla, a town seven leagues away. Reyna had wanted to stay in Cordoba where her family had lived for many generations. She was also still looking for the table that her grandmother had so valued, having been told the reason for its importance. She pleaded with Fernando, telling him about the table and how it was lost without, however, disclosing why it was such an important heirloom in her family.

"You mean to tell me that we should not move to a better and healthier place just because of an old table? For all I care, it could have gone for firewood after you grandfather disposed of it. Do you know that back some seventy-five years ago Friar Francis Solano cured a young virgin of the plague in Montilla? It is said that now the town is free of this terrible illness. I was told that the Friar later went to the New World to help spread the word of our Lord."

"It was a very special table. It was made of oak and was not rectangular like most, but with rounded edges, and had feet in the shape of animal paws. Somebody must have it and I am willing to buy it back, even if I have to part with some jewelry."

Fernando was adamant and they moved to Montilla. It was a growing place that had been declared a city by Phillip IV just fifteen years earlier.

The beginning in the new city was difficult. Even though Fernando had brought with him several exquisite pieces of jewelry, which he displayed in the little shop he had opened near the main square, very few of the inhabitants were wealthy enough to purchase them.

Fernando decided that he must, at least for a while, make the most basic jewelry, like plain rings, earrings, and simple bracelets, before returning to his beautiful creations. As he only had a very small stock of raw gold left, he melted down some of his early, complicated designs, but he did that only when they were almost going hungry for lack of money. Reyna, at the beginning of her pregnancy, went out to pick the Pedro Ximenez grapes that were just then ready for harvest. It was hard work, starting early in the morning before the sun was high up in the sky, and carrying the heavy basket on her back containing those beautiful golden bunches of grapes. All this labor for just a few coppers, hardly enough for the daily bread.

After a long and nearly fatal labor, Reyna delivered a daughter, whom she called Blanca on account of her fair hair. Considering the difficult economic situation, she despaired of ever being able to look for the table as she did not have enough money to feed her now growing family. She could not consider taking time off from work or paying for it, even had she been able to find it. From an early age, Blanca was told of the family history and was impressed in the importance of keeping some Jewish customs while taking care of being externally a pious Christian. Reyna also made sure to inculcate in her the importance of finding the table in order to recover the precious memento.

Montilla was indeed almost spared the plague with only a few inhabitants dying because of it. By the time

Blanca was eight, the disease had subsided in all of Andalus and the economic situation had improved. People started to buy fancy expensive jewelry for weddings, engagements, and births, and Fernando's business began to prosper. As precious stones were now readily available coming from the new lands in the West, Fernando incorporated these in his new designs for earrings, brooches, and pendants. Very desired were emeralds of which he made a great deal of use. At the age of fifteen, Blanca was married off to carpenter of a good family. Not having sons, Fernando had desired to see her married to a jeweler, but none besides him lived in Montilla or the nearby villages. With two other daughters to be married off, they could not afford a large dowry and had to accept a carpenter from a decent family as their son-in-law. Before she agreed, though, Reyna made sure that Manolo, the prospective groom, was from a *Converso* family. Blanca did not have much say in the matter. She was satisfied, as he was reasonably good-looking and had even finished his apprenticeship.

Blanca and Manolo got along well, as Manolo turned out to be good-natured and went along with many of Blanca's requests, as long he could afford them. In order to augment his meager income from his carpentry work, he came up with the novel idea of renewing old furniture, going from door to door both in Montilla and the nearby villages. He was quite successful in this enterprise, especially in the poorer homes and farmhouses. He repaired, cleaned, and polished tables, chairs, and cabinets and sideboards, the latter ones he enlarged. It was in one old farmhouse that he came across a table that seemed to be the one that Blanca was desperately looking for. He realized the reason for it and was willing to pay a small amount for it to make his wife happy. He told the owner that to repair and make it presentable would require a great deal of work and would thus be very expensive. He would nevertheless give him eight maravedi for it. This amount, with a small addition, would enable him to buy a modern table. The man agreed and Manolo took the table home.

Blanca was ecstatic when she saw the table and asked Manolo to check whether it appeared that the feet had been tampered with. He had already done so, he replied, and noticed that the wood at the bottom of one of the feet was of a different kind than the others. He added that it was not very obvious, and only he, with his carpentry experience, was able to see the difference. Blanca went immediately to her mother, who lived nearby, to tell her of the near miracle, and ask her what to do with it.

"God in heaven!" Reyna cried upon hearing Blanca's story. "There is someone who is watching from above. I can't believe it, after so many years! Come Blanca, I must see it! Tell Manolo to open the hiding place so that we can see for ourselves what our ancestor placed in there. It must be very precious."

With that, she grabbed Blanca's hand and pulled her along, running the short distance without caring what the neighbors would think. The first thing she did upon entering Blanca's house was grab Manolo and kiss him on the cheek. The poor man did not know what happened, as never before had Reyna showed such affection for him.

"Please, Manolo," she said breathlessly, "do open that leg of the table where something is hidden. I must see it right away."

Manolo went to work, and soon enough he had a silvery-black piece of metal in his hand, which he handed to Reyna, with Blanca too looking at it eagerly.

"What is it?" he asked. "What is so precious about this old piece of metal to have been hidden so carefully and passed down through all these generations of your family? I hate to think that I have paid eight maravedi for it. It does not seem worth even one."

"It is an heirloom that was handed down from generation to generation. From what I know, our ancestors converted to Christianity, back some two-hundred years ago, at the time when Jews were forced to leave their homes in all of Al-Andalus unless they converted. Now, this meant that no sign of Jewish custom or religion could be in the home of those that converted. How well do we know what happens to families if the Inquisition find any trace of adherence to Jewish religion in their house? It must have something to do with our heritage. Come, let's clean this thing up and look at it."

Fernando joined the others after Reyna told him of the find of the table and the strange piece of metal hidden in it. They all crowded around, each waiting their turn to look closely at the odd piece of metal. "It looks to me like a coin, don't you think so Fernando?" Reyna asked.

"But what are these strange letters on this side of it? And look at the other side – maybe it is a house?"

"Now I am sure it is connected with our old religion, it is possible that these letters are in the holy tongue and may contain a blessing of some kind. Why else was it so carefully hidden? I think it is also very valuable, since you said that the word was passed in your family from mother to daughter to take good care of it."

"That sounds right, father," Blanca interjected. "But who will be able to tell us what it is? I understand that we must be careful not to show it to someone who might report us to the Inquisition."

"You are very right, Blanca. I think that we should not endanger ourselves and rather bury this thing somewhere around here, in case it is a blessing, and then forget about it."

"How could you say something like that, Fernando?" Reyna sounded angry but was careful not to raise her voice to her husband. "You know that it has been in our family at least these past two-hundred years and most likely much before that. I am sure that we can find someone with knowledge of old coins without jeopardizing us. You are right; we should bury it for now, but only until we learn what it is, and then decide what to do."

Fernando agreed reluctantly, thinking that they might not find anyone appropriate, and then it would remain buried and forgotten.

It was nearly a year later when Manolo came home one evening that he excitedly told Blanca that he had found someone who he thought might be able to tell them about the coin. "I did some work in nearby Aguilar, for a pawnbroker who is one of the wealthy ones there. He was rather friendly, I would not be surprised if he was a *Converso*, I just had that feeling."

"What gave you that impression? Were there any signs to justify that he really is? Even if he is, who is to say that he might not report us to the Inquisition?"

"I think we are safe with him. I told him that I found a piece of round metal deep in the ground when I was digging for a new latrine and that it had some inscriptions on it that I could not make out. Maybe, I said, it is of some worth. He said that it may be a coin and that he would have to see it to be able to tell us. Some generations ago, one of his ancestors was a money-lender who also exchanged different currencies. The family converted later, becoming good Christians, thus not able to continue lending money at interest. The knowledge, however, was passed from father to son."

"I am still a little worried, Manolo. Even if he comes from a *Converso* family, why would he not tell the Inquisition about us having this coin? What is his name?"

"It is Jose Maria Gonzales Alvares. I doubt that he will turn us in. Look, once it is in his hand, I could just as well claim that it is his. I am sure that it will turn out all right. Maybe he will give us a good amount of money for it. As far as I am concerned, he may just as well keep it and good riddance."

"Manolo! How can you say something like that when it has been in my family for many generations and must be passed down? Please, bring it to him and see what he has to say; maybe it is not worth that much anyway."

Manolo took his time, afraid of being caught with the coin on his way to the pawnbroker. It was a month or so later that he went to him. The man welcomed him cordially, offering spiced wine, which for Manolo was a great treat. Jose took the coin, pulled out a magnifying glass, and looked at both its sides for a long time. He finally looked up at Manolo and said, in a measured voice, "Do you want to hear the true meaning of this coin? It may mean something very difficult for you to accept. I assume that you really found it by accident like you told me. You may want to get rid of it like a burning cinder that accidentally fell into your open hand."

"Why, of course I want to know. If it is such a dangerous object, then I can always bury it again in some God-forsaken forest."

"I am quite sure that this is an old Jewish coin that was minted almost a millennium and a half ago in Judea, as the writing is Hebrew and the picture may represent the Temple of the Hebrews. As for its worth, I really do not know if one can put a value on it. It may be very valuable to *Marranos* who wish to have something to remind them of their Jewish past. The metal seems to be silver, although is not worth that much, maybe a little less than one maravedi de plata, if it is at least eleven grams of silver. You won't get rich on it."

"Thank you, Jose. I will take it back and dispose of it, I guess."

"Glad to help you, Manolo. And do not worry, I will not say anything about it to anyone and I know that you will not mention my name in this connection. We both have to be careful. Go with God."

Manolo returned home, not sure if he could convince Blanca to get rid of the coin. *She will have to do what I tell her, I do not want to quarrel with her about it, but I cannot let her have her way in this matter, it is too dangerous*, he thought. Blanca was just attending to the baby, but quickly put her into the crib when she saw Manolo entering, regardless of the ensuing howl.

"What did the pawnbroker say when he saw the coin?" she burst out. Manolo was wondering what to tell her, and took his time before answering.

"He did not say anything of importance. He said it may be an old Jewish coin, that it maybe of silver, and worth one maravedi."

"Well, we have to hide it someplace where our offspring will know where to find it and pass it down through the generations. Some day, I am sure, we will again be free to worship and live in peace and honor."

"No, Blanca. We cannot risk it. There is no need for this old coin to remind us of our heritage, we can pass it on to future generations very well without it. Look, the coin was hidden in a table leg for years, and for many more years the table itself was lost, and still we remembered what we were without seeing it or even knowing where it was."

"But Manolo, a solemn promise was made to one of our ancestors and renewed every generation. How can we break this pledge? Please, think about this."

"I thought about it, it is too dangerous for us to keep it around here. Either we bury it somewhere in the woods and forget about it, or we give it to someone who would be willing to assume the risk involved and hand it down to his future generations."

"Manolo, I am your wife and must do what you demand, but this is too cruel. Do you not have any feelings for our heritage, the one that so many of our brethren went to their death for on the stake?"

"I do, but I have to look out for my family so that no harm will come to it. We have a child and more will hopefully follow. Come to think of it, I have a feeling that Jose will take the coin and promise what you want of him. Is not this the most important idea here, that at one time the restrictions placed on us will be abolished and we will again follow our religion in the open? The coin will be proof of us not forgetting our heritage during these many years. I hope that you are satisfied with this."

Nothing more was said and Manolo waited for an opportune time to go to Jose.

It was a dreary morning when Manolo finally found the time and the willingness to ride over to Aguilar to see Jose. The sky was overcast with the threat of rain, which added to his foul mood. He just wanted to get rid of the stupid coin. Only because of his consideration for his wife did he finally go to Jose. He felt a little better once he arrived at his destination without being stopped and searched. Jose received him cordially, assuming it was in connection with the coin.

"I presume you have come because of the coin, Manolo. I am glad to see you for whatever reason and hope all is well with you and your family. Do tell me what is on your mind."

Manolo did not know how to start, thought for a while and said. "I trust that I can be honest with you and tell you about my family. I gathered from what you had said that you come from a family of *Conversos*, as do many here. None, I am certain, will admit to still having some, how shall I say, nostalgia for the old religion. What say you?"

Jose looked long into Manolo's eyes and said, "Well, yes, my family and I do have some longing for our heritage as, I imagine, does yours. Both of us will, of course, not talk about that with anyone. Now that this is out of the way, what is it you really want?"

"I am not a very brave man, Jose; I just wish to support my family quietly and safely. My wife, however, is more attached to our heritage than I am and wants to keep the coin. I am strongly opposed to that because of the danger of the Inquisition. I had planned to bury it somewhere and forget about it. However, in order to please her, I suggested that I would try to find someone who is willing to keep it and pass it on to his descendants until such time as we will be free to keep our religion openly. It would thus show our adherence to our faith in spite of the long persecution of our people. I thought about asking you to do that. Would you be willing?"

Jose asked Manolo to let him have the coin for a moment, he took it and looked at it for a long time, turning it over and over.

"You took me by surprise, Manolo. Let me think about it some more. Have some wine in the meantime." Manolo, gratefully sipping the wine, was getting impatient when Jose failed to say anything for a while, pacing back and for in the small room. Finally he sat down and said. "The danger for me is as great as it is for you, Manolo. Nevertheless, I have decided to agree to your request. It is because of the great value of such a coin for our people. We do not have many other memorials of the time of our independence in our land. This little piece of metal would fetch practically nothing here on the market, but I find it actually an honor to have it in my possession, and will guard it as best as I can. I will instruct my eldest son to hand it down to his, and so on through the generations. Please tell your wife what I have said and, if she wishes, I will tell it to her personally."

He stood up and shook Manolo's hand, who thanked him profusely. Back home he told Blanca what had transpired. She was pleased, but still harangued her husband bitterly for showing such little regard for their heritage.

PART IV
CHAPTER 18

2006

The drive to Malaga, in the South of Spain, was fairly short as it was only some eighty miles. Both Michael and Caroline kept to themselves. At one point, Caroline tried to sound a little more conciliatory, but did not get much of a response from her husband. Michael was still thinking about their meeting with Joanna, hoping to see her again somehow, yet afraid of just that. *It really shook me up good. I had not thought about her for a while, but now I can't put her out of my mind. I don't even know if she's still married. And even if she isn't, what would I do? Also, neither she nor I are the same as we were all those years ago. I can't just wish to be with her as if nothing happened in the meantime. Has she possibly come to Spain to search for Jewish roots in her ancestry? Maybe I should've given her more time to think of how to placate her parents while we could have occasionally seen each other. I was too abrupt, just told her it was finished and hung up on her. How stupid could I have been? Come to think of it, though, marrying Caroline was not such a bad idea. We have been married, what, nearly five years now, and it has been good. It all started with Helen's birthday party.*

CHAPTER 19

2001

Michael arrived early to Helen's surprise birthday party that David had arranged at the Red Barn in Westport.He had invited about thirty people and asked them to be there before the scheduled time of his arriving with Helen. Michael was sitting at the bar when a nice-looking blonde girl sat next to him and ordered a martini. It took a while before he turned to her and asked if she came for Helen's birthday party.

"Yes, I work with Helen at the office and have known her for quite a while. She's a terrific girl and so is David, who called to invite me. How about you?"

"Oh, Dave and I have known each other since the time we went to Boston Latin High and were in the same class in Sunday school. I quite agree with what you said about Helen."

"So you come from Boston? I've always lived here in Westport, except for the time that I was at NYU and lived in the dorms there. Would you believe it, I still live with my parents? It's very comfortable – they have a big place and I have my own suite. We belong to Temple Israel here. But please excuse me, here comes someone else from the office." With that, she got up and went to greet a young man who just came through the door. *She seems quite nice and she let me know that she's Jewish. I don't even know her name, I'll ask Helen*, thought Michael.

The party was nice. Helen, when she and David came in, acted very surprised to see all her friends and colleagues assembled, singing "Happy Birthday." The dinner that followed the drinks and hors d'oeuvres was quite good, the mood was jovial, and it was fairly late by the time the celebration broke up. Michael had a chance to ask Helen about the girl he had talked with.

"Oh, that's Caroline Goodman. She lives here in Westport and has been with the firm about a year and a half, after she graduated from NYU. She's nice and very smart. She graduated in computer science and works as a systems analyst. I don't know why it never occurred to me to introduce you to her. I should have. Why don't you call her now that you have met her here? As far as I know, she has no current boyfriend."

Michael called Caroline about a week later. She seemed glad to hear from him and said that Helen had told her some good things about him in the meantime. They made a date to go for dinner the following Friday. Michael decided to make an impression and splurge and suggested the Dressing Room. He did not know what made him do it, as it was not his usual nature. As always, he was a little early with Caroline sweeping in breathless about fifteen minutes after the time they had agreed.

"Sorry for being a little late. Somehow I couldn't get myself together. This is a great place, I'm so glad you picked it; their food is always so wonderfully fresh. I think they use organic stuff. I've come here with my family a couple of times." The food indeed was good, and with the wine Michael ordered, the conversation flowed smoothly over a range of topics, from their studies to politics, and on with the latest discoveries in science. They parted in the parking lot with Caroline kissing Michael goodnight, saying that she hoped they would see each other again soon. Michael drove home quite impressed with his date. *She is not only good looking but apparently also very intelligent. Only with Joanna did I get that impression at the beginning of our acquaintance. I will certainly call her and hope to get to know her better. Maybe we can meet up with David and Helen.*

Only a few days later, David called Michael and told him that they would love it if he would bring Caroline over to their place for dinner. Helen had spoken to her and she had said that she would gladly come if Michael agreed.

"Thanks, David. I would like that very much. You guys are acting like matchmakers, but just don't push it. The start was good but let's sees how things develop."

The following Friday evening, the start of the long Memorial Day weekend, Michael drove to Caroline's place. As there was no reply when he rang the bell at the door with her name, he took the few steps to the main entrance where a woman, with some resemblance to

Caroline, opened the door.

"Come in please. You must be Michael. Caroline asked me to entertain you for a few minutes until she was ready. It won't be long."

Michael followed her to the living room, which was huge. Gilt-framed paintings hung from one wall with another covered with two old large tapestries. A grand piano stood in a corner, the elegant furniture, and Persian rugs showing wealth, if not a feeling of a warm home.

"Where do you live, Michael? Caroline told me that you have known Helen for quite some time. We have met her, and found her a very nice young woman."

"Yes, she is indeed. I live in Norwalk and work in Stamford. I'm an engineer."

"That's nice. Ah, here comes Caroline. I told you it wouldn't not be long."

Michael got up to approach Caroline and turned to say goodbye to her mother, who invited him to come again.

As usual, the dinner cooked by Helen was excellent, the wine pleasant, and the conversation relaxed. Michael, feeling comfortable in this familiar environment, led the conversation with Bush's election and other current affairs as the main topics. All four voiced their unhappiness with the defeat of Al Gore, Clinton's vice president. They, like many of their fellow Jews, were liberals and usually voted Democrat. The steam leak in the Indian Point II nuclear power plant came up and the girls voiced their objection to the continued use of nuclear power.

"It's too dangerous – look what happened at Chernobyl. A whole city was nearly wiped out," they said. "We don't want it to happen here." Michael objected, saying that technological progress was not only inevitable but also desirable, in spite of occasional disasters.

"The world will soon run out of fossil fuel and will need alternative energy. Do we want to go back to live like in the Middle Ages?" he said.Caroline seemed well informed and contributed a great deal to the conversation. She brought up the topic of Condoleezza Rice's selection as the first black and first woman National Security Advisor. Nobody had expected Bush to do that. The brandy after the meal helped the four let their hair down, with Helen prodding Michael and Caroline to talk about their mutual impressions. Seeing Michael somewhat hesitant, Caroline said, "I don't want to push things, seeing that we met only a short while ago, but it looks good to me. We do, however, need to get closer before we can be sure."

Michael, looking a little embarrassed at hearing that, thought for a while before saying, "It's a good start, anyway. But I asked you, Helen, not to push things. The makings for a permanent affair are either there or not. Time will tell."

Their conversation petered out until Caroline said that it was getting late, and thanked their hosts for a wonderful evening. Michael joined in and they left after a great deal of hugging all around.

Both were rather quiet on the way to Caroline's house. Only when they had almost approached it Caroline turned to Michael and said, "Why don't you come in for a nightcap? My rooms are separate from my parents' and we won't disturb them."

Michael understood and felt aroused. "Sure, I'd love it, even if we have drunk quite a bit this evening."

Caroline had a whole apartment to herself. After they entered, she suggested they have Benedictine and relax for a while, which Michael readily agreed. She went to a cabinet, got the drinks, and said that she would just go for a moment to put on something lighter and less fancy. It did take only a few minutes, and she was back, wearing what seemed to be a light robe and sat down on the sofa next to Michael. Caroline raised her glass and said "To us." Michael followed, and before he realized it, their glasses were on the table and Caroline was on his lap. He felt her warm body beneath the thin material, kissed her passionately, and opened her robe feeling her firm breasts. Caroline, highly aroused, tried to open the zipper of Michael's trousers and, as she did not succeed, took him by the hand and dragged him to her bedroom where Michael frantically looked for a condom in his trouser pocket and put it on his fully erect member. He entered Caroline forcefully, her arms outstretched to pull him closer unto her. The climax came quickly. As they lay exhausted side-by-side, Caroline suggested that Michael stay with her that night as they did not have to work the following day. It took only a moment for

Michael to agree. They made love twice more during the night and did not wake up until late in the morning. After showering and dressing, Caroline fixed a quick breakfast, after which Michael said that he'd better leave as he arranged to meet a friend for lunch in Norwalk. They first agreed that she would pick him up on Sunday morning, the weather forecast looking promising, and go to the Norwalk beach. A minute later Caroline suggested that he come that evening to her place and stay the night. On second thought, she suggested that she come to his place in the late afternoon, as she wanted to see how he lived. Michael agreed, if somewhat reluctantly.

Wow, that is some girl. Michael thought as he drove to Norwalk for his meeting. *I better go home early to fix up my place and get a few things to put in the refrigerator. It certainly cannot compete with hers. I wonder what her parents are like. Her mother looks well; supposedly daughters take after their mothers in later years. Wait, why the hell am I thinking how Caroline will look in twenty-five years? Am I going to marry her? And what about her feelings?*

Caroline arrived at six. Michael hugged and kissed her as she entered, with Caroline responding ardently. There was no time to see the apartment as their passion mounted and within seconds, they were in the bedroom, their clothes off, making love as if it was the first time. Only later did Caroline look around the apartment, and even inspected the refrigerator, which, luckily enough, Michael had the sense to stock up the previous night. Caroline voiced her approval of what she saw. She asked

Michael where he thought they might dine that evening as it was getting late. He suggested the Kazu Japanese restaurant on North Main Street, not far from where he lived. She agreed enthusiastically.

It turned out to be a great weekend. By Sunday, after spending the morning on the beach, the weather sunny and warm, Michael felt as if he had known Caroline for the longest time, and she, in turn, seemed to feel comfortable and sure that Michael made a good partner with whom she wanted to go steady, if not more than that. They had finished the lunch that Michael prepared and sat relaxed in their bathrobes when Caroline said, "Why don't you come over for dinner at my parents' sometime this week? I'll ask them when they'll be home. My dad has odd hours, sometimes coming back late. He has an insurance business and often sees the big clients in the evening. I'll give you a call and let you know. Would you mind? They are OK and we don't have to stay with them too long." Michael agreed readily.

Dinner with Caroline's parents went off quite well. They asked the usual questions about his work, his future ambitions, his parents, what temple they belonged to, and more. Michael's answers seemed to satisfy them; at least that was his impression. Caroline became somewhat impatient at this lengthy interview and put a stop to it, suggesting they eat their dinner since she and Michael had plans to go to a movie. Instead, they went to a local bar that had some entertainment. Michael felt it quite natural to go back to Caroline's apartment later that night. At breakfast the following morning, Michael suggested they go up to Boston the nearest weekend that his parents were free. Caroline happily agreed.

They took the train to Boston on a Saturday morning, two weeks later. The ride was pleasant except, as they neared Back Bay, Michael had an uneasy feeling about introducing Caroline to his parents. *What's the matter with me, why do I feel this way? Sure, it's not the same as when I came up with Joanna; but Caroline is also a nice, smart girl. My parents might actually be pleased that I'm bringing a Jewish girl this time.*

Things turned out to be rather pleasant, the welcome was warm, and dinner, again with Esther and Robert Serman, was very enjoyable, conversation flowing easily. Caroline seemed pleased with the visit, and enjoyed being taken to see some sights by Michael. She did notice that, at times, Michael seemed to be preoccupied with some thoughts, which he always explained as thinking about problems at work.

One thing led to another, and they were married just six months after they had met the first time. The wedding was magnificent. It took place in great style in Temple Israel in Westport, with several hundred guests invited; the families of both sides, friends, and colleagues. For their honeymoon, the couple went up to Canada, first to Quebec and then to Newfoundland.

PART V

CHAPTER 20

2006

Arriving in Malaga, Michael and Caroline spent the day shopping, seeing the Moorish fortress of Alcazaba, with its gorgeous views of the city as it's situated on top of a hill, visiting the Roman theatre, and touring the Picasso home that served as a museum. The hotel was comfortable and at the end of a satisfying dinner Caroline, a little awkwardly, said, "You know Michael, I really was rather bitchy concerning Joanna. She does seem like a nice person and you were right that I had no right to feel jealous as I did. I had several boyfriends before I met you and I think I was smart enough to wait for you. Spain is pretty big, so I don't think we'll run into her again, but if we do, I won't embarrass you again, OK?"

"I'm so glad you said that, darling. I love you. I may have acted a little miserable too. So let's forget it. Here's to us." With that, they lifted their wine glasses and clinked them together. Two days in Malaga was enough and early the following morning they set out for Seville, a distance of about one hundred and thirty miles away.

Arriving at their hotel, the Fernando III, they were pleasantly surprised at its unexpected luxury. They rested for a short time and then left the hotel anxious to see the sights. They went to the cathedral and saw the Treasury, the unbelievably rich Sanctuary, the Chapel Royal, and thought of going up the Giralda that used to be a high minaret, nearly three hundred feet tall. Caroline, looking up, decided to skip the excellent view of the city from the top and stay down. Michael went up, coming down excitedly describing what he saw. They went to the Alcazar and its gardens, took a carriage ride to the huge park, went to the fine arts museum, and just wandered around in the gorgeous weather. One evening, they went to hear flamenco music and dance in a small nightclub. It was very close to the hotel at a small plaza hidden within the narrow streets. The place was jam-packed, people excitedly talking, a drink in their hand waiting for the performance to start. Noise and cigarette smoke filled the hall. Things calmed down as a guitarist came on stage, sitting on a stool waiting for the first dancer to appear. It was a young woman holding the hem of her long flaming red dress in one hand. She acknowledged the audience with a slight nod of her head and nodded to the guitarist to start. She danced to his powerful rhythm, carrying the audience with her in the interpretation of a tragic story conveyed by the music. The audience cheered and clapped vigorously after she finished. She was followed by both male and female dancers, dancing alone or in couples. The show finished after midnight, with Michael and Caroline going to the hotel deeply engrossed in the experience they just had.

A little weary from two days of exploring this interesting city, Michael and Caroline decided to take it easy the following day and went up to the large roof pool to relax. There were no other guests there, so after a refreshing swim they were able to lie side by side in the warm sun, cuddling, fondling, and kissing until they hurriedly put on their bathrobes and went to their room for more privacy. Later, going out for dinner they found the town alive with people strolling through the quaint narrow streets. The evening was still warm and the sidewalk restaurants were filled with customers. They looked at the menus posted and picked one that seemed to meet their desires. Michael had seafood paella while Caroline preferred the grilled sardines. That, with a bottle of Vino de Tierra, a good local wine, complemented by a strong cappuccino and sweet pestinos, made for a perfect meal. They sat for a while looking at the people walking by. Wishing to get an early start the next day, they decided to go back to their room. It was after midnight when Michael woke up with severe stomach cramps and nausea, leading him to run quickly to the bathroom to throw up. Caroline awoke hearing the commotion and went to Michael's side leading him back to bed. He felt a little better but still nauseous.

"What could have happened?" asked Caroline. "The food seemed to be good at that restaurant, there were so many other people eating there. I normally do not like fried food, which often doesn't agree with me. We both ate the pestinos and still I feel perfectly well. Maybe it was the paella? What do you think?"

"I don't know, dear. Normally I would not pay much attention to it as these things usually get better quickly, and with eating carefully for a day or two it'll be all right. Right now, though, I'm a little worried. The paella had a lot of oil in it. Do you not remember that we read in the Malaga paper the news about the machine oil that was added to olive oil and sold all over? It caused about a hundred people to die lately here in Andalusia? Please call downstairs and see if there is a doctor that can come up."

Caroline called the front desk to ask whether a doctor was in the house but was told that one would have to call from the outside and it would take a while for him to arrive. The clerk suggested that, if possible, they to go to the clinic nearby where a doctor was available at all hours. They got dressed, Michael still feeling poorly and worrying that he may have ingested some of that machine oil.

They found the clinic easily, as it was no more than a few hundred yards from the hotel. A very nice young doctor received them, the clinic otherwise empty at such an early hour. There was only one problem: The doctor spoke only Spanish so that no verbal communication was possible. Pointing to his stomach, Michael made himself understood through sign language. The doctor made a thorough examination, at the end of which he smiled and gave them to understand that it was nothing serious. He sat down to write what seemed a prescription and handed it to Michael. After they left, they looked over the note and saw a few words in Spanish with the word *manzana* underlined. On the way back to the hotel, they passed a pharmacy that had opened by that time and went in to have the prescription filled. The pharmacist looked at it, then at them and said something. Seeing that his customers did not understand, he tried German but again without success. Giving up on verbal communication, he took his pen and wrote on the prescription the words 'hotel restaurant' and gave it back to Michael. Very puzzled, Caroline and Michael went back to the hotel, waited some twenty minutes for the restaurant to open and sat down, the first guests there. When the waiter came to take their order Michael gave him the doctor's prescription which he took, a puzzled look on his face, as well as Caroline's order, and went to the kitchen. After a rather long wait he appeared, placed Caroline's order on the table and then, with a flourish, put a green apple on a small plate before the astonished Michael. "Is this on the prescription?" he asked the waiter, who nodded and left with a bow. Caroline smiled, saying that it was well known that apples are good for upset stomachs and that the doctor apparently did not believe it was anything serious. Michael seemed a little skeptical but ate the apple, chewing it well, feeling somewhat relieved.

They decided to take it easy that day and went up to the roof, taking with them a local English newspaper, the *El Sun News*. Michael looked first for world news but found very little. However, when glancing at news from around Andalusia, he was astounded to see Aguilar de la Frontera headlined, which he immediately associated with Joanna's last name. Looking at the article he excitedly showed it to Caroline. They read the following:

Aguilar de la Frontera, 20.9.2006

This little quiet town is in an uproar at the unheard of episode that occurred here yesterday. A young American lady tourist was kidnapped by two young men in broad daylight, had her hair shorn, and was left in a locked basement. She was fortunate that it was not entirely underground, so that she was able to knock on the narrow high window and draw the attention of a passerby. She was rescued with no physical injury but suffered from shock. The municipal police have requested the assistance of the National Police from Cordoba in solving this crime.

Michael and Caroline looked at each other astonished by the news.

"Do you think that it was Joanna?" asked Caroline. "I don't believe that there are so many single American women tourists in what must be a small town. Do you know where it is?"

"I don't know exactly, but it must be near Cordoba. Joanna's maiden name is Aguilar and, as she has said, she has come to look for her family's roots in this country.

They must have come from this town having the same name. We cannot be sure, but it does seem like it's her. We should get in touch with her, but I don't know how."

"We planned to go to Cordoba tomorrow anyway," Caroline said. "Maybe we can get in touch with the police while there and get some more information."

"You are so right. I hadn't thought of that. To think that something like this could happen here to an innocent tourist is pretty awful. Everything seems to be so pleasant and safe. Why, in heavens name, was she attacked? There was no mention of a robbery. You know, cutting a woman's hair reminds me of the stories I read about the French resistance against the Nazis during World War II. The resistance fighters cut the hairs of any woman suspected of having affairs with German soldiers during the occupation. Doing it to Joanna, if it was her, really does not make sense to me. Well, we'll try and get to the bottom of it."

As the drive to Cordoba was only about an hour and a half, they decided to leave after an early lunch and see the synagogue and possibly the Zoco, the market. The visit to the synagogue – the only one in Spain besides the one in Toledo – was a short one. It dated back to the 14th century and consisted of a small square room with a balcony on one side for women. The market was exciting. Colorful and noisy, they saw stalls heaped with fruits, vegetables, an endless variety of fish on beds of ice, meats in glass refrigerators with roasted chickens hanging from hooks over the display. On one side of the market there was a patio on which several craftsmen were working making engraved brass plates.

The drive to Cordoba was indeed only a bare seventy-five miles, so that Michael and Caroline arrived quite early at their hotel, the Las Casas de la Juderia. It was well situated, quite near to the Mosque, and was in the old Jewish quarter, as the name implied. As their room was not ready, they left their luggage and, after receiving directions, went to the National Police station to inquire about the article they read. It was an exercise in futility. At first they waited for quite a while until an officer who spoke English was found. Unfortunately, he was not the proper authority to speak on current inquiries and suggested they come back the following day between eleven and twelve, at which time the officer in charge would be available. On the way back to the hotel, they picked up an English newspaper, which had only a small article about the kidnapping stating that the police had a few leads and were hoping to soon find the culprits.

Returning to the hotel, they received their room and then visited the Mosque, which was astounding with a forest of pillars connected by red and white Moorish arches. With the conquest of Cordoba by the Christians, the mosque was converted to a cathedral with some architectural changes made to reflect the new religion.

The next morning, Michael and Caroline visited the Jewish quarter, the *Juderia*, with its narrow streets and brilliant flowers spilling over the white walls. At some places, the doors were opened onto cool patios filled with greenery. In one of those streets, a large bust of the Rambam had been erected, commemorating the great Jewish philosopher, scientist, and physician. They then managed to arrive at the police station just at a quarter before twelve. Luckily, the senior officer was still available. He politely listened to their questions, telling them that Aguilar de la Frontera was very near Cordoba and that his department was responsible to find and arrest the culprits. When Michael asked if it was their friend, Joanna Aguilar, who was the victim, he hesitated for a moment before confirming that it was she. He further said that such an attack was extremely rare not only in Andalusia but in all of Spain. As to the culprits, he added that they had not been found as yet but, with some of the leads they had, they would soon be apprehended. Michael asked if he could tell them where Joanna was staying, to which he said that he was not certain but thought that she was in the only hotel in that town, the Malvasia. His parting words were that they should feel perfectly safe there and wished them a pleasant vacation.

CHAPTER 21

Despite running as fast as she could, Joanna's pursuers caught up easily with her. They grabbed her roughly by the arms and pulled her around trying to lead her back. All the while, Joanna resisted vigorously while screaming for help. No savior appeared and the two ruffians dragged her to a nearby courtyard of a dilapidated building, apparently abandoned. Because of Joanna's fierce resistance, they had to practically carry her down several steps into a basement. She gave in only when she realized that continuing resistance would cause her injury or worse. It was then that she was able to look directly at her captors. They seemed to be men in their mid-twenties, one rather tall with the other of medium height. They wore baseball caps and had their faces covered with pieces of cloth tied in the back. Both wore jeans and identical black tee shirts and sneakers. Joanna tried to gather something that would assist in eventually identifying them later, but could only see their eyes. Those of the shorter one were a dark brown while the tall one had blue eyes and, as his face cloth slipped some during the struggle, she saw that he had the start of a fair beard. What impressed her as rather odd were the fingers of the shorter man, which were very stubby but had long nails.

The basement reflected the condition of the building. The walls and ceiling paint was peeling, the floor dirty with what seemed to be ash, food remnants, and several broken syringes. It was graced by a small rug the color of which was barely discernible. An old sofa was standing in one corner, bereft of pillows, although one of which was on the floor. That and a couple of old kitchen chairs and a small rickety table made up the furniture. All this was barely illuminated by light trying to enter through the narrow, filthy, high windows on one side of the basement.

"We see you got the point that resistance is futile," said the taller one. "We will show you what we do with dirty dogs like you. Maybe that will teach you not to spread your filthy religion among us good Catholics. I don't care if you are *Marrano* or Jew. Neither one should be here."

"It seems you are too dumb to have learned something during five hundred long years," the shorter one butted in. "Wasn't the expulsion enough for you? You *Marranos* have poisoned the well you drank from, doing your vile things in secret. Come on Jose, get out your scissors and start the haircut, see how she likes her new look."

The tall one gave his buddy what seemed a warning look, took a pair of scissors out of the small shoulder bag he carried, and grabbed hold of Joanna's hair. She tried to move her head away, but felt the tip of the scissors pricking her scalp so that she held still for the inevitable.

With a voice strangled in tears and frustration, she shouted, "Stop it you cowards, you hoodlums, pick on someone your size! What do you want from me? I'm neither Jewish nor *Converso*. And if I was, you can't do such a thing. Let me go, now!" Fearful for her life, she was careful not to threaten them with the police and submitted to the painful cutting of her hair with the dull scissors. When he was finished, he told her that if she behaved they would come that night and release her. With that, they turned and left, locking the door.

It took a while for Joanna to calm down; her sniffles gradually disappeared and clear thinking was slowly restored. Her immediate reaction was to try the door that was locked with an old fashioned key. She remembered vaguely seeing some crime movies in which locked doors were opened by slipping a thin object into the crack between the door and the frame where the lock is. She still had her bag, which the two had left her after rummaging through it and looking at her American passport. She thought at first of using a piece of stiff cardboard, but the only thing she had that met her need was the cover of her passport. She inserted it as she had seen but nothing happened. Thinking that maybe it was not sturdy enough, she took one of her credit cards and inserted it instead. Again nothing happened, however, as hard as she tried to push the card. Failing this, after many tries, she turned to the windows, trying to reach them in order to bang on them and attract attention. There was no way for her to know if these windows were facing the street or the inner courtyard. If the latter, there was little chance that she would be heard. With nothing better in mind she nevertheless decided to try and break one. She moved the one chair that still looked sturdy enough under one of the windows, climbed on it, and started to hit the window with the heel of her shoe. It did make some noise but not very loud. As hard as she hit, the glass did not break as she had hoped. She kept at it for some time without a response. Seeing that, she decided to find a suitable tool. Looking around, the only possibility was to break the other chair, the rickety one, and use a piece of it. It took some effort, but she finally succeeded in breaking free a leg. By this time, however, Joanna was exhausted, feeling her mind not functioning properly. It was not only the physical effort she had made. It was mostly fear – bordering on panic – of being incarcerated in this prison, without food or water, not knowing when and if she would be released. She rested for a while on the sofa, as uncomfortable and dirty as it was. Only after quite some time did she feel her physical and mental strength returning, so she got up and stepped on the chair with the chair leg in her hand. This time her efforts were successful. After repeated attempts the glass broke and she started to shout as loud as she could. There was no reply, but now she could see clearly through the opening, hoping the leg of a passerby would appear at which time she would shout for help thus saving her voice. It was tiring to stand on the chair for what seemed like hours until she finally spotted someone passing. Joanna immediately shouted as loud as she could. There was a moment of despair when the legs seemed to have passed on, but then she saw the face of an older man looking at her, asking what happened. She told him quickly, asking to have the police come and open the basement door. He promised to do so and left.

It took the better part of two hours until there was knocking on the door, and the word "Police" heard, muffled by the heavy door. Joanna shouted, asking to be let out. She heard some noise at the keyhole, after which the door opened showing two policemen standing, looking at her curiously. It was mid-afternoon by then.

"Who are you, what happened here?" the older of the two asked. "How long have you been in this place?"

Joanna told them what had taken place and started to describe the two men, when the officer interrupted, saying that they would take her to the station where she could make her report.

During the short ride to the police station, Joanna felt as if she had just woken up from a terrible dream, her hunger notwithstanding. The sergeant at the desk eyed her suspiciously as she came in escorted by the two officers. One of them made a short report, at which the sergeant gruffly directed her to the third door down the hall where a detective would interview her.

"Could I have at least a cup of coffee, please?" Joanna pleaded. "I have not had anything since early morning."

Ask the detective, maybe he can get you something," was the only answer.

The detective, a fairly young man, rose up from behind his desk as Joanna entered and motioned her to sit in the chair opposite him. He looked at her, a curious expression on his face, and said, "Please, tell me what happened. I see that your hair was shorn, I gather involuntarily. Do start at the beginning please." Joanna related her harrowing experience, including the disgusting expressions used by the two men.

"The kidnapping was well planned," she said. The men had had access to the basement in which she was held and ready scissors for her hair. Upon questioning, she described the two men, including the fact that the tall one was apparently named Jose. She also asked for at least a cup of coffee, as she had had nothing to eat since morning. The detective wrote everything down before he went out for the coffee. With it, he brought also a stale hard roll. Joanna devoured it rapidly and made a motion to get up and leave when the detective requested a few more moments of her time, saying, "We shall try and apprehend these two criminals but it may take time. We have no idea if they were locals. They might have come from out of town, in which case we will have to involve the National Police. How long do you expect to stay here?" "Just until tomorrow," replied Joanna. The detective looked disappointed. "It might be a good idea if you could delay your departure for a while. If we do catch two men who fit your description, we would want to have an identity parade so that you could identify your kidnappers. That is the usual procedure. You are the only person we could call upon. It is really very important."

"OK, I can postpone my departure for a few days, but I can't stay indefinitely. You can reach me at the hotel. But wait, something just occurred to me. You said that they may be out from out of town. I don't think that's likely, unless someone from here has brought them. You see, during my stay here I talked to a number of local folks, mostly concerning my wish to know something about my ancestors who might have come from here. These talks touched upon the possibility that my family is of *Converso* origin. Now most of us in the US are not prejudiced against Jews or other religions, but that does not seem to be the case here. I don't wish to accuse anybody, but there is, for example, this Mrs. Lopez here who seemed rather upset at my liberal views. She may have talked to others about it, who knows? You might want to look into this. I hope you find those bastards soon."

Joanna asked for a taxi to be ordered and went to the hotel and the privacy of her room. It was evening by then. She had hoped to sneak unobserved into the hotel, but just this time the proprietress of the Malvasia was at the reception desk as she entered. She took a look at her, exclaimed loudly, "What happened to you? Your hair!"

"You have some hoodlums here in town, I am afraid. Frankly, I thought this was a nice peaceful little place. It seems I was wrong. Can you recommend a decent beauty parlor? And, yes, could you fix me a sandwich and a cup of tea? I don't wish to go out looking like this."

"I'll be glad to do it. As for a beauty parlor, there are a couple right near the central plaza. Look for the one on the street nearest to the Rosales bakery. You cannot miss it."

As tired as she was, sleep did not come for a long time. The awful occurrence of the day kept returning and with it an awareness of the deeply ingrained hatred against Jews of at least part of the population. She knew that prejudice was common everywhere, but that she would be a victim of it here in the town from where her ancestors apparently came – that was absolutely shocking.

After rising early the following morning, still tired from lack of sleep, Joanna waited impatiently until the opening hour of the beauty parlor. She went straight there, skipping breakfast, as she wanted to minimize her exposure. Entering the store, she was welcomed by the two girls working there. They looked at here for a few moments with both bursting out in unison: "Why, you must be the lady that was attacked and held prisoner for a day! Right here, not that far from our shop! It was on the front page of our newspaper."

"Do you have it here?" Joanna asked, and when she saw her nodding she added, "Please let me see it."

One of them ran to the back of the store and brought the paper. Joanna read it and reread it, and said, giving it back to the girl, "Well, I guess it is good that people here will know what kind of prejudiced thugs they have here. It sure does not add to the good name of your town."

"What do you mean by prejudiced?" the younger girl asked in surprise. "Wild young guys like that are everywhere. Looking for kicks I guess. Maybe they were on drugs, who knows? They overdid it in your case for sure, but such things happen in your country too. You're American, aren't you?"

"What are you talking about? These men thought I was a *Converso* who wanted to spread the Jewish religion here. That's what they said. That's why they cut my hair and imprisoned me in that basement. And even if I was, what is wrong with it? Our Christian faith was born in what is now Israel. Jesus was a Jewish preacher. The fact that the two religions developed in different directions do not make theirs any less legitimate. Sure we have hoodlums in America, and prejudice, but we must fight it, not excuse it."

The older of the two, wishing to stop the argument, pulled at Joanna's hand, urging her to sit in one of the old-fashioned barber chairs, "Don' t worry, my dear. You will look gorgeous, just wait. There are some very fashionable short haircuts. I know just the one that will suit you."

They went to work. The younger girl washed her hair, the older did the cutting and setting. Joanna looked at the mirror hardly recognizing herself, but admitting that they did as nice a job as was possible. She gave each a generous tip and left for the nearest coffee shop for some late breakfast. Still being very self-conscious, she stayed reading in her room for most of the day.

Later that evening, her telephone rang. It was Mr. Gonzales. "How are you my dear? I was shocked to read just now in the paper what happened. Do come over whenever you feel like to unburden yourself. How long do you expect to stay here?"

"It is so good to hear your voice, dear Mr. Gonzales, thank you for calling. At least I know there's somebody I can talk openly with. I haven't decided how long to stay. The police asked me to be here for the identity parade if they catch these two horrible men. Obviously, I can't remain indefinitely. Will it be OK if I come tomorrow in the morning around ten?"

"That will be fine. And please, do not bring anything. Just come."

Joanna waited until after nine thirty in the morning before going to Mr. Gonzales, again skipping breakfast since she did not want to be recognized and questioned in the nearby café. Arriving at Mr. Gonzales' home she knocked softly, fearing he might still be asleep but then heard him come shuffling to the door. He was in his usual old worn-out clothes, his face seemingly more wrinkled than before, possibly due to the early hour. She could see the great pleasure in his eyes when he saw his visitor. Joanna hugged him, with tears in her eyes.

"Do come and sit down while I prepare coffee and a few rolls so that we can have a bite before talking. I would like to hear details of what happened to you."

Joanna could hear him doing things in the kitchen, so she got up and went to help. Mr. Gonzales had put rolls and croissants on a tray, together with milk, sugar and butter, and was just pouring coffee into two mugs. Joanna took the tray while Mr. Gonzales came with the mugs. Both sat down at the coffee table with Mr. Gonzales looking at Joanna, "You are looking as beautiful as ever, my dear. The short haircut suits you well. I assumed that you have not had breakfast yet, not wishing to meet people. Is that not so?"

"You are right, Mr. Gonzales. I was accosted yesterday several times by people who made a big fuss over me, some in a rather friendly way while in others I sensed a somewhat hostile manner. I guess I can't remain in my hotel room all the time and will have to continue to face this kind of encounter."

"You should not worry about people here. On the contrary; face them proudly as you stand for the correct liberal way against this ancient prejudice; no matter how horrible some people might be. I know them well; I told you that I am ostracized by many here but I will not give in to them. It will not hurt them to hear from you what you think about those that did this awful thing to you. But come, eat something."

Feeling a bit more relaxed after having a croissant and coffee, Joanna told Mr. Gonzales the entire story, starting with the encounter with the two men until her release and the talk with the detective.

"I don't know what to do now. I can't stay here indefinitely until such time as the two will be apprehended. On the other hand, I want to see them in custody and want to help convict them by identifying them. What do you think?"

"It all depends on your schedule. I understood that you are a High School teacher. When do you have to be back?"

"Since I taught during summer school I was able to take a leave of absence for a month and a half. I don't have to be back in school until October 12. A substitute is covering for me. I have about two weeks left. Speaking of my school, I just want to show you how we relate to the different faiths we have in the US. Our school has a majority of African-Americans and Hispanics with only about twenty percent whites. Most of them are Christians. Yet the school is closed on the two major Jewish holidays that usually fall in September. I bet this kind of thing does not happen here."

"No, indeed not. But then we have only a very small Jewish population here. I guess you are correct in implying that we are still a prejudiced country. If it were not so, I believe many *Conversos* would come out and declare their old faith in the open. You see, I am one of those. I was fearful to do so in my younger days and now I am too weary to do what I believe I should have done."

"I can understand that. You see, right now I'm quite certain that my family has *Converso* roots, yet I am afraid of talking about it with my parents. I'm sure that they will refuse to even listen to what I have to say about their own history. I can't really blame them; they were most certainly brought up in an environment of prejudice. Nothing will make them understand that there are better, more humane, ways. I'm very grateful to you for letting me unburden myself. It helps to have someone that I can talk freely with."

"Dear Joanna, it gives me a great deal of pleasure to have you, a young woman, come and share things with me. You have no idea how much this means to this lonely old man. Now, as far as your stay here is concerned, I still know some people in the police department and will try to ascertain if any progress is being made. I will call you if I have any word as to when they think it will be possible to have this identification parade. In the meantime, take care and do not worry about people here and their gossip. Just try and ignore it."

Joanna felt much encouraged on the way back to the hotel and walked leisurely not caring if people turned their heads to ogle at her as they passed. When she returned to the hotel the proprietress told her that she had received a phone call about one hour previous. *Who could possibly call me?* she wondered, and asked if there was any message. The proprietress turned, took a piece of paper that was in her key box and gave it to her. She looked at it, slowly deciphering the scribbled handwriting, seeing the following: Someone by name of Michael called from Cordoba, said that he will call again at nine in the evening. *My god, Michael of all people. I did not even know that they were still here. I bet he must have seen something in the paper, I suppose even the local English paper would have something about my case in it. Well, I will be in my room anyway.*

Joanna made sure to be back from her dinner before nine o'clock. She was getting very impatient as no call came and had almost given up when, after nine thirty, the phone finally rang.

"Hi, Joanna, it's me, Michael. It's good to hear your voice. I'm sorry to call you so late. I had a problem here with the hotel switchboard. We read in the paper about an American tourist being abducted in Aguilar and immediately thought about you. Was it really you?"

"Oh Michael, I'm so glad to hear your voice. Yes, it was me alright. It was a pretty bad experience. Cutting my hair was the least of it. At one point I didn't know if I would ever get out from that basement. It was pretty horrible. But I am OK now. I even got a nice-looking haircut! I wonder what you will think of it. But tell me what your plans are. I gathered that you are in Cordoba, which is very close to Aguilar. It's only about a thirty-minute drive."

"We arrived here only yesterday afternoon, after a stay in Seville. Our plan is to be here for two more days and then leave for Madrid and home. I think we should be able to come to see you for a little while. Just hold on a second while I talk with Caroline about it."

Joanna could hear them talking without being able to make out details of the conversation. Michael came on after a short while.

"OK Joanna, we thought we would come see you tomorrow late in the afternoon, say about six, if that's convenient. It will give us a chance to see things here during most of the day, as we don't have that much time left. We can have dinner together if that suits you."

"Any time will be fine with me. I don't have anything to do since I'm waiting for the police to catch suspects so that I can identify them. I would have already left otherwise. I don't feel very comfortable here anymore. I will wait for you at the hotel; the Malvasia, which is the only one in town, it is right on the A-45. See you then."

CHAPTER 22

Caroline and Michael spent the morning visiting the archeological museum that had, amongst others, Andalusian sculpture and decorative arts from the eight to the fifteenth centuries. Caroline was very interested and spent an inordinate amount of time looking at the exhibits. Michael was getting impatient, saying that the Moors had actually no real influence on later western art. The sculpture, he pointed out, was never meant to be stand alone but served primarily as architectural ornaments. Their religion did not permit representation of the human face or figure so that they developed only calligraphy, jewelry, and textiles. Caroline pointed out the magnificent architecture they had seen during their visit, mentioning especially the Alhambra and the Mosque right there in Cordoba. As it became time for lunch, their arguments were cut short when they found a place to eat. The afternoon was spent walking leisurely around, admiring old Moorish mansions until it was time to return to the hotel, relax a while, and drive to Aguilar de la Frontera.

They found the hotel easily enough. "It looks like a pretty shabby place," Michael said when they entered the lobby. As nobody was at the reception counter they rang the old fashioned bell, waiting for a while until the old lady appeared, asking for their wishes. Upon hearing that they came to see Joanna, she went upstairs to her room to announce the visitors. Joanna came running down breathlessly, her face shining from the pleasure of seeing them, kissing Michael and Caroline. "My, I am so glad to see you, finally familiar faces," she exclaimed. "Please, do come up to my room where we can have some privacy, only I can't offer you any refreshments. We'll have to wait for that until we go out in a little while to eat. There is one place here, not a bad one, that opens early for dinner. That's ok, I hope?"

They went up the one floor. Looking around the room upon entering, Caroline admired the view, while Michael asked why she had to stay in this dilapidated place as there must be better and more modern hotels around.

"Yes, Michael, there are better places, but all are several miles from here. This is the only one in town and I wanted to be here to get a feel for the place and try to meet people. I did, some actually very nice with others not so. I also looked up the old records in the church and the town hall. How have you been? Are you pleased with your trip here and was it interesting?"

"Yes, very much so." It was Caroline who answered. "I really had no idea of the rich and varied cultural history of Spain. I found it fascinating. Being in France before coming here was also an eye opener. Not so much Paris, about which we have read and seen in movies and on TV, but the old small towns, the cathedrals, the prehistoric caves, and so much more. I really envy you having studied history and now teaching it. I work as a systems analyst; I do come into contact with people but I have no understanding of different cultures, of historical processes, what it is that leads to changes, to outbreak of war or to positive developments."

"What exactly do you do? I have heard about systems analysts but it is so foreign to me."

"We have to do all kinds of things. In short, we research problems, plan solutions and coordinate development to meet the particular business need. As such, we interact with customers, with designers, with programmers, and finally deploy the complete system."

"That sure sounds complicated. What did you have to study for such a profession?"

"Computer Science and I also did an MBA."

"You girls seem to want me to starve," Michael interjected. "Why don't we go out for dinner? We can talk there, too. We'd like to hear from you details of the whole episode. Let's go."

Much to Michael's surprise, the dinner was quite good, even though the place was somewhat shabby and the service mediocre. Apparently not many foreign tourists came to dine there, so that the chef, who turned out to be the owner, came out to make sure that they were satisfied and brought three small glasses of licor Cuaventa y tres. Joanna said that for her alone he had never done that. The liquor, she added, was the best after dinner drink available in Spain. She told them in great detail the story of the kidnapping and that she was now waiting for a possible police lineup. "Here they call it an identity parade," she said.

"You know," said Michael. "I never asked you how come you have been able to travel at this time of the year. I thought you taught in high school; the term must have started a while ago, right after Labor Day. When do you have to be back in Bridgeport?"

"I was able to get a leave of absence as I taught during the summer and now must be back by October 12."

"That means that you can't stay here very much longer. Who will be able to identify any possible suspects? Do the police have any evidence such as finger prints and what not?"

"I really don't know, they weren't very forthcoming when I asked them about that. There is a very nice old man here, with whom I have become very friendly, who promised to look after this matter after I leave and will be in touch with me. By the way, he's the only one of all the people I have met and talked with, and there were quite a few, who admitted that he is of a family of *Conversos*. Others seemed to hint of such ancestry. One knowledgeable doctoral student told me that, according to present estimates, about twenty percent of all Spaniards are descendants of Jews. There were also others, biased ones who I talked with. One in particular stands out. I suspect she may have been the one behind this attack on me but, of course, I have no proof. That reminds me; I just mentioned the one who said that he is a descendent of *Conversos*. Well, he gave me something so precious that I am still awed by it. Here let me show you." At that she reached down into her handbag and extracted the ancient coin and placed it on the table.

"It seems to be an old coin. Let me take a close look," said Michael and picked it up. "Wow, those are Hebrew letters. I don't believe it. This must be a coin dating back to the Jewish kingdom. It's like one w... *I* saw in the Metropolitan Museum. This is a real treasure! And he gave it to you, why?" he said, handing it back to Joanna.

"He said that he has no offspring or close relatives to leave it to and thought that I would know what to do with it. I think that he is quite sure that I also am descendent from *Conversos*, although he never said it outright."

Caroline looked at it too and handed it back to Joanna. They sat for a while longer in the restaurant until Caroline exclaimed how late it had become and that they must start on their way back to Cordoba. They parted, promising to get together back in Connecticut.

During the next couple of days, Joanna was extremely bored waiting to hear from the police department. She went for long walks, always, however, during daylight and on busy thoroughfares. She also went to the public library to read books on the history of Spain, concentrating on the years after the conquest of Andalusia by the Christians. It was on the third day after Michael and Caroline's visit that she received a call from the police department asking her to come to an identity parade that was to be held the following day at eleven.

Joanna appeared promptly at the noted time but had to cool her heels for the better part of half an hour until she was asked to enter a large room and sit on one of the chairs lined up towards the back of the room. The detective to whom she had reported her story, as well as another officer, was sitting there. Not much time passed and a side door opened with six men, all dressed in a similar fashion having baseball caps on their heads, coming out led by a young policewoman. The men lined up before the white wall opposite where Joanna was sitting. Two of them were rather tall with the others of various heights. The detective turned to Joanna and told her that she may question any one of the men, but that he will tell the man to answer provided he approved the question. Joanna turned to one of the tall men and asked for his name. Having seen the nod of approval by the detective, the man replied that it was Jose. The second tall man to whom Joanna turned replied that it was his name too. She then looked at their eyes, seeing that one of them had blue eyes with the other brown. Turning to the detective she said that that one could be dismissed. He was escorted out by the policewoman, who returned after a short time. Joanna then asked the remaining tall one to remove his cap. He did so showing his black hair cut short. Joanna asked permission to get close to him, which was given. She got up and saw that although he was close shaved it appeared that his facial hair seemed blond. It also seemed to her that the roots of his hair, where it had been parted, showed a trace of light hair. Next, Joanna turned to the remaining four and asked them to show their hands. They all stretched them out, with one having notably stubby fingers without, however, the long nails she had noticed on one of the kidnappers. He did have the brown eyes she remembered but so did all four. For a moment she was at a loss of what next to ask, but then remembered vaguely their voices, and asked each one in turn to say the following sentence which had been impressed in her mind: 'Maybe that will teach you not to spread your filthy religion.' They all said it, which made her sure that the tall man was one of them. She thought for a moment and asked for permission for the four shorter ones to say something else, even though she did not remember exactly what it was the other man had said. It was granted and she asked each of four to say: 'You are too dumb to learn anything.' One after the other they all said it, which strengthened her opinion that the man with the stubby fingers was the second one. She turned to the detective and said that she was now sure who the culprits were. He asked her to point them out, which she did. Thereupon the detective told the officer to remove the two to a holding cell while the rest could be dismissed. He then asked Joanna to accompany him to his office.

"Well, I think we may have something here," the detective said after they were seated. "Now comes the hard and extended part, I am afraid. I can tell you that we had our eyes on these two. They are known to be unsavory characters. The tall one has had a minor conviction while the other one was remanded for assault but had to be let go as the judge did not find the evidence to be sufficient.

They now will be remanded for up to seventy-two hours, which is the maximum allowed by law, during which they will be brought before a judge who will decide on bail or held for trial. I trust that bail will not be allowed, as the charge of kidnapping is severe. They will be held in the Cordoba jail with the trial also conducted there. I must tell you that our judicial procedures are very slow so that I cannot say when the case will come to trial, it can take quite a while."

"I certainly won't be able to stick around here, as you know. Who will inform me as to what is happening while I'm in the US?"

"I suggest that you hire a local lawyer who will look after your interests. I know that is costly. If you cannot afford a lawyer, at least get a person here who you can rely on to do that."

"Well, thank you. I'll let you know before I leave to whom to provide the information."

Joanna shook hands with the detective and left. That evening she called Mr. Gonzales and told him all that transpired at the police station, including her talk with the detective. She asked him if he knew a lawyer whose fees would be minimal and who could represent her after she returned to the US. He said that he would think about it and call her back the following day.

It was getting close to evening the next day and Joanna thought that Mr. Gonzales, being such an old man, may have forgotten. She nevertheless waited patiently until the hotel proprietress called her to the phone. It was Mr.

Gonzales, who said that he had an old acquaintance in town, a retired lawyer, with whom he spoke. "The man's name is Antonio da Pina and he lives on Calle Lorca 5, not far from the Plaza San Jose. You will have no trouble finding it. He is very nice and will be glad to have something to do. He said that he expects you to come tomorrow about five, unless you call him to tell him you prefer another time, or have changed your mind."

"Thank you so much, Mr. Gonzales. You've been so helpful and supportive all along; I don't know how to thank you. I will be in touch and let you know if I have come to any agreement with Mr. da Pina."

Promptly at five o'clock, Joanna knocked on the door of Mr. da Pina's apartment. It was in one of the more modern apartment blocks in town, apparently well kept but without the charming courtyards of the old houses. Mr. da Pina was a man about seventy, well dressed with a coat and tie, with his gleaming white hair brushed back and falling to near his shoulders and a small white moustache adorning his ruddy face. Smilingly, he extended his hand to Joanna in greeting, inviting her to come to his book-lined study.

"Gonzales, my good friend, told me that you might need some legal assistance. I understood that you are here for only a short time and will need a contact to look after the trial of the two who attacked you. It was shocking, indeed, to read about it. Such a thing has not happened here for many years. I read in the paper that the two young men have been apprehended and will now appear before a judge to set bail or have them held for trial. Can you tell me a little more about the case?"

"First I want to thank you, Mr. da Pina, for receiving me. Let me describe, in as few words as possible, what happened, the identity parade, and subsequent talk with the detective, if I may."

"Please, go ahead. I am retired as you may have heard, and have plenty of time. I like to keep my hands in legal matters, something I have done both as defense counsel and as prosecutor for the State for many years."

It took a good twenty minutes for Joanna to tell her story, at the end of which Mr. da Pina nodded sagely and said that he would be interested following the case and would be in touch with her by fax. He wished, he said, that he were computer knowledgeable but that at his age he no longer felt capable of it.

"And what, if I may ask, are you doing besides looking for your roots in this town, as old Gonzales has told me? This, if I may say, is a very admirable thing to do. We have not seen American tourists doing that."

"I teach history in high school at home in Bridgeport, having graduated from college seven years ago. I have started on my master's degree, part-time, and should finish next year. I am divorced with no children. I would like, of course, to know what costs I would incur, should you agree to follow my case and, if needed, try to see that it is concluded with the jailing of the two for as long as possible."

"That, my dear Joanna, is difficult to say at this point. As long as there is no trial there will be little for me to do except to keep you up-to-date as to the expected time. I realize that you cannot afford substantial fees and I will try and hold expenses to the absolute minimum. For the time being, there should be hardly a financial burden, as all I will do is correspond with you from time to time. Once the trial begins, I will have to interact with the prosecutor and be your representative. For that I will need a power of attorney from you, the content of which I will prepare. A retainer of, say, two-hundred-and-fifty Euros should be sufficient for the start. Whenever the trial will begin, I will advise you as to any additional costs and you can agree or not, as you wish. How does that sound? And yes, are you as good at reading and writing in our language as you speak?"

"As to the latter question, I am afraid the answer is no. Still, I can read fairly well and my writing should at least be understandable. I hope you will excuse my mistakes. I certainly appreciate your willingness to take on this assignment. I can leave here knowing that I'll be apprised of the situation here. Frankly, I really shouldn't have taken this matter so personally. There are prejudiced people everywhere, people who will stoop to violence and crime. Still, I can't let go; this has affected me deeply, bringing home the depth to which prejudice can sink and the effect it has on both the perpetrators and the innocent peaceful majority."

With that, Joanna thanked Mr. da Pina again and gave him the 250 Euros from her purse. She also told him that she expects to leave in two days, and gave him her address and phone number in the US.

The following morning, Joanna called Mr. Gonzales, told him about her meeting with Mr. da Pina, and thanked him for the introduction. She told him that she was leaving the following day and said again how grateful she was for his constant support and understanding. At his request, she gave him her home address and phone number. She then called Mrs. Benavides telling her that she was leaving for home shortly and that she wanted to thank her for her hospitality and kindness. Mrs. Benavides asked if she had the time to come for dinner that evening. She told Joanna she had meant to be in touch with her all the time since the article about her abduction had appeared in the local paper. She had not done so, however, because of her husband's sudden passing a couple days after her visit. Joanna expressed her condolences and accepted gratefully.

Joanna, carrying a bunch of flowers, arrived at the agreed time and was embraced by Mrs. Benavides, who was dressed in black, her face haggard, and her wrinkles deeper than before.

"I am so glad you called before leaving town, my dear. I thought about you a great deal after reading the awful thing that was done to you. I am very anxious to hear all about it after we have a bite to eat. Do come and sit down at the table and I will bring out the food."

Mrs. Benavides had prepared seafood paella, which, together with the wine, made a very satisfying dinner. After they had finished, Joanna recited the whole kidnapping episode as well as the fact that two suspects had been apprehended.

"That must have been very traumatic. I see that your hair is now quite short, but still very becoming. What will happen now that you are leaving? I wish you could stay longer, as I have become rather fond of you and would love for us to spend time together. Once you are gone I will never see you again unless you will return quite soon. I expect to follow my dear husband before long."

"Now, now, Mrs. Benavides, I am sure that you still have a good number of years before you and, who knows, I may be back. I have come to know and like the country. What happened to me here is not going to affect any future plans. I do hope, of course, that gradually there will be less prejudice against those that have different opinions and religious preferences. I am going back with the thought that my family may very well have had *Converso* roots, as my research here has shown. This, certainly, does not trouble me. On the contrary, it makes me more open to the belief of others."

"What you just said, my dear, makes me admire you all the more. I do not know if you may have guessed, but I will tell you now that our family is definitely of *Converso* ancestry. As long as my husband was alive I did not say so since he preferred to let sleeping dogs lie and not draw attention to us. He was a town employee and was afraid that Jewish ancestry might have an adverse effect on his position. Now I do not care anymore, I'm not afraid that someone will do me harm. I have lived here for such a long time and a lot of people know me. You, being an American tourist, an outsider, became a convenient target for these horrible men. I hope they will be soon brought to trial and given a good long jail sentence."

"I say amen to that, Mrs. Benavides. I appreciate it what you said about your *Converso* ancestry. I hope more and more people will feel they can express it openly. There have been a few signs of this happening in some Portuguese towns as well as in Majorca. So there is hope. I'm very grateful to you for having me in your house and the long talks we have shared. I learned a great deal from going to the church you recommended and seeing their records. Your late husband was also very helpful inasmuch as I was able to see the records in Town Hall. There, too, I found valuable information. Thank you so much for everything."

Joanna was about to leave when Mrs. Benavides retained her, telling her that she had just remembered something she had wanted to tell Joanna a while ago but had forgotten.

"My memory fails me very often these days. Some time ago I read that at the beginning of the nineteenth century there lived in England a woman by name of Grace Aguilar who was a famous author. It is said that she was a descendant of *Conversos* from Portugal who arrived in England sometime during the eighteenth century. She was apparently attached to her Jewish roots, her books reflected that. Is that not interesting? I had to tell it to you that since you are wondering about your own roots. Not that it proves that all Aguilars are *Conversos*, but I think that you might want to consider it. Well, go now my dear, I hope that you will find what you are looking for and much happiness in your life."

Joanna embraced Mrs. Benavides and left.

Michael and Caroline were rather pensive on the way back to their hotel in Cordoba. Each immersed in his own thoughts until Caroline broke the silence.

"I'm beginning to feel uneasy. If such things occur here, it could have happened to us. So far I've enjoyed our trip immensely and believe that we could not have planned it better, but now this. I'm glad that we'll be leaving the day after tomorrow, drive up to Madrid and fly home."

"Sure, this was very upsetting, but it could have happened at home too. We have, unfortunately, plenty of crime, including kidnapping. I think we're especially affected since we know the victim and identify with her. Don't take it to heart, darling. We'll still walk around tomorrow, see things, and enjoy the place. I'm so glad that you've enjoyed our vacation, as I have."

"Michael, are we going to see Joanna after we go home? She seems to be a nice person, but... will it be wise to do so?"

"If you're worried that she'll come between us, forget it. We love each other and have a wonderful marriage. I hope you have stopped taking your pills and we should just look forward to having a family. That was our understanding, wasn't it? Frankly, I am curious to know if she really is of *Converso* ancestry, but we'll be in touch with her only if you are perfectly comfortable about it."

As much as it was anticipated, Michael and Caroline's return home turned out to be somewhat of a letdown. It was natural, of course, after such a marvelous vacation with many new experiences, free from the daily problems at work or home. It took a few days to adjust, visiting family and friends, the first ones being David and Helen. At dinner at their house they described the marvels they had seen, the varied experiences they had. Caroline also mentioned their encounter with Joanna in Madrid, and described in some detail what had happened to her in Aguilar. "What an awful experience for her. She seemed like a very nice person."

"Did you ever meet her, Helen?" Caroline asked it with a slight edge to her voice.

"Oh no, never." There was a slight pause while Helen thought how to correct the faux pas she had made. "I know Michael went out with her once or twice, and we know Michael well, he is such a choosy person who would never go out on a blind date. Only with a girl he had seen or was recommended by a friend." Caroline seemed somewhat relieved, with Michael shooting an appreciative glance to Helen.

On their way home, Caroline asked Michael if he thought of getting in touch with Joanna and if he know her phone number.

"We talked about that, didn't we? I said that I wouldn't be in a hurry to call her. Anyway, I have no idea where she lives. Look Caroline, I knew her, like I said, some six years ago. She got married in the meantime and I don't know her married name. So how can we find her? Let's see if she'll get in touch with us. She knows my last name so that she shouldn't have any trouble finding us. And please, stop insinuating, or thinking, that I have any special feelings for her, OK?"

CHAPTER 23

Reyna and Eleanora were waiting in the international arrivals building at Kennedy for Joanna to come out. As it was, the Iberia plane was almost half an hour late in arriving, with Eleanora impatiently asking her mother what might be causing the delay. Joanna finally arrived, pulling her heavy suitcase, embracing first her mother and then her sister.

"It's been a marvelous trip," Joanna said breathlessly, "I've seen and learned so much, meeting interesting people. I'm so glad I went; it had been on my mind for so long. But it's good to be home. How are you? How is Papa? Still working so hard?"

"We are so glad you are back, darling. We all missed you. Vanessa also wanted to come but could not take off from work. Papa and she are going to be home by the time we get there. But look at you! What happened to your hair? It is so short; I have never seen you like that. Will you be staying with us for a few days now?"

"I think I better stay only tonight and then go to my place. You know that I have to start teaching in a couple of days and still have to go over some things. As to my hair, well that is a long story which I'll tell all of you when we are home."

"I rather like it that way," Eleanora broke in. "Do keep it short, it's very becoming and makes you look younger."

"If you say so, maybe I will. I have gotten used to it by now. But come, let's go and find the car. I hope you remember where you parked it. Kennedy is such an awful airport. I once looked for my car for 45 whole minutes."

The car was found easily enough and the ride home to Bridgeport was relatively quick with hardly any traffic problems as it waslate in the evening. Manuel and Vanessa jumped towards the door as Reyna and Joanna just opened it, both wanting to embrace the returning traveler. Manuel was given the honor and he held his daughter tightly until he looked closely and exclaimed, "What happened to your hair, you should never have had it cut so short. You look like a boy; I do not like it."

"She said she'll tell us all about it, Papa," Eleanor said. "Why don't we all sit in the living room, have a drink and some of Mama's cookies. Joanna can then tell us all about her trip. Tomorrow is Saturday and we can sleep a little later."

After Vanessa had her hug they all sat down, raised a glass to honor Joanna's return, and listened to her story.

"Actually there is so much to tell that I think it will be quite late before I finish. But first of all, I must say how marvelous a trip it was, a journey into what seems a natural part of me. I was in Madrid, Toledo, Granada, Cordoba, and, most important of all, in Aguilar de la

Frontera. Let me start there since I think I found the names of my great grandparents there. I've never asked you if you remember them, did you, Dad?"

"I remember my grandfather's, it was Juan. My grandmother passed away when I was still quite small and therefore I do not remember hers." He turned to Reyna and asked if she knew. "How could I? When I married you both were long gone. I am sure you girls remember my telling you about my grandparents, Isabel and Miguel Iglesias. Did you also look for them, Joanna?"

"No, why should I? I remember you telling us their names and stories about them. Yours, Dad, I found in church and town hall records in Aguilar. They were Juan Aguilas Mendez, born on June 4, 1891, and Maria Aguilas de Calderon, born on February 20, 1900. How do you like that? Now we know for sure the place in Spain where our ancestors lived."

"But why did you say Aguilas? That is not our name," asked Manuel.

"These are the names I found. One old gentleman, whom I got to know in town, told me that he heard some things about Maria who married Juan Aguilas. He was a baker. The old man said that most likely my great grandparents changed their names slightly to remember their hometown. I think that the dates of their birth seem right."

"What were the things he told you about them?" Reyna asked Did he say anything about why they left the old country?" Joanna hesitated before answering.

"He didn't know very much. He was a seven- or eight-year-old boy when he heard his mother talking about them. He said that Juan was known as a very taciturn and short-tempered man. I talked to someone else who also had heard of a Maria Calderon. She said that Maria was married when they suddenly left town. It was soon after the end of World War I. She said that they didn't get along well with people in town and may have left because of that. That, too, fits since you told us that they arrived here in 1919."

Reyna agreed that the names Joanna found, with their birth dates, were most likely those of the great grandparents on her father's side and said that she was very impressed with Joanna's detective work. Manuel wanted to know if the woman had given a reason that they weren't accepted in that small community. Joanna again hesitated before saying "That was all the woman had said." Vanessa and Eleanora both cried out to know why Joanna had cut her hair so short.

"Well, that too is a long story. It appears that not only here, but in Spain, too, there is crime on the streets. One day I was walking along in broad daylight when all of a sudden two men came up from behind, held me and threatened to do me harm if I do not come quietly with them. They dragged me to a nearby empty basement where I was locked in without food or water. They cut my hair before they left, having come prepared with scissors. As the basement was not entirely underground, but had narrow high windows I was able to break the glass in one of them and shout for help until a passerby heard me, called the police who came and released me. The next day I went to a hairdresser and the result is not too bad. That is the story."

"That must have been pretty horrible," said Manuel, "but what did they want from you? There must have been a reason for holding you captive and cutting your hair."

Reyna nodded in agreement while Joanna tried to think what best to say.

"… It seems they did not like Americans with our liberal tradition. They seemed to be fascists, reactionaries, wanting Spain to be a totally Catholic country with no foreign ideas allowed. I have been in company with people prejudiced against Jews for example."

"So what has that got to do with you?" asked Manuel. "You are obviously not Jewish. Why this attack on you? What did the police do? Did they tell you about the possible motive of those criminals?"

"Yes, I forgot to tell you that two suspects were caught and I identified them in a police lineup. There they call it an identity parade. Now they are awaiting trial. I hired a local lawyer, who was recommended to me to follow up on the case and will let me know of any progress. As to the possible motives, the police said nothing except that the two were known to them as small-time hoodlums."

"Very strange indeed, I wasn't concerned at all about your safety in Spain, and now this. It's getting very late; you must be very tired from the long flight. So let's go to sleep." Reyna sounded very perturbed. Vanessa and

Eleanora voiced their disappointment at not hearing more and went reluctantly upstairs.

The following morning, Joanna came down rather late; the rest of the family had had their breakfast and were waiting to hear more of Joanna's exploits. Reyna served her breakfast and all waited for her to finish.

"Ok, so where do I begin? Like I said, I felt a deep affinity for the place and its people. I was in Toledo where history comes alive. I once saw El Greco's View of Toledo in the Metropolitan museum. Now, when I approached the city this painting came immediately to my mind. Changes have not been too great. Mind you, the painting was done at the very end of the 16th century. It is an experience to wander in the narrow streets, see ancient churches and synagogues, the El Greco museum, the Alcazar, the Cathedral. I was there just overnight, much too short."

"Did you say you saw synagogues in Toledo?" Manuel asked. "I did not know Jews lived there. When was that?"

"Jews made up a large portion of Toledo inhabitants, from the 12th century and up to the expulsion in 1492. Toledo is not far from Madrid, where I spent four days, so much to see there. Life still seems to be much more leisurely there than it is here. In the early evening, you will see lots of people walking on the main streets, often groups of girls and boys ogling each other as they pass. Most good restaurants will not serve dinner before 9 PM and you can see people dining as late as midnight. Those who can take a siesta from one to four and then return to work until seven. Imagine that when I was at the Plaza Mayor, the great old center of Madrid, I met there, of all people, my ex-boyfriend Michael and his wife Caroline! You remember him, don't you? She is very nice. They had a car and invited me to drive with them to Granada. We both had tickets for the Alhambra for the same day, but not the same hour as one has to get tickets in advance to view that marvelous place. It is said to be the most magnificent fortress ever built. It is beautiful. It dates back to the 14th century and was built by the Moslims who ruled there at the time."

"How about taking a break and having some coffee and danish?" Reyna said. "Dad and I have to go to the restaurant in a couple of hours, so we still have time to hear more."

Vanessa and Eleanora had sat all that time quietly absorbed in Joanna tale, but now Vanessa exclaimed that it was such a general overview that she received no feeling of the place. It was more of an advertisement to visit Spain, except for the abduction, which did not make her feel like going to such a country.

"I guess you are right, Vanessa. You really must visit Spain to get a real feeling for the country and its history. I'll try to tell about some of the people I met in Cordoba and Aguilar. As to what happened to me, I am sure it was a one in a million occurrence and there is no need to be afraid of it happening to you. Don't we have incidents like that here in our town?"

After a short pause for the refreshments that Reyna put on the coffee table, Joanna continued with her tale.

"From Granada I took the train to Cordoba, which also is rich in history. The most remarkable place there is the Cathedral that formerly was a mosque, and before, that at the end of the eighth century, a place of worship shared by Moslems and Christians. It's breathtaking, the forest of pillars, the red and white Moorish arches. When the Christians conquered Cordoba in the thirteenth century they made changes adding the grandeur and richness one finds in the great cathedrals. In Cordoba I met a young man, a doctoral history student, from whom I learned a great deal. He also took me to a couple of restaurants where I greatly enjoyed the food. I think that you, Dad and Mom, should visit Spain. I am sure you'll enjoy the sights and also might want to bring back some of the dishes to add to your restaurant menu. While in Cordoba, I also visited a very nice older woman who invited me for dinner. She told me about her family who were descendants of the Jewish converts who remained in Spain after the expulsion. She's a practicing Catholic, like most of Spaniards." Here, Joanna hesitated realizing that the mention of Jewish converts might not sit well with her father. Sure enough, his face took on a disturbed look and he exclaimed, "Why are you telling us all about expulsion and Jewish converts? What has that got to do with your trip? You wanted to explore the land that was the home of our ancestors and possibly learn something about your great grandparents. Why bring in all kinds of extraneous things?"

"…I am afraid, Dad, that this is part of the history of Spain and you can't escape it. I got to know quite a few people, also in Aguilar. All kinds, some prejudiced against Jews, others very nice, and some had stories similar to those of the woman I just talked about. Look, I teach history, I am not afraid to learn things that happened in the past. I think it's my job."

"Your father is not afraid, Joanna. He just thought that this matter of Jewish conversion is of no interest. We haven't had the opportunity to learn history like you, so some things are of little importance to us. You do seem to have had a wonderful trip and we like to hear about it. I am curious, though, why you, of all people, were subject to this attack, especially in what appears to be our ancient home town."

"I certainly can't be sure, but I have an idea who might have been behind it. The two culprits are probably just hired hoodlums. Maybe after the trial, my lawyer might be able to enlighten us."

"You speak in riddles, daughter. Why would anyone, or any organization, want to do you harm? How many American tourists come to this town? How big is it anyway? You should have been appreciated, spending good dollars there."

"I think I really should finish now. I will only add that Aguilar de la Frontera is a small town. It's a very old place like a lot of other places in Spain. It has its charm. I spent a great deal of time there, meeting people and going through the records in the main church and town hall. It certainly was worth the visit."

CHAPTER 24

I should have been more patient, especially with Dad, thought Joanna when she was back in her apartment ready to go to bed. *Why was he getting upset when I mentioned Conversos and Jews? How can I tell them what I found out and that I now believe that we have Jewish blood? I can't even show them that precious old coin. I'll have to tell them eventually about my findings, but will I be able to do so? Who can I get advice from? Maybe a psychiatrist or psychologist might be a good idea. I could call Michael and Caroline, but she might think that I want to start with her husband. I sure don't. I'll get in touch with Megan; I should have called her, anyway.*

Megan and Joanna met for lunch the following Saturday. Megan wanted to hear all about Joanna's trip. It took quite a while for Joanna to tell all she had seen and especially about the kidnapping and its aftermath. It was then that she came to her findings concerning the possibility that her family had Jewish ancestry. She also mentioned the ancient coin she received and the deep impression it made on her.

"I wanted to tell my family about it, but when I even as much as mentioned that Jewish converts to

Christianity lived in Spain, my father became angry and said that he's not interested in hearing about it. I did not even say that back in 1492 Jews were either expelled or had to convert if they wanted to stay. I was told that about twenty percent of today's Spaniards are of Jewish extraction."

"So what exactly is your problem? Just don't talk about it at home."

"Look, Megan, from all I have learned there, I am quite sure that my family also has Jewish roots. I want to delve deeper into Jewish history as it was in Spain and in general. From the little I know, I have great respect and admiration for their religion and have a high regard for their adherence to it during all the terrible persecutions they suffered throughout the ages."

"Come on, Joanna. You sound like you're considering converting, if I follow your thinking. That certainly will upset your parents a great deal. Would you want to do that? Tell me, you mentioned that you met Michael, your great love before you married Tim. Are you thinking by chance to revive that old affair? You said that he was married."

"You're nuts, Megan. I met Michael and Caroline just a few days before I left for home. By then I had learned everything I could in the towns I visited. I had more or less formulated my thoughts about Judaism, conversion, and my family well before I saw them, without coming to any conclusion, as you see."

"I really don't know what to advise. All I can say is be careful. You are stepping on mines, both as a far as your parents are concerned and Michael. I love you anyway."

Both had tears in their eyes as they kissed goodbye.

Not knowing where else to turn, Joanna decided to call Michael. It took nearly a week, though, before she got up the courage to do so. Caroline answered, sounding surprised to hear Joanna's voice.

"How've you been? When did you get back and were there any further developments with the kidnapping?"

"I came back just four or five days after I saw you in Aguilar. I think I saw you before I was at the police lineup, where I identified the two bastards. I hired a lawyer to follow the case for me and he faxed me just the other day that a judge had remanded them for trial. That may take place in quite a while, though. They are worse than us in that respect; he said it could take a year or two before there is a judgment. How about you? Did you visit any other places in Spain after Cordoba? I want to go back and see further areas, like Catalonia and the Basque region. But that will have to wait."

"No, we drove back to Madrid, stayed overnight and flew home the following day. It was a marvelous trip for us. Better than anything I imagined," said Caroline. "Don't you think so, Michael?"

"He agreed that it was. By the way, I have great news. I am pregnant. So tell me, what's with you? Have you started teaching?"

"That is wonderful. When are you due?"

"Oh, not for a while. I am just in my second month."

Joanna hesitated a while until she said, "I think I told you that I found some indication that my family has Jewish roots dating back to the time of the expulsion.

I'm now in a dilemma as to what to tell my parents. I didn't, for example, tell them of my being positive that the attack on me was a result of anti-Semitism, as people may have thought that I was encouraging Catholics to revert to their Jewish roots. As you may know, there has been lately a movement, in some communities in Portugal and Majorca, of small numbers of people to reconvert. I thought that you, being Jewish, might know of a Rabbi or a learned person to whom I could turn. I also need advice as what to do with that old coin I showed you."

"We would be glad to do that, Joanna. Michael might know someone suitable and we'll also make inquiries. Where do you live?"

"I am still in Bridgeport, but not at my parents', of course. I will certainly appreciate it; do call me whenever you know of someone. I assume you have my phone number now from caller ID. Many thanks."

She sure didn't want me to talk with Michael. He must have told her, after our meeting, in Madrid of our friendship. I can't blame her being suspicious. I just need some help now, who else could I turn to?

Teaching and studying filled Joanna's life to the fullest. She taught European history to the four parallel junior classes as well as Greek civilization to the sophomore classes. She also continued attending the University of Connecticut, where she had started the previous year on a Masters Degree program in medieval history with possible admission to a Ph.D program if she met all the requirements. She travelled to Storrs two afternoons a week, no small effort, as it required a drive of one-and-a-half hours each way. She had also applied to Columbia and NYU and was accepted to both. UConn, however, offered much greater financial aid than the other two, based on her undergraduate record, which made her choice easy. Her financial situation was actually satisfactory, though she had made a substantial compromise during her divorce proceedings concerning both alimony and division of wealth. At the time, all she wanted was to terminate the marriage.

More than two weeks passed since her telephone conversation with Caroline and no word from her or Michael. *I guess Michael thinks it's better not to start seeing me again. I can understand him. I should have been more mature and made it clear to my parents that I would decide what is best for me. Michael's relationship with Caroline seems OK, but I've lost what could have been a wonderful life. I guess I haven't changed much, though I'm a mature woman now. I'm still afraid to possibly offend my parents. Why didn't I tell them about the likelihood of our Jewish ancestry? Or why I think I was attacked in Aguilar? Will I never grow up?*

Nearly another week had gone by when, finally, Michael called. His voice sounded restrained as he asked her if she'd made as yet any contacts concerning her quest. Joanna answered that she knew no one and was waiting to hear from him.

"I can't say that I know anyone who is well versed in Spanish-Jewish history or someone who is an expert in numismatics and Jewish history. The closest I have come is my Dad's friend Robert Serman, the history professor from Harvard. We met when we visited my parents. Remember him? I am sure he will be glad to talk with you. If you want, I can call Dad and ask him to arrange an appointment for you. Then there is this Rabbi in the Spanish synagogue in New York. It is actually one of the oldest Jewish congregations in the US; it was founded in the seventeenth century by a number of Jews from Portugal and Spain. My friend David told me that he once visited the place and had a talk with the Rabbi who very much impressed him with his liberal outlook and apparent wide-ranging knowledge. I suppose you can call the synagogue and make an appointment."

"Gee, that sounds like a good beginning. Thanks a lot, Michael. How are things with you and Caroline? She told me that she's pregnant, that's exciting."

"We are good, Jo. But do tell me why are you so anxious to find out about you possibly being of Jewish origin? Supposing your notion is supported, then what? And that old Jewish coin, what's the big deal there? Any museum will be glad to have it, together with the story that the old guy told you. There is a Jewish museum in New York, and of course the great one in DC."

"Oh Michael, I don't know. Ever since we were at your parents, and maybe even before that when we had those long talks, I have felt a certain attraction to the Jewish religion. It has now, with the trip to Spain, come to the surface with a great deal of force. I wish I knew. Please let me have your Dad's friend phone number. After I will talk to him and the Rabbi in the New York synagogue, I will get in touch with you; maybe we can get together and discuss the whole thing."

"OK Jo. I look forward to hearing from you. Be well."

First thing the next day, Joanna called the Spanish synagogue and reached the Rabbi, one David Moreno, and told him why she wanted to meet with him. The Rabbi sounded very interested, and suggested that she come to see him the following Monday morning. He added that in the meantime he would also speak with two of the scholars in residence and try to make an appointment for her with one or both. She then called Robert Serman but was told by his secretary that he was away at a conference and would be back next week. She left a message, asking him to get in touch with her.

The meeting with Rabbi Moreno went very well. She had expected to see a long-bearded older man and was surprised that he was youngish, had no beard, had glasses, and with his small *kippa* on his head could have been taken for any Jewish teacher or lawyer. She told him about her experiences in Spain and her exposure to *Conversos* and their history in that country. She added that she was looking for personal religious direction and mentioned her present religious affiliation. Rabbi Moreno's interest became even more obvious and asked about her family's attitude to her discoveries. She described her father's biased attitude towards Jews and his objection to her erstwhile Jewish boyfriend. As her father was unwilling to even hear about *Conversos*, she did not mention to him her notion of believing that the family had Jewish ancestry.

"Do I detect that deep down you are thinking of the possibility of converting to our religion? Did your boyfriend try to influence you to go in this direction?"

"As to your first question, I admit that I had thought of converting for quite a while now, but am far from being ready to make a decision one way or another. I feel that I don't know enough to do that. No, my boyfriend did not influence me; not directly. Maybe visiting his family, seeing their lifestyle and customs, may have had something to do with it."

"You told me on the phone that you are a high school teacher of history. How much do you know of our history in general and what happened in Spain in particular? To our way of thinking, that experience can be thought of as a forerunner of the recent European Holocaust, even as it had less severe results for our people. We are, as you may know, not a proselytizing religion. In fact, we try to make it difficult for the prospective convert in order to test his or her sincerity. Generally, for example, we will not be ready to accept someone who only wishes to convert in order to please his or her spouse. What I suggest is that you talk with one of our scholars in residence, Rabbi Aaron Perez who is of Sephardic heritage and is very knowledgeable in Sephardic customs as well as is in spirituality and life. I've already talked to him about you.

He is the Rabbi and spiritual leader of a congregation in New Jersey,and shares with us his wide knowledge. I expect him to be here for several days at the end of the month. I'll let you know when he can see you. Does that sound OK?"

"Yes, thank you very much. As for my knowledge of Jewish history, it's rather superficial. I did pick up a great deal while recently in Spain concerning Jewish history there from the thirteenth to the sixteenth centuries. That, by the way, alerted me to the injustices done on the one hand and the fortitude Jews displayed in keeping their religion on the other. As I learned, many went to their deaths rather than forsake their fate while others accepted exile in order not to convert. Many of the converts actually kept their old religious practices a secret, even at the risk of being discovered and punished severely. I look forward to meeting Rabbi Perez and will wait for your call. Thank you again, Rabbi."

Joanna had arranged to visit Robert Serman in his office at Harvard University on a Wednesday, the day she taught only the first two morning classes. She took the train to Boston, which brought back memories of her and Michael going up to meet his parents. *What am I doing here going to meet this professor? What can he tell me that I don't already know? That I am stupid to have let a wonderful prospect for a life with Michael slip out of my fingers? How can he tell me what to do now with regard to my parents? I shouldn't have bothered him with my trivial quest.*

Robert Serman sat in his small, book-lined office as Joanna opened the door. He got up to meet her, a big smile on his face.

"It sure is a great pleasure to see you again, Joanna. It has been quite a while. We were very sorry to hear that you and Michael are no longer together. You seemed such a nice couple. You also mentioned that it was Michael who recommended that you come to see me. So you are still in touch, which is nice. Well, you told me a little about your quest on the phone, please enlarge upon it a little as I am very interested to hear more."

"First, thank you again, professor, for receiving me. I know your time is valuable."

"Come on now, girl, my name is Robert, as you know, and we in academia can make time as we see fit. There is no external pressure. Once you have tenure you can sit and do very little. For most of us, though, this would be very boring, so we research things that are of interest to us and publish the results to see our name in print. The latter, by the way, is also important to obtain promotions, as that is dependent on the number of good publications in your name. You are a history teacher, if I remember correctly, Isn't that so?"

"Yes I am. I have started going for my Masters at UConn and hope to continue for the PhD, if I am good enough." Joanna thought for a few moments how to continue and then said, "I don't know if you remember that my family is Seventh-Day Adventists and that we have some, what seem to be, Jewish customs. While in Spain, I spoke to quite a number of people, some of whom told me that they are of Jewish ancestry and their families apparently kept some of their ancient customs in spite of the danger of the Inquisition. I also met others, obviously prejudiced against Jews. I spent a while in the town, the name of which I carry, and found records in a church and in town hall of what appear to be my great grandparents. They might have been *Conversos*, since they were ostracized by the community and came to the US soon after World War I while still young. For some reason, all this strengthened my latent feelings of wanting to convert to Judaism. Strangely enough, this feeling was strengthened by the fact that I was attacked in that town by two hoodlums who incarcerated me in an abandoned basement. I believe that they were employed by some prejudiced people who thought that I wished to have local people of Jewish ancestry convert back to their roots. I'm still not sure what I would want to do. Anyway, my own father is very prejudiced, and would not even hear me talk about families of *Conversos* whom I met in Spain. That's my dilemma. I also wanted to show you this," Joanna pulled the ancient coin out of her purse and handed it to him. "This was given to me by a lonely old man who had no one to leave it to. It was considered an heirloom handed down from generation to generation. His *Converso* family received it from another who was afraid to keep it lest the Inquisition would find it. Who should I give it to?"

"Look, I'm certainly not going to give you advice. I can talk about Judaism and history, which might give you more things to consider. Converting to Judaism is not an easy thing as you may have heard. Not like converting to Christianity or Islam. To become a Jew one needs to study for a long period and show a sincere reason for doing so. You see, Judaism is actually a nationality first and a religion second. The Jewish nation was established by a covenant of people with God. In other religions, you belong because you believe, in Judaism, you believe because you belong. Once a Jew, you cannot renounce it. Take the case of Cardinal Jean-Marie Lustiger who was the Archbishop of Paris. He was a Jew who converted to Christianity at the age of thirteen. Still, he was always considered by us as a Jew. I suggest you study a little, maybe with a Rabbi, to understand the emphasis Judaism puts on morality, on the relation between man and man, and man to God. I imagine you know that there are various streams in Judaism, ranging from Ultra-Orthodox to Reform. You can also be completely secular, as many are especially in Israel. You see, one of the major commandments, or *mitzvoth*, is to live in the land of Israel. By satisfying that one, one has fulfilled a *mitzvah*. Unfortunately, most Rabbis would expect you to be much more observant before they agree to a conversion. I am afraid that I am not very helpful."

"Oh, but you are. You have clarified certain things for me. I know I'll have to work hard to really understand what it is I'm looking for. I know that one of the ten commandments Moses brought down from the mountain is to honor one's parents. How can I do that if it turns out that I might be doing something that is against their wishes?"

"My interpretation of honoring one's parents does not mean that you have to go against your values, provided they are morally justified and you're not doing something just out of spite, or getting back at them for something they did not to your liking. I think you certainly can explain to them your feelings and reasons for your opinions, and of course make sure they understand that you continue to honor, love, and support them."

"I understand what you're saying. I'll try and get into this more deeply. Now, can you comment on the coin? I don't know what to do with it."

"Here at least I'm on firmer ground. My teaching and research interest is the Roman Republic and later Empire. This covers a great deal of ground; say, from five hundred BC to three hundred AD. It is definitely a Jewish coin minted around 133 AD during the Bar-Kochba revolt against the Romans. The coin shows on this side the Temple façade while the other side says 'to the freedom of Jerusalem'."

"Wow that is interesting. It agrees with what the man who gave it to me said; he mentioned that to the best of his knowledge it was minted in the first century AD, but that is all he knew. Has not Roman history been researched over and over again? What is there left to find?"

"There are constantly new finds that one can discover. Even if there are no more big stories to tell, one can come up with a particular interesting item. True, it may not attract a wide readership, but suffice if it is good for the fewer devotees to the subject matter. You'll find it once you advance to your thesis topic. Let me get back to Bar-Kochba, who was based in the province of Judea. His was the last of three revolts against the Romans and as always it was based on religious reasons. There was, apparently, the fear that the Roman emperor Hadrian wanted to put a statue of Jupiter on the temple mount, to which the Jews objected. The revolt lasted from 132 to 136 AD. It had disastrous results for the Jews. They were no match for the six Roman legions. They suffered enormous casualties; cities and villages were destroyed. Hadrian expelled all Jews from Jerusalem as punishment and ordered that Judea be named Syria-Palaestina. That, by the way, is the reason why the area now occupied by Israel, the Palestinian authority, and Jordan was called Palestine in the Franco-British border agreement of 1920. As to what to do with the coin, you'll have to decide. I'm sure it would fetch a good price on the antique coin market, or you could donate it to a suitable museum, and there are many of them."

"I definitely will not sell it. Depending what I decide to do about my future religious affiliation, I may either keep it in my family, handing it down to future generations as it was apparently done, or, as you said, donate it to a museum. I certainly appreciate the time you devoted to me, I've learned from you a great deal. Thank you so much."

Both got up, shook hands cordially, a wide smile on Professor Serman's face when he said that he was glad to be of some help, and asked Joanna to give Michael his best regards.

CHAPTER 25

It took Joanna several days before she called Michael to tell him about her visit to the Spanish synagogue and her talk with Professor Serman. She could not decide whether to call him at home or at work. *Caroline might answer if I call him at home. She might be upset thinking that I want to start with him. On the other hand, calling Michael at work could give him that impression, which I don't. Or do I?* She finally called him at work.

"Hi Joanna, good to hear from you. Have you done anything with the suggestions I made concerning your dilemma?"

"I followed your advice, Michael, but am not much closer to knowing what to do. I went to that Temple in New York and had a very good talk with the Rabbi. He was a youngish guy who impressed me a great deal. My session with him was rather short, as he suggested that I speak with one of the Temple's scholar in residence, a Rabbi from New Jersey who will be there at the end of the month. I had a good long talk with Professor Serman, from whom I learned a great deal. He is a very nice man and received me as if I was a long-lost acquaintance. He asked me to give you his regards. So your suggestions were very good. How are things with you and Caroline? How is her pregnancy going?"

"We are fine and there are no problems with the pregnancy, just the usual morning sickness and things like that... Tell me, when are we going to see you? You're always welcome."

"I don't know how wise it is for me to visit you guys. How would Caroline feel about that? I know it was OK to be together in Spain, but that was a temporary kind of thing for a short time. Let me know, I would be very happy to come, or maybe go to a movie or play together. Speaking of Spain, I heard recently from my lawyer who said that the trial is still far off. The two criminals are out on bail and are forbidden to leave the province of Cordoba. Get in touch with me to let me know how and when we can see each other."

Several days after her talk with Michael, Joanna heard from Rabbi Moreno that she was invited to come and meet Rabbi Perez on the following Sunday at the Temple. Rabbi Perez, too, was a man in his forties; a small black beard surrounded his smiling face as he welcomed Joanna warmly.

"Rabbi Moreno told me a little about you. He was under the impression that you are searching for a more meaningful religious life. It appears, he said, having been exposed a little to Judaism and learning about our history in Spain, you would like to explore our religion and way of life more deeply. Am I right in thinking that you are considering the possibly of converting?"

"I have thought about it, especially lately after my trip to Spain, but certainly have a long way to go before I decide. Did Rabbi Moreno tell you about my family's present religious affiliation? That's what started me thinking; I learned some Jewish customs and saw their similarity to some of ours. I understand that there is a vast difference between the two religions."

"Well, yes and no. All major monotheistic religions believe in God. We certainly cannot conceive that there is more than one God; according to our bible all of us are the children of one God. We believe that the righteous of all nations have a place in the afterlife. A major difference is our emphasis on the relationship between man and man and yours on that between man and God. We are more concerned with life on earth while I understand that Christianity concentrates on the life hereafter. Then, of course, there is the matter of the Messiah. You believe that it is Jesus who has appeared, but was killed only to be resurrected and appear on earth again. We are still hoping and praying for the coming of the Messiah. There is the story of Rabbi Nahmanides who appeared before King James I of Aragon back in the thirteenth century. His confessor wished to prove the truth of Christianity over Judaism. His appointee for the debate with Nahmanides was Friar Christiani, a convert from Judaism who was well versed in the Talmud. It was a long debate that can be summarized with Nahmanides' conclusion. He said that all believe that with the coming of the Messiah everlasting peace will come on earth. This proves that the Messiah has not yet arrived as wars still continue to plague us and therefore Jesus cannot be the Messiah. The king gave Nahmanides a prize and supposedly said that he never heard an unjust cause so nobly defended."

"That certainly is food for thought, Rabbi, but I am troubled by the saying that Jews are the 'chosen people.' What are your thoughts on that?"

"The meaning of being chosen should not imply superiority. In fact, it is a burden. We should live morally and spiritually pure and thus act as an example for others. True, unfortunately all of us cannot claim to live like that, but our religion mandates it."

"In Christianity we have different divisions, for lack of a better word. There are Catholics, Protestants, Baptists, Seventh-Day Adventists, and more. I understood that Jews are divided into Sephardim and Ashkenazim. Can you tell me their differences?"

"Throughout the centuries of exile these two developed slightly differently. Sephardic Jews are from Spain, Portugal, North Africa, and the Middle East. The Ashkenazim are from France, Germany, and Eastern Europe. Different prayer books evolved, which are essentially the same with some dissimilar customs. Hebrew pronunciation of the two streams is also slightly different. By the way, I am of Sephardic heritage. I was born in Morocco but my ancestors went there with the expulsion of the Jews from Spain and Portugal, which occurred in 1492 and 1497 respectively."

"Well, you enlightened me a lot. How difficult is it to convert? Mind you, I certainly haven't decided what to do."

"It may seem simple when you learn what Rabbi Hillel, who lived in the first century BC, said. According to him, the whole Torah is not doing to others what is hateful to you. The rest, he said, is commentary. But you must know that we do not make conversion easy. It is much simpler to convert to Christianity or the Moslem religion. We want to be sure that the motive of the applicant is purely religious. I will add that this requires a good amount of study. One has to know the various commandments, the *mitzvoth*. And, of course, the convert is expected to live a religious life after he is accepted. By the way, Jewish history has many famous converts. Did you know that King David's great-grandmother was Ruth the Moabite? I hope that I was able to clarify things for you. Do not hesitate to come again if you feel like it. Here, take my card so that you can reach me directly. I was very happy to meet you."

"Thank you so much. I might just do that."

Joanna waited for another week and a half hoping to hear from Michael. *Maybe he's afraid that Caroline would object*, she thought. *I wonder if I should call him. I better not.* Sure enough, a few days passed and Michael called. "Sorry for not calling sooner, Jo. I was very busy at work and we had a lot of obligations to see people. How have you been? Have you seen that Rabbi from the New Jersey synagogue?"

"I'm good. Yes, I went to see him in New York and it was certainly very worthwhile. I learned a lot, but now I will have to do some hard thinking. It's not only about my religious conundrum, but also what to do about my parents. What's with you and Caroline?"

"We're fine; Caroline had to fly to Chicago yesterday and will be there for a week. She's in charge of a project her company has with one of the big diesel engine companies. They want to introduce greater efficiency into their production line and have contracted her company. She went there with one of her senior programmers. So I have some time now. What do you say we have dinner together?"

"I could make it on Wednesday or Thursday. How is that?"

"Great, let's meet on Wednesday. I can come up to Bridgeport and we can eat there and maybe also go to a play or movie. Do you still live with your parents? I wouldn't want to come to their house; we would have to meet somewhere."

"No, I haven't lived at home since I was married. I took a small place of my own after the divorce. I am in downtown Bridgeport, on Gold street number 12, it's right off Main. You have to come from Main, since it's one way. How about seven, is that OK?"

"Sure thing, I look forward to seeing you, Jo, and would like to hear all about your plans. See you then."

Wow, he is afraid of having Caroline see us together, even at a purely social event. Yet he seems eager for us to get together. I wonder if he has any long-range plans for us or if this is only something on the spur of the moment. Well, I won't have long to find out, I like being with him, it does not have to have romantic implications."

Joanna was getting worried as Michael still had not shown up; it was a quarter past the hour. She remembered him being always very punctual, something she used to joke about, telling him that he was compulsive. Finally the doorbell rang and he stood there, a sheepish grin on his face, saying how sorry he was being late, there had been an accident on the Post Road, which caused the delay. Joanna didn't know whether or not to kiss him and he in turn also looked hesitant until he kissed her demurely on the cheek.

"So, you know Bridgeport, where do you recommend we go for dinner?"

"It all depends what kind of food you are in the mood for. Here, take your pick of three pretty good ones that I know. There is the Taberna Food and Wine Bar for Mediterranean and Spanish food, Lenox Cuisine for Jamaican, and the Captain's Cove for seafood. What will it be?"

"I guess we both had plenty of Spanish food not so long ago, and seafood can be had in so many places, so what about that Lenox place? OK with you?"

"Sure, why don't you leave your car here and I'll drive, as I know where it is? Would you like a drink here before we go?"

Michael hesitated a little before he said that it would be better if they forego it and leave now. *My God,* went through Joanna's head, *he is afraid that one drink may lead to another and we will end up making love. That wouldn't be so terrible, actually. Am I trying to seduce him?* "Let's go," she said and got her jacket.

The Lenox Cuisine was a medium-sized place, with checkered tablecloths covering tables for four. The main decoration consisted of a few large colorful posters of Jamaica on the wall. It was fairly empty and after being seated, a waitress came over immediately to give them their menus and take their drink orders. Joanna looked questioningly at Michael, letting him decide. He asked for their wine list and selected a bottle of California Pinot Noir after asking for Joanna's agreement.

"I believe you said that you've eaten here before. Everything looks interesting but rather strange. What do you recommend?"

"To start with the soup called 'mannish water.' It has goat meat and is supposed to be an aphrodisiac. But it's not for that I recommend it, it really is very good. If you do not mind a bit of spicy food, then I suggest the jerk chicken and for dessert there is bulla cake. I bet it's a little different from cakes you know. How does that sound?"

"Very good, I'll order it."

The food and wine were good and had their effect; their shyness evaporated. Michael placed his hand over Joanna's that was flat on the table. He looked at her for what seemed a long while and said: "You know I really missed you. Being here brings back so many wonderful memories of the time we were together. I have often thought about what went wrong, what I should have done to prevent the split. I concluded that I acted a bit childishly, insisting you decide immediately between me and your parents. I ought to have been more patient and have tried to get us to work it out together. Other times I wondered what would have happened if I had one day taken you by the hand and driven to some far, outlying, motel and stayed there. You would have had to call your parents to tell them why you were not home and maybe would have told them that we planned to get married. A crazy fantasy, I suppose."

"Maybe it was and then again, maybe not. If we are on the subject of confessions, I should say that, in hindsight, I acted very childishly, too. I suppose I was not mature enough to do what I knew would have been best for me. Now, after a failed marriage that I went into for the wrong reasons, I think I have learned some lessons. But you know what, even that is not quite true. Look how I can't face my parents with what should be a simpler problem, the matter of telling them about my findings that we are possibly of Jewish ancestry? I'm certainly not consideringtelling them that I am considering conversion."

"We sure screwed things up, didn't we? Come let us order those desserts you had mentioned, what are they called? Ah yes, bulla cakes – funny name – and coffee."

They lingered over the dessert and coffee for some time until Michael asked what they should do next.

Joanna suggested they come to her place for a drink and listen to some music. Michael said that he would love to do that but wanted to be home as Caroline usually called around ten. For some reason she didn't like cell phones. "Why don't you come to my place if you do not mind the drive to Westport?" he said. She agreed to that but added that they should each drive their own cars so that he wouldn't have to take her back.

During the drive, Joanna was a little apprehensive, feeling rather sure that it might lead to their love-making but worried about the consequences of such an act, both from her and Michael's point of view. *Could I really be responsible for breaking up their marriage, even if he would want to? Oh to hell with it, let's see what happens, we are both adults now and can take responsibility for our actions.* When entering Michael's home, Joanna commented on how she liked the living room and added that Caroline had very good taste. Michael made a face as if he was insulted, and said that he, too, had a say in it. He then asked what she wanted to drink and brought two glasses of Benedictine. Sitting comfortably on the deeply cushioned sofa, they raised their glasses in a toast. There was a small pause until Michael asked about Joanna's future plans concerning her studies with the Rabbi in New York.

"The little I have learned so far drives me to delve deeper into your religion. I must admit that a conversion procedure seems quite difficult. The demands made of the prospective candidate are very high. At this point, I don't know what to make of the requirement to live a religious life. I suppose nobody would come and check up on you, but still they expect your promise to do so. You sure make it difficult, no wonder there are relatively few Jews in the world!"

"You are right there, but think what all the persecutions have done to our people throughout the ages. Think about what happened in Spain and Portugal. All the generations lost that could have been were it not for the killings and forcible conversion that took place. More recently, the Holocaust took six million of our people, A million and a half of those were children who, had they lived, by now would have had children and grandchildren; millions more. But come, let's listen to some music. I know you like Chopin. I'll put on his first concerto. I like it too."

They sat primly side by side on the sofa listening until Michael turned to Joanna asking if she would like another drink. "I'll have some cognac; I have a very nice Remy-Martin, try it." Joanna agreed and they continued sitting and sipping quietly until Joanna said that it was getting late and she better drive home, as she had to teach in the morning. Just then, the telephone rang and Michael got up to answer. It was Caroline; it was a short conversation since apparently nothing newsworthy was exchanged. Michael seemed relieved and came to sit next to Joanna, placing a hand on her knee.

"It's not quite ten yet, stay awhile, when was the last time we were together this way?"

Joanna turned to Michael, looked him deeply in the eyes, and said: "Oh Michael, how many times have I thought about being with you and now that I am I am utterly confused." Without any reply Michael leaned over, with his arm over her shoulder he pulled her to him, kissing her softly at first but with increasing force. Joanna, a groan escaping her, yielded her lips, which she opened looking for his mouth with her tongue. They held each other for what seemed an eternity until Michael groped under her sweater opening her bra and cupping one of her breasts, gently pulling on her erect nipple. Joanna felt herself bursting with desire and clawed on Michael's belt. He obliged, and standing up, he relieved himself of his clothes while Joanna quickly did the same. They stood looking at each other with wonder but quickly pulled each other close, their mouths joined. Michael tried to pull Joanna in the direction of what must have been the bedroom, but Joanna resisted, whispering, "Here, here." She stretched out on the sofa opening her arms to receive Michael who kissed her body passionately, forcefully entering her at the same time. She pulled his buttocks down strongly wanting him to stop while they were thus joined together and savor the feeling of warmth and peace that had come over her. Michael was not able to hold himself back and quickly started on rapid rhythmic movements that increased in force and speed. He came rather quickly with a convulsion that shook his body and left him limp on Joanna. She, her body wet with sweat, felt herself coming down slowly from the never achieved peak, started to cry softly; not so much because of the unrealized orgasm but because she understood that in back of her mind she had imagined that here she and Michael were free, continuing where they had left off so many years ago. Reality now came back with a vengeance. Michael, meanwhile, felt guilty and said: "Jo, darling, I acted like a schoolboy who was with a woman for the first time. You are so beautiful, so exciting. I had forgotten how it was when we were together. Then our love grew gradually, ever deeper. It was so sudden now, maybe only a one-time opportunity, although, right now, I don't know and don't want to think about the future."

"Let's not talk about it now, Michael. We need time to think. Whatever we do now will cause problems and heartbreak. Maybe it would have been better had we not met in Spain. Now we can't escape and will have to act like the adults we are and take responsibility for whatever we do." Joanna had dressed in the meantime, not wanting to shower as Michael suggested. "I'd rather do it after I get home, dear," she said. Michael, too, had put on his trousers and a T-shirt and stood holding Joanna's hand, unwilling to let her go. "Yes, let's not be hasty making final decisions that we may later regret. Promise we'll be in touch soon."

"Why, of course we will. We'll always be friends, even if we leave the romantic attachment behind. I'll always value you as a person regardless of what we do, stay well and take care of yourself."

"Bye, darling Jo. I'll always treasure you too. How can I otherwise?"

It took several days for Joanna to get back into her normal routine. She tried to concentrate on the preparation of her lessons, her interaction with pupils and staff, but did not wish to see family or friends. Thinking about being with Michael had shaken her up since she came to realize the pent-up desire she had to be with him. At the same time, she appreciated the price both would have to pay for achieving that. The imperfect coupling of that evening didn't leave her with less affection for Michael, since she recognized it as his frustration for the unnecessary breakup and all the time they had lost.

Joanna finally called her friend Megan and made a date to meet her in their favorite coffee shop. She told her all about her being with Michael and the problem of telling her family what she had discovered in Spain and her continuing to see Rabbi Perez to explore Judaism. Megan, in her usual straightforward manner looked at Joanna in amazement. "Are you completely nuts, or what? Do you want to break up a marriage and be responsible for the possible dire results? I understood that Michael and his wife have a good stable marriage with a kid on the way. I think Michael is a little immature. He should have talked about how he views that possibility and the consequences before seducing you."

"I don't know who seduced whom, to tell the truth. All the old feelings we had for each other came out before we knew it and there we were. I really do not want you to tell me what to do. I'll have to work that out. I just wanted to share all this with you, my dear. You don't mind do you?"

"I'm glad, Jo, that you did. Now what is this about you and your family? First of all, though, are you really serious about converting to Judaism? Why in heaven's name would you want to do something like that? You are not a religious person as I know, how come this involvement with religion, and not the one you were born and brought up with?"

"Look Megan, what I found in Spain points to the fact that we are very likely descendent from Spanish-Jewish stock. Also, I have learned a great deal about Jewish religion, their customs, and beliefs and found their emphasis on life on earth rather than our concentration on the life hereafter very appealing. It means more attention to morality on earth. Also, I understood that Judaism is a community first and a religion only second. That means they have a feeling of brotherhood. The fact that they have survived these thousands of years against all odds says something, too."

"Well, if you join them you may meet unpleasantness in the form of anti-Semitism. It's still prevalent even here and more so in many countries. Look at the trouble Israel, and all Jews, has from those Moslem extremists who now spread it all over the world even more than before. As for your family, you are a big girl now and should live according to the way you feel is best for you. Telling your parents may be uncomfortable but they have to accept you as you are, and I am sure that they will. Best of luck my dear."

It was nearly a week later that Michael called to ask Joanna how she was, and if she had thought about their possible meeting and talking about how they felt.

"Yes, to a certain extent, Michael. I believe that the one who has to make the hardest decision is you. Obviously, if we do decide to be together, you'll have to decide if you're willing to leave your wife and future child for that? If you answer yes to that I'll still have the problem of always feeling guilty about breaking up a family. We don't have to make any immediate decision, so let's be in touch again."

Joanna waited until Thanksgiving to continue talking to her parents about her findings in Spain, delving into what seemed problematic subjects for her father. She wanted to do that in the morning before Vanessa and her husband and young son would arrive at noon. She thought that her parents would be in a good mood and wouldn't want to spoil the festive meal. Eleanora was home on vacation from college but Joanna did not mind her presence at the conversation. Her mother noticed her nervousness when they prepared breakfast in the kitchen and asked what it was that bothered her. Joanna, trying to sound nonchalant, said that she just now remembered that she hadn't told them all about what happened in Spain and now was a good time for it. Her mother looked somewhat perturbed but did not say anything more.

At the breakfast table, after they had eaten and were drinking their coffee, Joanna said: "I believe I didn't tell you all that was in Spain, and in particular in Aguilar. By the way, I recently received word from my lawyer there that the two criminals who attacked me are going on trial scheduled for next April. He spoke with the police, and thinks there is a good chance for conviction. What I didn't tell you is that I think there is a connection with what I found in the archives and what I discussed with various people in town."

Eleanora and her parents looked with expressions of curiosity on their faces as Joanna continued. "I don't know how much you know of Spanish history and in particular that of the late Middle Ages. Spain had at that time a very large Jewish community who was involved in science, literature, and trade and were also in high government positions. This community was persecuted at times, which culminated in 1492 with their expulsion or forcible conversion to Christianity by Ferdinand and Isabella, of whom you might have heard. The thinking in Spain today is that about twenty percent of the population is descendent of those converted; they are called *Conversos*. Many of those, it is said, kept their original religion in secret. As I told you, I found the names of my great grandparents, including their birthdates, in the archives. The name of your grandfather, Papa, was Juan Aguilas Mendez and your grandmother was Maria Aguilas Calderon. As I said, they apparently changed their name to Aguilar when they arrived here to better remember their birthplace. I was told that Juan, the baker, was rather short tempered. They were apparently ostracized by their neighbors who thought they might have been *Conversos*. It seems they left Spain for that reason. Did you know that?"

Manuel looked up and said in a subdued voice that he knew that he was a baker but not much more. "Anyway," he said raising his voice angrily. "Why do you bother us with all this crap about Spain of the Middle Ages and *Conversos*?" He looked at his wife and said, "Sorry about this word, but we are not Joanna's students that we have to sit here and listen to all this."

"You are so right, Manuel," said Reyna and turned to Joanna asking her to show how this connects with the attack on her. "But please do not go into all the little details, try and make it short."

"OK Mama, it's like this. The matter of *Conversos* came up in many of my conversations with people in Cordoba and Aguilar. There were those that admitted to have *Converso* ancestry, others seemed to try to hide it; a few were very biased against them. I suspect that one of the latter organized this attack on me since those hoodlums said something that I am a dirty *Converso* trying to spread an ugly religion in 'this good Catholic town.' So there you have it. Naturally they were wrong; I never did any such thing. Was that short enough?"

There was a minute of silence around the table until Manuel said that it sounded as if Joanna was mixed up in this business. She should not, he emphasized, have done so. It appeared to him that she received what she deserved. He got up from the table without looking at Joanna and stormed out.

Later in the day, Joanna and her mother were alone in the kitchen, when Reyna said, "Don't take it to heart, darling. You know your Papa. It might have been better if we had talked about it before. Do not worry, he will get over it."

"But Mama, does he not realize that we, too, are very possibly of *Converso* stock? Did you know that we, as Seventh Day Adventists, have some customs that are very similar to those of practicing Jews? Why should Papa be so upset with what I said? I'm sorry he feels that way but I don't have to live according to his criteria. I will, to the best of my ability, try not to be biased against anyone's customs or religion."

"OK dear, let's leave it be. Today is Thanksgiving; we do not want to spoil a nice family dinner."

Several weeks later, it was late afternoon while Joanna was sitting at her desk, the ancient coin prominently displayed, preparing her lessons for the following day, when the phone rang. As quite a while had passed, Joanna assumed that she would not hear from Michael, thinking that he could not face talking to her.

"Hi Jo, I know that I should have called much sooner but first I did not know what to say and then I was afraid of hurting you. You will always be dear to me... What I want to say is that I can't see myself starting divorce proceedings and I don't think that we should see each other in secret. I doubt that you would want to do that either. I have a good life with Caroline and am anxious to see my child and be a father. I am sure you understand that. I see no reason why we can't remain friends. If and when you will find your love it would be easier for

Caroline to accept you as she now sees you as a rival. What do you say?"

"Of course I understand you, Michael, and do not fault you. I, too, think that it is best if we do not see each other, at least for a while. It was fate that we met in Spain and maybe it was unfortunate. We would not have been in such a situation as we found ourselves had we missed being in Plaza Mayor in Madrid at the same time. Keep well, my dear." She said the last part with her voice about to break. She hung up, kept staring at the coin, and watched history, with its tragedies and jubilations, unfold in her mind. *What a big deal I am making of my little affair. I have grown up and will find what I am looking for. Things will work out the way they should.*